BEST DAY EVER

KAIRA ROUDA

BEST DAY EVER

GRAYDON
HOUSE

GRAYDON
HOUSE

ISBN-13: 978-1-525-81140-1

Best Day Ever

BookClubbish.com

Printed in U.S.A.

For my daughter, Avery Robinson Rouda

Continue to write the stories that speak to your heart and never stop believing in your power to change the world for the better.

MORNING
9:00 A.M.

I glance at my wife as she climbs into the passenger seat, sunlight bouncing off her shiny blond hair like sparklers lit for the Fourth of July, and I am bursting with confidence. Everything is as it should be.

Here we are, just the two of us, about to spend the weekend at our lake house. Today represents everything I've worked for, that we have built together. The sun blasts through my driver's side window with such intensity I feel the urge to hold my hand up to the side of my face to shield my eyes, even though my sunglasses are dark and should be doing the job. Under any other circumstances, on any other day, they would be, I know. But today, something is different between us; some strange tension pulses through the still air of the car's interior. I cannot see it, but it's here. I'd like to name it. Discover its source and eliminate it.

Sure, this morning has been hectic. It's a Friday, and Fridays always seem the most frenzied when you have kids. Getting the boys up and dressed, and then dropping them off at their immaculately landscaped and highly ranked redbrick elementary school where they will no doubt excel, in first and third grade respectively. Truth be told, though, I usually have little to do with the scenario I just outlined. Mia, my wife, handles all the tasks pertaining to the boys each morning. We're a traditional suburban household in that respect. In the morning, I make coffee, shower, dress and leave for work before the boys awaken. Yes, mine is quite a selfish and single-minded pursuit on most days.

That's another reason why today is so special. I drove the boys to school, reminded them that the babysitter would be picking them up afterward. When I returned to the house, I put the dirty dishes in the dishwasher. I can be helpful when I want to be, although I don't want to remind Mia of this fact as she may come to expect it. Dishes finished, I had called up the stairs to Mia, urging her to hurry. We haven't had a weekend together, just the two of us alone, for more than a year. This day was going to be just for us, and it was time to go.

She called back, her voice floating like a butterfly down the stairs, asking for my help with her luggage. The next moment, I found myself lugging two huge suitcases down the grand main staircase of our home. She followed behind me with a laundry basket filled with who knows what.

"Staying awhile?" I teased. She blushed, embarrassed by her notorious overpacking. But I didn't complain. It was her day. She was free to overpack away. Once we got everything loaded into the trunk of the car, just as Mia was starting to relax, the packing part over, that was when my phone rang. I shouldn't have answered it. But onward. Taking the call was just one small mistake in a day that's destined to be brilliant.

From the driver's seat, I finally finish syncing my phone with the car's system. I find the playlist I created for my wife. All her favorite songs will play during our drive. Music is such an important part of keeping romance alive.

And now we're getting on the road. Mia turns toward me and smiles. She has a perfect smile: half-moon-shaped, with glistening white teeth. My smile is more of a rectangle; no matter how hard I try, I appear to be smirking, I know that. But my teeth are perfect, thanks to the cosmetic dentist. I grin back.

She loves me so much, and of course the same can be said for me. We've been together almost ten years now. We know each other's best qualities, and we know each other's dark sides. Although to be quite honest about it, I'm not sure Mia has what you'd call a dastardly alter ego. Her dark side is simply grumpy, and it typically only appears when she is tired, or when one of our boys faces a rough patch. For my part, I wonder if Mia thinks I have a dark side. Most likely, as far as she knows, I am just her dear loving husband.

Today, though, this morning, right now, she is exuding energy; it oozes from her pores, from her flawless face. It's the cause of the strange pulsing between us, I decide.

"You seem wound up, honey," I say. I want to pat her leg and tell her to relax but I don't. Despite her odd mood she is still beautiful, almost perfect in every way.

"Do I? I guess I'm just excited," she says, confirming my assessment while stretching her hands toward the front windshield. The diamond from her wedding ring flashes in the overbright sunshine as if imitating her energy.

"Me, too. But we've got a long drive ahead of us, so try to relax. Let's make today the best day ever." I attempt to add the proper lilt to my voice. I need her to believe I am just as happy and carefree as she is. That driving up to our lake house for the first time this season is the most exciting thing I could ever imagine doing on any day, ever.

"In that case, can I request a small detour? There's a little bakery in Port Clinton, just before the turnoff to Lakeside. I'd like to stop there on the way in. For croissants for tomorrow morning. Do you remember the spot? We won't arrive in time to grab croissants for breakfast today, of course, but tomorrow's almost as good," she says. Thankfully, her bright blue eyes are hidden behind dark sunglasses that match mine. When I glance at her, we cannot make eye contact. Not really.

I wonder if the comment about not arriving in time is directed at me, and realize it is. Of course. I am the one who took the phone call just as we were packed up, ready to hop in the car and drive away. I shouldn't have. It wasn't anything new, but I had still held out hope that it would be. Instead, I spent thirty minutes on a worthless call with a headhunter, and, I know, made us late. The croissants will be gone by the time we arrive at the bakery; I know this, too.

"Yes, I remember the place. Ugly strip mall, but sure, we'll stop. Not worried about gluten anymore, I take it?" I say. For a while, Mia and her doctor du jour thought her upset stomach, weight loss and other intestinal issues were caused by gluten. I was relieved when she decided not to hop on that fad after giving up wheat for a few weeks with no change. She still insists on a vegetarian existence, leaving her with few choices when we go out to dinner and endless questions for the waitstaff. It's annoying. But I push those thoughts away. My wife is just doing her best.

"Turns out gluten isn't the culprit," Mia says. She smiles. "So yes, I'd love to stop. If it's okay with you, of course."

Stopping on our way to the lake house at a bakery that will

no doubt be out of croissants was not on my agenda today. She knows I'm a man of action and when I have a plan, I follow it. I just want to get up there already. But today, Mia's every wish is my command.

"As you wish, my dear." I am the perfect husband. I smile as one of the songs from our early dating days comes on. There's an art to crafting the perfect playlist. This song, "Unforgettable," was the soundtrack to our first night together. Innocent Mia, a virgin even after four years of college, somehow untouched by all of those lecherous fraternity guys. She was waiting for someone older, someone sophisticated, someone who could take care of her. She found that in me.

I had reserved a suite in the finest hotel in downtown Columbus, with views of the river sparkling below. We'd been dating a couple of months by then and I'd waited as long as any man could be expected to. Mia was nervous, uncomfortably sitting on the edge of the red-and-white-striped upholstered chair, gripping her champagne flute like a weapon she'd use for protection. She wore a light blue dress that matched her eyes. The dress slipped easily over her head once I'd pulled her to me, asked her to dance. The memories of that night are vivid. It took me until the sun was coming up to convince her to go all the way. She worried about the promise she'd made to her mother. I told her if a tree falls in the forest but no one is around to hear it, then did it really fall? She laughed and I slid on top of her, pinning her arms gently above her head, pressing my mouth firmly against hers. And, she fell. I lick my lips at the memory and shift in my seat.

"Who were you talking to on the phone? The office?" she asks as I back out of our driveway.

"Who else? Sometimes I think they can't last a moment without me," I say. Some sort of emotion crosses Mia's face before she turns toward the passenger side window. I guess we're finished with that topic. I should apologize for the delay, but I don't. An amicable silence falls between us.

Personally, I have to admit I love the implied success I feel being able to drive out of my very nice neighborhood, my wife by my side, on a Friday morning on my way to my second home. I am driving a Ford Flex, navy exterior, by choice. Supporting America while demonstrating that my ego does not require a fancy sports car or luxury sedan. No, I am secure in my status and a family man, all rolled into one. The American dream, that's what we're living right here.

My wife is still looking out her window. She seems to be taking in the signs of spring around us. The lawns are greening up nicely and the trees, so stark for the long, dreary months of winter, are budding and flowering. Our suburb is becoming a lovely place to live again, just in time. We pull onto the freeway heading north through downtown Columbus, and I feel a pride for my hometown that extends beyond the college sports franchise. It's growing up. People from all over consider us a sophisticated, cosmopolitan place now, not just a college town or a field of grazing cattle. I don't have to say Columbus comma Ohio anymore. We are on the weather maps internationally as *the* city in Ohio. Our weather matters more than Cleveland's or Cincinnati's does. That, to me, is a sign we have arrived as a great city.

Ironically, as we zip through the periphery of downtown, skyscrapers slicing the clear blue sky, we are headed to farm country. Most of Ohio still is agrarian, it seems, no matter how much Columbus has changed. My wife and I, we spend our time in the bubble of suburbia mostly, cutting through the city on our way out of town. We really should explore downtown more, I realize. There always seems to be so much more to do in a day than you can ever accomplish. That's why I make plans.

Mia shifts in her seat, angling her body toward me as much as possible for someone strapped in by her seat belt, and asks, "Do you really think the strawberries will take hold? I mean, they looked like they were from the photos Buck sent me. They might even have grown a little. But things can change." I notice she holds her phone in her hands now; her lovely fingers, accented by a cheery red—strawberry red—fingernail polish, move quickly across the small keypad. She was a copywriter at the advertising agency when I met her, and she has amazing keyboard speed still.

"It says strawberry plants should be bought from a reputable nursery. I'm just not sure I picked the right one. And they need deep holes, wide enough to accommodate the entire root system without bending the roots. Very persnickety plants," she continues. Her lips are pursed together, as if she has eaten a sour berry.

"I'm sure they're fine," I reassure her. "No one will nurture them more than you." A black sports car passes us on our right, only a flash of metal actually, because it's moving so quickly. I hadn't even seen it coming in my rearview mirror. It's funny how things can sneak up on you, appear out of nowhere.

"It's like having babies again, or puppies," she says, ignoring the race car as I turn on my blinker and slide us out of the passing lane. "Don't plant too deep, it says. The roots should be covered, but the crown should be right at soil surface. I should call Buck and ask him to check on the crowns."

She glances at me, no doubt catching my smirk. First, what kind of name is *B-U-C-K*? I mean, really. But despite his ridiculous name, Buck Overford is a nice enough guy, I guess.

He's our neighbor at the lake, a widower even though he's about my age, who likes to talk gardening with my wife. I should be clear. I'm forty-five, and Mia is only thirty-three. Buck is closer to my age than hers, maybe even a bit older. I look younger anyway. Not that we're old geezers by any stretch. Buck does have this affinity for gardening, which to me is a woman's thing, so that makes him older, weaker than me in my book.

At least gardening is what Mia tells me she and Buck have been talking about since we met him last summer. It was just after our moving truck had left. He brought over a bottle of Merlot, a nice one if memory serves, and the three of us spent a pleasant evening together on the screened porch until it was time for us to find our boys and get them ready for bed. The boys were free-range chickens up at the lake, had been every summer we'd rented. Now that we were owners, members, they'd increased their span of wandering, it seemed.

There were countless wholesome activities at the lake to draw their attention, from sailing lessons to shuffleboard, skateboarding to bike riding. Sometimes, we'd find them sitting by the edge of the water, skipping rocks, like they'd stepped out of a Norman Rockwell painting. It was all perfectly safe, these endless summertime activities that delighted our boys and made them beg us to head to Lakeside whenever possible. When it was bedtime, though, finding them, corralling them and then getting them into bed was a process best left for family only. We never wanted witnesses to that exhausting exercise.

"Right, I don't need to bother Buck. I can check the crowns as soon as we get there," Mia says in my direction before returning her attention to her phone screen.

"Good call." I check the rearview mirror for any more

speeding sports cars. I had an expensive sports car before, of course. I'll likely have one again one day when my lifestyle dictates a change, I muse, taking in the interior of my sensible Ford Flex. Room for the whole family, and as many strawberry plants as Mia could handle planting. I can haul as much of the boys' sports equipment as they can throw my way. It is a sensible, practical car. For a responsible family man. It fits me perfectly, this car. Me and my hot, newly skinny again wife. If she loses any more weight, though, she'll disappear. It's a real shame about the nausea she's been struggling with. The latest doctor is convinced it's stress-related. He told her to meditate.

"Did you know my strawberry plants' runners are called 'daughter' plants?" she asks. The air between us pulses, I feel it. *Ping.*

"No, I didn't," I say, taking a deep breath before I realize I am doing it. It's funny how the absence of a daughter catches your breath at the strangest times, over the silliest topics. "No 'son' plants? How sexist."

"I still wish we'd tried," Mia says quietly, stirring the age-old pot. Just that topic, that old leathery shoe of a stew makes me swallow something bitter. I cough, trying to clear my throat, my dark mind.

"Can we not have that old discussion today, of all days?" I ask. I focus on the farmland beginning to open up on either side of the road. We're finally out of the reaches of the city, finally free from the responsibility, the shiny office buildings, bespoke suits and country clubs that that part of civilization values. I would miss golf if I had to live in the country, of course. And many other things. Country visits are for weekends, a touch-base with our more rural and simple selves. Not a place to live full-time. I hope we aren't going to disagree this early in our country excursion.

Mia turns to me and I can hear her gentle, agreeable smile in her next words. "Of course, no fighting. This is our happy day, the start of a wonderful weekend. I just didn't realize until this moment about strawberry seedlings and 'daughter' plants. I should have grown peppers." Her voice is soft, a stealth dagger to my heart. This statement, the peppers, is a jab. Sure, we could have tried to get pregnant one more time, but I was convinced it would be another boy. We had two of those, perfect little specimens, each a miniature version of me, as they should be. I realize Mia would enjoy seeing a little version of herself walking around this world, following in her footsteps. But why tempt fate?

I glance at my wife. Did I see Mia wipe under her eye? No, I'm sure it must be an errant eyelash. This topic is almost as old as Sam, our youngest, who is six. We have been arguing, disagreeing let's call it, over our phantom daughter—her name would have been Lilly, Mia had said over and over again—for six years. The whole thing is absurd. She should be counting her blessings, like her strawberry daughters at her beautiful lake house, for example. She should be thankful for everything she has, everything I've provided, not missing something, someone who never existed. I feel myself squeeze the steering wheel, watch my knuckles whiten.

"Or beans. Green beans. Those would be fun to grow," I say in a concerted effort to play along. I have a passion for green beans and have since I was a child. I've learned not to question why. It's just a fact, like the impossibly blue May sky or the brown-green fields stretched out for miles on either side of the car.

I remember when I was a kid and my parents took us to a

fancy restaurant in town—this was long before their tragic
accident, of course. Before everything changed. Just goes to
show you, one thing can happen and poof, all bets are off.

People said it was an odd twist of fate, bad luck that both
of my parents had decided to take a nap in the afternoon.
Mom's friends in the neighborhood told the police my mom
hardly ever rested during the day. But she had Alzheimer's,
early stage, so things changed all the time. Bottom line was
she did take a nap that day. My dad was slowing down in his
old age even though he was stubborn and wouldn't admit it.
He napped daily. While my mom's disease was progressing,
she still functioned, still had more energy than he had. Sure,
she forgot little things like her neighbor's name, but until then
she hadn't forgotten big ones—like turning off the car when
she had parked it in the garage, most notably.

But my dad always napped, from twelve thirty to two every
afternoon. He'd pull out his hearing aids, put the golf channel
on the television and commence his obnoxiously loud snor-
ing. He sounded like an uncontrolled train screeching down
the tracks. I can almost picture my mom returning from her
errand, pulling the car into the garage and pushing the button
to close the garage door. She'd walk inside the house, accidentally leaving the door connecting the garage to the house
open, the car running. She would have heard my dad's freight-
train snores coming from the bedroom and for some reason,
that afternoon, she'd decided to join him in bed. Maybe she
had too much to eat at lunch that day and had a stomachache,
maybe that's why she decided to take a nap? The investigators
found a bottle of Tums on her bedside table.

It comforts me to know they both slipped into death, like
when you have anesthesia for a surgery. The nurse slides the
IV in your arm and before you can count backward from ten,

you're out. But in their case, they never woke up. The silent killer, that's what they call carbon monoxide. I made sure to install detectors in our house after it happened, even though only about four hundred people a year die from the colorless, odorless toxic gas. Still, you have to be cautious, consider every threat. Be one step ahead of everything, everyone. That's how the universe is working these days.

But before the tragedy, back when I was a kid, my parents would sometimes take us to the fanciest restaurant in town. It would only be when my dad was in a good mood, when he got a bonus and hadn't blown it yet on booze or whatever. We'd dress up in our little suits and ties, and Mom would beam and tell us we were the most handsome men ever and then we'd drive to The Old Clock Tower restaurant. All the staff would dote over my brother and me. That's where I had my first taste of perfectly prepared green beans, sliced thin and painted with a buttery mustard sauce. I remember the beans glistening in the light from the candle on the table. I can still taste that first bite, the smile it put on my face. Those beans weren't anything like the ones we had at home.

Mia and I don't have a family restaurant we take the boys to on a regular basis. Not one with flickering candles and crisp white tablecloths at least. We manage to sit down together fairly regularly at the kitchen table. Never at the dining room table, not yet. The boys are too messy to be dining above our fine Tabriz rug. A gift from Mia's parents, a souvenir from one of their exotic vacations, of course. I checked online one day. The rug is worth almost $70,000. So we stick to the kitchen for family meals, though neither Mia nor I would be considered a good cook, not by any stretch.

Sometimes I'll help throw something together, but usually Mia is in charge of meals, truth be told. Obviously this makes sense: she is the housewife. I'm uncertain why, then, after all of our years together, she hasn't grown and developed her cooking expertise. I know she's invested in cookbooks, and cooking classes even, but still, her best efforts can only be awarded a C. Barely edible, actually, when compared to fine dining. The boys and I struggle through "Momma Mia's Lasagna" every week on Italian Tuesdays. Every week, it's soggy and almost tasteless. It's a shame, really.

On the rare occasions when I'm in charge of mealtime, I like taking the boys to Panera. It's not quite like going to McDonald's or Wendy's for dinner—although I've been known to do that, of course. Please don't tell Mia, though. No, Panera is almost a sit-down establishment, a step above, say, a pizza joint or fast food. Sometimes I try to talk the boys into eating green beans there, you know, for tradition's sake. They don't have the taste for them, though. Mikey actually grabs his throat and makes choking, gagging sounds at me. He doesn't eat anything that's the color green, Mia says. She says he'll come around, his taste buds will mature. In my day, those taste buds wouldn't really have a choice, thanks to dear old dad. You ate what was served to you. But I love my kids. Those little guys. Despite the family resemblance, sometimes I like to wonder aloud if they're mine, they're so perfect.

"Green beans," Mia echoes, pulling me from thoughts of parents and offspring and crumbs on expensive rugs. Her back is to me; she seems fixated, fully focused on the farmland rolling by the window. Even though I cannot see her face, I detect a tone in her voice, something that sounds like the feeling you get when you can't understand a joke. Like you are the joke, like you are an idiot. Only someone you love can make you feel that way. "I can ask Buck if that's possible, over the summer." I notice she's nodding, the landscape is rolling and the overall effect is dizzying. I turn my eyes back to the road.

Since when do we consult with good old Buck on all things garden-related? I wonder. And what else do Buck and Mia discuss: The weather, the pros and cons of fertilizer, our marriage? Soon the road will narrow, and it will be down to one lane, each direction. That's when I'll really need to pay attention. That's when it gets dangerous. If you make a mistake, there is no forgiveness on a two-lane country road.

10:30 A.M.

2

This monotonous stretch of highway, the section between Columbus and, say, the big Pilot Travel Center
where we typically stop for gas, is boring: flat, semi-
green farmlands, and few sights out the window to feed your
imagination. Usually when we hit this point in the journey, I
start daydreaming about the destination, thinking about that
first moment when I'll see the lake again.

I know what you may be thinking: Is this guy really daydreaming about Lake Erie? Yes, I am. If you've never been
you're probably envisioning the dead lake of the late 1960s
fed by the burning Cuyahoga River. By that point, Lake Erie
had become a toxic dump thanks to the heavy industries lining its shore, the sewage flowing into it from Cleveland and
the fertilizer and pesticide runoffs from agriculture. Dead
fish littered its banks. This poor lake was the impetus for the
Clean Water Act in 1972, thank goodness.

Or, more recently, you may have heard of the toxic algae blooms that turn the lake water into green goo that looks like the slime they spray on people during that teen awards show the boys like to watch. But that doesn't happen all the time. Sure, there are invasive mussels and some nasty, dead-fish smells in the air sometimes. But mostly I find, if I sit on a bench near the lake and just listen to the water playing with the boulders along the shore, I feel at peace. It's hard to explain, I suppose, to someone who has never seen a Lake Erie sunset. But they're beautiful. And, if you don't turn your head too far left or right, you can almost imagine you're at the ocean. It's almost possible to believe that you could start your life over again, just as the sun drops into the water. And then everything would be simple, just like the little lakefront community where our lake house is nestled under a big oak tree. Sounds romantic, doesn't it?

Our lake house is part of a special, gated community appropriately named Lakeside, a Chautauqua community started by Methodist preachers more than 140 years ago as a summer retreat for adult education and cultural enrichment, with a heavy dose of religion sprinkled in. Not that there's anything wrong with religion, of course; it's just that I didn't grow up with it, and we're not raising our kids in it. That doesn't mean we don't enjoy the amenities these fine Christian souls have blessed the community with. Even an atheist like me can appreciate its many glories.

At one point or another, Presidents Ulysses S. Grant and Rutherford B. Hayes stayed at Lakeside. My wife likes to note that Eleanor Roosevelt stayed here, too. Mia quotes that woman a lot. I don't. I find her to be too ugly—I mean, that face of hers is hideous. I could never wake up every morning to a face like that. But Mia doesn't care about that. Says Eleanor Roosevelt inspires her to do one thing every day that scares her. I'm paraphrasing but you get the idea. I tell her seeing that woman coming at me in a dark alley would have scared me and Mia doesn't laugh.

The point is, it's a great little community, and it's located on a peninsula, halfway between Toledo and Cleveland. But don't think of those big, dirty cities that the weather maps have forgotten. Imagine instead a place right out of Mayberry RFD. Remember that TV show? No, I'm not old enough to have watched it, of course, but just think about Ron Howard and freckles and simpler times—that's this place. Its wooden cottages were originally designed to use the lake as the only air conditioner. Now with global warming, most of them have central air.

There's a little main street with a pizza parlor, a shop selling the best glazed, potato donuts in the world, T-shirt stores and the rest. We have a historic inn built in 1875 that sort of seems haunted to me, what with its old, uneven wood floors, squeaky screen doors and musty smell others might call charming but that gives me the creeps. The windows are too tall, too narrow in my opinion, like inside there is something to hide. The place was supposed to be bulldozed in the mid-1970s, half of its rooms as unusable as the lake was polluted. It was saved from demolition by a group of Lakeside residents and they've been sprucing it up, slowly, ever since. Good for them, although I doubt they ever actually stay there. But it is right on the lake and it's what they call gracious.

My favorite spot in the whole community is the dock and the boathouse. It's so all-American with its decorative Victorian scalloped roofline, its prime position in the heart of the place. I can just imagine the important visitors arriving by boat back in the day. I like the way I feel when I stand at the end of the dock. The backdrop complements me like a movie set: oh, look, there's handsome, wealthy city-dweller Paul Strom enjoying a carefree day of leisure at his lakefront community. Very presidential.

Not sure any current-day presidents even make it to Cleveland, our distant neighbor to the east, let alone to our little haven by the lake. But that's just fine with me. Enough people have discovered it already. When the boys were tiny, we'd come up once a summer and stay with the Boones, our neighbors two doors down back in Columbus. That lasted about three summers or so, and then we started to rent our own place. When we saw the Boones at the pizza parlor after, it wasn't even that awkward. They'd moved on, invited other neighbors to take our place at their huge cottage. We weren't able to buy a place of our own until last summer and when we did, it was a cottage on the very same street as Greg and Doris Boone's stately second home. Not as big, of course. Ironically, though, because we're up the street we're on a higher lot so we look down over their property now. It was a dream come true, especially for Mia.

We like visiting Lakeside best just before and after season. Season is the ten weeks in the heart of the summer when the place is crazy packed with tourists and the gates are down. Even homeowners have to pay the stupid gate fees during the summer. That doesn't make any sense to me, but it's the way it is.

But, on the plus side—and today is a day for positivity, I remind myself—Lakeside is wonderful, especially during the relatively deserted off-season times like now. I remember our first trip up here, back when we were newly married, the Boones having invited my wife and me up to stay for the weekend. We were thrilled for a chance to leave baby Mikey at home with my parents and have a weekend on our own, just the two of us and some other young parents. It was the start of the good times at Lakeside, and it was all thanks to the Boones. We'd play card games, especially euchre. Drink too much, eat too much, and then the guys would smoke cigars on Greg Boone's back porch while the women relaxed in over-size white wicker chairs with pink cushions on Doris Boone's front porch and gossiped. We could hear them, laughing and making fun of things, probably us, from the back porch. Us guys all rolling our eyes; women will be women, you know.

If you ask me, I'd tell you I'm still not really sure what hap-pened, why the Boones stopped inviting us up, but it doesn't matter. We managed to take ourselves up here every sum-mer, no invitation necessary, and rented great places all on our own. And now we actually own a cottage, perched on a grassy lot above the Boones' place. If I sit on my screened-in porch at night, I've noticed I can even watch Greg on his back porch, with his male guests du jour, smoking all his smuggled-in Cuban cigars. But who needs lung cancer? Not me. No, I think it all worked out beautifully.

Like the Boones', our primary residence is located in the highly coveted Grandville suburb of Columbus, the city's nearest northwest suburb, and is approximately two hours south of Lake Erie. All of what we own in the world is in Ohio, in this politically decisive, coastally deprived state. I am a native, born in the suburb we are raising our family in. Don't tell anyone, but it wasn't considered upscale back then. No, Grandville has grown into its—well, grandness, to use an apt term—as the Ohio State University and Columbus grew in prominence and wealth. Before, Grandville was a com-munity filled with butchers and factory workers and the like. Now it's filled with country-club brats and men like me who don't ever have calluses on their palms. It's like my dad and me, actually. Callous versus refined. But as far as picking a place to call home, not only did the apple not fall far from the tree in my family, but our crab apple tree was actually started by a seed from the apple tree in the next yard over. Literally my parents had lived right next to us. Before the accident.

Yes, I bought the home next to my parents, even before I met Mia. I knew where I wanted to live, and when it became available, I was there. Life requires planning, don't you agree? My wife had grown comfortable with the arrangement, though of course, like any new bride, initially Mia had her concerns. She wasn't from here, so she didn't understand how close family can help you out, how nice it would be for the kids to know their grandparents and be able to toddle over to their home. She came to appreciate the setup, after our home was whipped into shape. Naturally, I let Mia and her mom completely renovate the place. You wouldn't even recognize it from my primitive man cave days. But that was all part of the plan. I provided the shell, a "fabulous 1931 masterpiece," according to the Realtor's brochures, "that just needs some TLC." Mia and her parents provided the TLC and much more. Our wedding gift. As a thank-you, I presented Phyllis, Mia's mom, with a vintage Italian Mosaic pillbox.

"This is fabulous, thank you. I'll add it to the collection, next to the other one you gave me. You are just so thoughtful. And I don't have any mosaics, how did you know that, Paul?" Phyllis's bony arms had wrapped around my waist. I tried not to flinch.

"Just a lucky guess, Phyllis," I managed, although of course I knew. I'd saved a photo Mia took of Phyllis's collection, the little trophies displayed on a mirrored table in Phyllis's dressing room. It's very important to keep your mother-in-law on your side.

On mornings like this, before my parents died, we would have walked the boys across the green grass of our lawn and then over to the front walk of my mom and dad's one-story house, depositing them for safekeeping for the weekend. My boys weren't old enough yet to notice how small their grandparents' home was, compared to the rest of the street. I'm just waiting for the new owners to smash it down, build a Mc-Mansion.

But anyway, back when the boys were little the smell of my mom's famous chocolate chip cookies would have greeted us at the door and the comforting sound of cheers from fans at some sporting event would be blasting from the television set my dad turned up too loud. The rocking chair my mom had used to calm me as a child had been returned to the corner of my parents' bedroom. The tub of wooden blocks I'd played with as a kid magically appeared in my parents' family room as soon as Mikey was old enough to start creating forts.

Sounds idyllic, doesn't it? Just as life should be for my privileged sons. Doting grandparents next door, a luxurious home to live in filled with pricey furnishings, a stay-at-home mom and a hardworking dad. My boys had it made. And they loved my parents, especially my mom. As for me, as long as my dad and mom both followed my rules everything was perfect. Family is family. Family first, and all that. If you aren't needed, then fine, make other plans. But grandkids come first. They only violated that rule once, my parents. In my book, you always make time for your favorite son's kids, no matter what. I'm sure you agree.

Of course, now that my parents are gone we rely on babysitters of varying skill levels. In retrospect, my parents, despite their age, probably would have done a better job of keeping my sons safe than the gangly teenagers we now employ and overpay.

My parents would have been a better choice for this weekend, for example, undoubtedly more effective than Claudia, who arrived this morning looking overwhelmed. Big dark circles hung below her wide eyes and her nails were bitten to the core. *Maybe she's on drugs*, I think suddenly, wondering if I should ask Mia her opinion. Better not, though. She'd want to turn around and rescue the boys. We need this time together, this great day together. Claudia isn't the only one who is overwhelmed; she just looks the most like it.

I'm pretty adept at covering my emotions. For instance, my wife always wonders if it bothers me, living next to the ghosts of my parents. She doesn't put it that way, just says things like it's odd seeing the new family painting the front door a different shade of brown. I think it's odd they haven't torn the thing down, but I don't say that. Things like that, the little things, don't get to me. Big things, those bother me, but still I might not show it. "Poker-face Paul," my friends called me growing up. I'm proud of that. It has served me well in sales.

A natural born salesman, that's me. I'm not bragging, not at all. I know, in fact, that many people don't even like salespeople. They think we're unsophisticated and lowbrow, no matter what we sell. Me, I don't care, not as long as I'm making the big money. And I have. It has been a great ride. Even Mia, when we first met, may have considered herself above me. She was a copywriter on the creative team and I was just a client services guy. Now she knows what's what. It didn't take long for me to teach her how the world works.

"Paul, I need to use the bathroom," Mia announces, closing the magazine on her lap as if she could just pop out of the vehicle and relieve herself along the side of I-71.

"Oh, okay, I'll pull off at the next exit and try to find someplace acceptable," I say. The facilities on this road are subpar at best.

"Make sure it looks clean," she adds as if I have X-ray vision capabilities. Typically, we do not take bathroom breaks on the drive to the lake house. The boys know this, Mia knows this. But in her weakened state, and on this, the best day ever, I will make an exception without shaming her. I'm in a loving, flexible mood.

"Right. Gas station or fast food? Your choice," I offer. I'm not about to be blamed for choosing the wrong bathroom for her. This I say with warmth in my voice although I do not want to stop at all.

"I'll let you know when we see the options," she says, re-opening the magazine. I'll let it go, my disdain for the fact that she isn't more appreciative of my willingness to stop for her. I glance at her, engrossed in the meaningless celebrity drivel opened on her lap.

She should stop reading that trash.

"You know that magazine is all gossip. The stories about celebrities are completely made up. Nobody is as happy or as sad as they make it seem in there. Life is lived in the middle. In middle America, like here, in the middle of nowhere, like now, and in the middle of life, like us," I say. I'm feeling poetic today, although I don't believe for a moment that I am normal, or in the middle of anything.

"Paul, I've never heard you call yourself middle-aged." I think Mia is teasing me but there is an edge in her voice.

"I'm not," I say. "All those guys are older than me in there. They get airbrushed. If you saw them on the street, you'd be disgusted at how old they are. It's not real. That's all." I'm tired of this subject. I've never been a gossiper, or a reader of tabloid magazines, of course, but I know how the world works. People are always talking. Heck, a few years ago Mia heard from somebody back home that people think we aren't happy. And just recently, the rumor has something to do with me flirting with a saleswoman at the mall. Ridiculous. I hate malls. As a rule, I shop at boutiques or online. Not that the gossips care to take a little thing like facts into account.

Anyway, back when the first wave of rumors started a few years ago, Mia launched what she called the "rebranding" effort on Facebook, posting photos of the two of us in various places, laughing and smiling together. Some of the shots are really old, but as long as I look good, I'm fine with it. She says it has worked, because she hasn't heard the rumors anymore. I don't tell her I have, and I certainly don't mention the mall rumor, because she'd ask me when and where, who and in what context and I wouldn't be able to tell her that, of course. I'm not a gossip.

I glance over and see my wife is reading an article about one of the late-night television hosts. Now, that's a job I could nail. I mean, sitting behind a desk, talking with famous people about nothing but fluff and getting paid like a king. I don't even know how you get a gig like that. As I look a bit closer, I realize the guy in the magazine looks a lot like Buck, our neighbor at the lake. Kind of a refined look, I guess you'd say. Lean but muscular build, dark brown eyes, a strong, manly jaw. It's the type of look you see in New York, on Wall Street, or on television, not something you see around here. That's what makes it odd that Buck lives at the lake year-round. Hardly anybody does because it's cold and miserable in the off-season and nobody else is around. It's like he's a spy and he's hiding from something or someone, that's what I think.

He seems successful, though. I heard through the grapevine that he sold his big home somewhere in Connecticut when his wife died, and now he's here "regrouping," whatever that means. The woman who told me doesn't know much, though she's the designated neighborhood gossip for our block up at the lake. Every street has one. She's just not very good at her job. Google knows a lot more about Buck than she does. And that's not much.

"McDonald's or BP?" I say as I pull to a stop at the stop sign. We're in the middle of nowhere. The town of Kilbourne is several miles west down Route 521. A right turn will take us to a McDonald's, a left is the gas station. And as far as I can see, there is nothing else.

"McDonald's," Mia says with that tone of disgust she uses for all things—people and situations—that are below her. Recently, Mia has become a firm anti-GMO, anti-fast-food mom. She was leaning that way before her recent illness, but now she's militant. I applaud her for the herculean effort it takes to say no to two boys who will, as soon as they are old enough to hang out with friends at malls or go to the movies alone, be the first ones in line at every fast-food restaurant in town, stuffing themselves with all things nonorganic and fried. I also have pointed out, at least once each year as we drive to the lake, the fields as far as the eye can see of Monsanto Roundup Ready corn and soy proudly framing the highway. It's almost un-Ohioan, Mia's stance on the issue.

We should embrace what we are, don't you think? We're a no-till farming, profracking, pro-GMO, pro-Monsanto state. It's our heritage, I tell her. Did you know Columbus is a fast-food mecca? It's true. We are the test market for most major fast-food chains. Us folks are the definition of America. We are the barometers of taste, at least the kind of taste that comes when you can buy an entire "meal" for under a dollar. We're the hometown of Wendy's and White Castle and of several others like Rax that have come and gone. Remember Arthur Treacher's Fish & Chips? Yep, that started in Columbus, too, thanks to Wendy's Dave Thomas, who made his fortune as a Colonel Sanders Kentucky Fried Chicken franchisee. Makes me hungry just thinking about that battered British fish. Not that I regularly partake in any of these low-class foods myself. When I do it's just a guilty pleasure. Everyone has his occasional vice.

"Do you want anything?" Mia asks, her hand already opening the door.

"Fries?" I ask, just to get a reaction. It works.

"Honestly, Paul? I meant do you want water or coffee or something. You know how I feel about this so-called food. A poor diet leads to a shorter life, all the studies agree. I've been reading a lot about this, remember? I'm trying to get healthy and it wouldn't kill you to work on that, yourself." She leans forward and points her finger at me like I'm a child. I feel her eyes on my stomach. I suck in.

The magazine ruffles in the wind from the open door and the blonde female singer on the cover looks as if she's waving to me. She's cute, I notice. I reach out and smooth the cover with my hand, touching the cool, glossy paper.

My wife softens her tone. "I'll get you a water. Hydration is key to health," she adds and then slams the car door before I can reply. I watch her walk away. From behind, she looks like the same woman I married a decade ago. Her hair still swings halfway down her back. Her butt is small and firm and perfectly toned. She looks very much the same, but she's not. Not at all. None of us really stay the same, though, do we?

My transformation is more apparent, I realize, as I look down at my middle-aged, small beer belly and sigh. It's comprised of something called internal fat, I've discovered, a fat that appears suddenly, like an army of ghosts, and then digs in to stay. It's distasteful to think that fat isn't just sitting in a layer on top of my belly, like I'd imagined, but is actually tucked in beside all of my organs, oozing around them like it's a part of the whole, not an addition to the top. It's in the ice cream, it's not the cherry. Basically, they can't liposuction it off and they can't freeze it away. The only way I can shed this thing is through hard work—less food, more exercise.

I plan to tackle this unwanted midsection addition soon. It's next on my list. I'll eliminate it as I do anything I set my mind on. It's just a matter of willpower and mental fortitude. I've got those, don't worry. When I suck in my stomach, as I did for Mia, it doesn't follow my command, not nearly enough. I'm on it, soon.

Unlike me, in the last six months or so, Mia has really thinned out. She's shed the baby fat even though I swear she eats more, and more often, than I do. And though she looks fit, she's also a bit worried about the weight loss. I tell her that's crazy, most middle-aged women would die to have their weight melting away despite eating anything they like. And she looks good. She took up jogging a year or so ago, but cut back on that. Just doesn't have the stamina these days. Mostly, she uses the free weights in our basement. Sometimes she'll still walk around our block, if she has the energy.

Maybe she's so thin because she stopped eating meat—excuse me, "animal protein." That could be, but I attribute it more to stress; you know how parenting can take a toll on your intestines sometimes. Worry ties your system up in knots, or so I hear, not being prone to worry myself. They checked for ulcers, but she didn't have any. Just a mystery, I guess.

She even went to this one doctor who had her hold different vitamins and minerals in her hand, and then pushed on her arm. I mean really? What does that do? Spend your money is what. Mia came home with hundreds of dollars' worth of herbal treatments. None of it has helped, of course. She's big on drinking water now, too. Staying hydrated. She tries to drink only from glass bottles. *Good luck with that here, honey.*

Mia has pulled her hair into a ponytail, I notice. I can see her standing at the counter, placing her order. The other thing I see is the other customers, the men, checking her out. *Yes, guys, she still has it*, I confirm with a nod to myself while watching them all watch her. She is walking toward the car now, a plastic water bottle in each hand and a big tooth-whitened smile eclipsing her face. She was voted best smile in high school, and it's still there, that smile. Although it's bigger now, I suppose. Our gums recede with age, making all of us long of tooth, and Mia especially. But don't get me wrong, only I would notice such a thing. Her bright blue cotton sweater, blue jeans, and white tennis shoes make her stand apart from the rest of the people going in and out of the McDonald's parking lot. Everyone else seems more muted, a black, gray and navy composite of people dressed for business, farming or trucking. It's an eclectic yet monochromatic bunch this morning, except for my wife and her bright blue.

Mia pulls open the car door and slips inside. "Good choice. Cleanish bathroom. Short line. Here's your water," she says as she hands me the cold bottle. The plastic is cheap and crackles in my hands. It's the type of water bottle that will spill out half its contents when I open it, I know it is. The bottle will have a label explaining why this cheap, shitty plastic is better for the environment than any other, more sturdy plastic. I know it's just cheaper. I also know I should have gotten out of the car to open the bottle. I should have gotten out, just to stretch. Perhaps I should have gotten out of the car and opened the door for my wife. I'll do that when we stop for gas in a little while. We have all day and she could use a reminder that chivalry is alive and well thanks to Paul Strom.

"So you think Taylor Swift is cute, huh?" Mia asks as I pull out of the McDonald's parking lot.

"Who?" I ask. I know who the pop starlet is, everyone does. I even like her song, "The Story of Us." But why would my wife ask such a random question?

"I saw you checking out the cover." Mia holds up the gossip magazine while tilting her head. Her eyes are shining as if she has caught me drinking milk out of the jug. I love drinking milk out of the jug, but alas, if my wife catches me, it's that same disappointed, shiny-eyed look I receive. Usually, she adds a hand on the hip, but that's hard to execute in the front seat of a Ford Flex.

"Why would I check out some magazine when I could be checking out my beautiful wife?" I protest, pushing the accelerator hard to merge back onto the highway. I'm glad they finally finished the fifty-million-dollar project to widen this freeway to three lanes on either side. I slide back into the flow of traffic without a problem. They have spent more than a billion dollars on this road since it opened in the 1960s. What I would do for a billion dollars. Taylor Swift has a billion dollars, I'm sure. "She's a very talented young woman, but I had no idea that was her on the cover. They all look the same with the makeup and airbrushing and all."

"You've got a point there," she says. She has opened the

magazine on her lap, to a different story now I see. She twists open her bottle of water and, as I could have predicted, spills a fourth of it on the magazine. "Darn it."

How adorable. Mia's ban on swearing in front of the boys has resulted in this childlike response from my wife, even though the kids aren't around. I should tell her to express herself freely in my company.

Before I can think to stop her, she has popped open the glove compartment and she's rummaging around in it. "I don't have any napkins in there," I say quickly. I feel my palms begin to perspire. I check myself in the rearview mirror and notice my forehead is shiny, suddenly damp. It's so hard to keep secrets these days. People can find out anything, ruin all kinds of plans. Sometimes, all it takes is just opening the wrong door. "Just close that back up. Here…" I know my voice sounds terse but I can't help it. I reach into the back seat to grab my gray cotton sweater, and toss it into her lap. "Use this." My voice has returned to its normal tone. That pleases me.

"You're acting weird," she says, instead of *thanks*. I'm going to let it go, though. She doesn't know I have a surprise hidden in there, part of our special day. I can't tell her that so I say nothing as she mops up the magazine with my sweater. She could have simply ripped out those two pages. Maybe there is someone important in there. All I see is another guy with a two-day beard, sparkling brown eyes and a thick head of hair. Another Buck look-alike. There really aren't any men in her magazine that look like me, not now anyway. Actually, that's not quite true. I could give George Clooney a run for his money, and I'm taller, too. When I was younger, watch out world. I would have been on the cover, you know, Sexi-

est Man Alive, if I had wanted to be. But I hate all that celebrity garbage, as I told you.

"I'm going to call Claudia. Can I use your phone so it's on
Bluetooth? I want her to have the boys call us after school,
just to check in," Mia says. We have been gone for about an
hour so far. This is ridiculous.

"We haven't been driving for that long. The boys are at
school, and I guarantee you they're having too much fun with
their teachers and their little friends to spare us a thought. We
can call them this afternoon. We don't need to talk to Claudia." Sometimes my wife acts like the kids are still babies in
playpens. That bugs me; them, too. They're big guys, both
in elementary school. They'll be men before we know it. My
parents started treating me and my brother, Tom, like grown-
ups as soon as we started school. Dad wanted us to toughen
up, fend for ourselves, especially me since I was older. Ah,
the good old days. Speaking of Tom, I wonder if I should tell
Mia that I think Claudia is on drugs, but decide not to rev
her up further. "You need to relax, let go a little." I pat her
thigh for reassurance.

I feel her eyes on me. "I know. But the thing is, they're my
life. You encouraged me, begged me, not to work outside the
home, so I quit my job at the ad agency, the job I loved, and
built my whole world around the kids. They just don't need
me so much now that they're in school most of the day." Her
voice is quiet, her eyes shiny but this time it's because they
are filling with tears.

"You raised them well. Now it's time for them to learn in-
dependence so they can tackle the world. Boys pulling away
from their mommy is natural. It's how they become young
men," I say. "You still baby them too much. But that's part of
what makes you a great mom, the kind of mom I knew you

would be when we first discussed your staying home. Don't cry, honey." *Honey*, such an interesting word to apply to a person. I guess she is dripping, sappy, syrupy, her tears like actual honey drizzling from a spoon. "This is our weekend. The boys are fine." *With their druggie babysitter*, I don't add.

I flash Mia my biggest rectangle grin, adding my signature wink, the account-winning combination. It's the smile that launched a thousand new accounts for the advertising agency—until it didn't. I swallow, holding the smile to reassure Mia that this is a joyful day filled with fun. "This isn't a day for tears," I tell her softly. I am a kind, loving husband. I understand her pain, I do. "This is our special day, a day for reflection and for being thankful for everything we created. A day to enjoy being together."

"Of course," she says, taking a big drink of water from the crinkly plastic bottle. *Hypocrite.* She reads my mind, a wifely skill I can't say I'm overly fond of, and says, "They didn't have any glass bottles, Paul. I need to start grabbing my glass water bottles for road trips. I don't even know if I have any at the lake."

"I don't think you realized the peril of plastic water bottles last season," I comment mildly, and now she smiles.

"Well, you know I'm right," she says.

"Every woman's favorite phrase," I tease. We're back to happy ground, I notice. She's even tapping her right thumb on the bedraggled magazine, keeping time to one of our favorite songs, "Still the One."

Until.

"So how is Caroline doing? Still flirting with you?"

I take a deep breath and squeeze the steering wheel.

11:00 A.M.

3

I check my expression in the rearview mirror, forcing my face into a blasé look of nonchalance: mouth relaxed, shoulders down. Poker-face Paul. I inhale a deep breath. I've got this, I do, but then I feel the heat on my cheeks. I pretend to check the driver's side mirror.

"Caroline?" I ask, stalling for a moment as a shiny silver frame holding a photo of a smiling young couple thuds into my awareness. I shake my head, erasing it. My brain has enough to do. I must recollect everything I've uttered to my wife about Caroline, and the Thompson Payne office in general over the past few months. Then, like for one of Sam's first grade projects, I must sort what has been said into one pile and what hasn't been into another. This is an important exercise, best done on my terms, not hers. Too late for that, though.

"Your jaw is twitching," Mia says.

It's true. I unclench my jaw, sliding it back and forth. I take a deep breath and force a smile. This is disappointing, her observation of me. My skills are slipping. Not so poker-faced, after all, these days. I glance at my wife, who is smiling, presumably at my discomfort with this topic.

She adds, "So Caroline is still bothering you, huh?"

"No, not anymore," I say, speaking slowly to find the right words. "She's young. It's her first job. She just didn't know what is appropriate and what isn't, that's all."

"Everyone knows it's inappropriate to call your boss at home at midnight," Mia says. "Especially when you've been drinking."

"She was upset, Mia. I explained all of that." I check the side mirror and pass the stupid green Honda traveling at a snail's pace in front of us. It's almost time for the two-lane road, so I need to get this menace far behind me. "Her father died. She didn't know where else to turn."

Mia gives me the look that says she doesn't believe me, still. "So you turned her in to HR, but she's still working at Thompson Payne?" she asks, her fingers drumming on the car door handle. I maneuver the car back into the right lane.

"We don't fire people who need help, Mia. That's why we have human resources. It's their job to explain policies and help make people better employees." I feel my eyes narrowing. I do not like this topic. Just the fact that I had to speak of human resources brings an unpleasant event to mind. I shake off the remembered smell of Miracle-Gro and old cat.

Mia isn't backing off. "And we suggest these people who need help, people like Caroline who we have turned in to HR, to our wives as appropriate babysitters, do we? As part of some employee rehabilitation program?"

"Sarcasm doesn't suit you, honey. We were in a pinch, you and me, remember? And that was ages ago. I'm not sure why you'd bring it up today of all days," I say. I feel my jaw begin to clench again and rub the back of my neck with my left hand. I'd rather be talking about the strawberry daughters. I feel like I'm being squeezed too hard, and all the air is gone.

"Right," Mia says. "Best day ever, I know. I'll drop it. She still bothers me, though."

"Honey, I never even see her at the office." This is the absolute truth. I feel my jaw calming down as if someone released the vise around my head, relaxed the grip around my chest. Good old Thompson Payne. I've spent an inordinate amount of my life at those gleaming suburban offices. Much of my job has been to make sure everyone looks good to potential clients. Are the women wearing heels and short skirts? Are the guys clean-shaven and friendly, nonthreatening but cool? Advertising agencies are all about the sizzle, all about appearance instead of reality. Making a good first impression. And that's why yours truly was a perfect fit for director of client services. I am like the man in the top hat at the three-ring circus that is an advertising agency. I am the person running the show, communicating with overbearing clients and the crazy creative team attempting to serve them. Running interference between the staff and the partners who are never satisfied even with our vast successes. Do they think it just runs itself? Without me, everything falls apart, as they have no doubt discovered.

When John Larson left three years ago, an exit I'll admit I had a hand in, I transitioned into his role with ease. And I learned from his mistake. He had trusted me, made me into his number two. I make sure I never elevate any of the account executives reporting to me. They are all equal in my eyes. In fact, I make certain they feel equally unstable, that their jobs are at risk all the time. That keeps me in control.

I don't have a right-hand man. Don't need one. Never have. I know what you're thinking, for a sales guy I sound like a loner. The irony is that I do prefer to be alone, most of the time. People in general, employees in particular, can be more trouble than they're worth. Just ask good old John.

"Have you heard from John?" Mia asks, reading my mind for the second time today. I mentioned, didn't I, what I think of that particular talent? I turn to look at her but her face is calm, almost friendly, indicating the topic of Caroline is behind us, for now.

"No, not at all. Why the sudden interest in Thompson Payne, past and present?" We've arrived at the turnoff for the two-lane road. Once I exit the highway, I'll turn left, passing one of the iconic old barns that was painted white for the Ohio bicentennial. I worked on that campaign for the state, back when I was a lowly account executive. It was a good campaign. Full of government-funded perks like fancy meals at the taxpayers' expense, and a lot of time spent driving around and identifying old barns across the state. Perfect for me. A lot of alone time.

"Oh, well, I actually ran into John recently, at Whole Foods of all places. He's a vegetarian now and he looks really great. He's lost the beer belly," she tells me.

I'm making the turn onto the two-lane road as she says this, and I cannot take my eyes off the road to stare at her. I sense, however, that something is up. The tone of her voice has changed. It's thin. It's hiding something. The air sizzles between us. How long ago did she run into John? I wonder. How much did they talk, do they talk?

She adds, "He looks great. Says leaving Thompson Payne was the best thing for him. He started his own advertising agency, did you know that?"

Interesting. His noncompete must be up. He won't be a real threat to Thompson Payne for years, I know. He'll start by knocking off the small clients who don't get serious attention from the big guys like Thompson Payne, and then he'll work his way up the client food chain. It will be a decade or more before he reclaims his status, flying to New York or LA for commercial shoots. I pity him, poor man.

"Good for him," I say. I do wish him well, of course. Nice guy, actually. He was simply in the way.

I hear my wife take a deep breath, an annoying sound, but I'm focusing on my barn. We're passing it now, two red silos behind it, green fields, no doubt Roundup Ready soybean, for as far as you can see behind it. Everything here is as it should be, orderly, symmetrical and productive. A beautiful farm. Perfection through pesticides and genetic modification. If only people were so easily controlled. Mia is droning on about John.

"After we ran into each other, he invited me to tour his agency. He even asked if I'd consider doing some project work for him, you know, copywriting and some press releases. Just something part-time since, as you said, the boys are in school all day and don't really need me anymore. Or as much, I should say."

This road is dangerous. I need to use my full attention to navigate. She knows this, and that's why she dropped this bomb during this stretch of the drive. I glance over and see her hands clasped tightly together in her lap, her ring sparkling like the edge of a knife when the light hits it just right. I have been holding my breath, I realize, and I let it out with a sigh.

Mia cannot get back into the advertising business—now is not the time. "No, that won't work," I say. I know my tone is firm, my voice deep and powerful. My stage voice, that's what I think of it as. When I was young, in high school, I loved performing in the school plays. Mrs. Belt, my drama teacher, said I had serious acting chops; she thought I would be a star someday. I guess I could have been. I had the looks, the talent. The road not taken, I suppose. "The kids do need you, honey. They're just acting as if they don't."

"I've decided I'm going to take him up on his offer. I'll work from home while the boys are at school," she says. Defiance is making her voice shake. "I need to exercise my brain again. I almost didn't tell you, but we're having such a nice drive, and it's a beautiful day. It seemed like the perfect moment. Don't let this bother you, okay?"

I don't say a word, a silent protest. Inside I feel heat, a flame igniting. We cannot ever predict what our supposed partner is really up to, can we? Even the best of plans can be ruined. That is why I must stay nimble, attempt flexibility. Not my strong suit. I'll remain calm and later I'll squash this foolish notion of Mia's like a cockroach. I'm sure she doesn't really mean this, that's why her voice shakes. She's in unfamiliar territory. This boldness is not like her. And I don't like it, not at all.

My wife clears her throat, and says, "John told me there's so much change in the advertising industry in town. He's heard all kinds of crazy things."

She pats my leg then and I almost jump. A chill runs through me and I grip the wheel. This is a challenge, I know it, but how and when did Mia become so confident? Where did she come from, this new Mia? And what, exactly, does she know?

11:30 A.M.

4

Mia's phone rings and she takes the call. From her end of the conversation, I know it is Claudia. They are talking weekend plans for the boys, I am sure. I tune her out and I take a moment to breathe.

If she already knows the truth, then why isn't she just coming out and asking me about it, demanding the information? This new, confident Mia certainly seems like she would just blurt it out. This is a surprising development, a stronger Mia. This is not my typical Mia—I know my wife. Therefore, she's poking around the edges of things she doesn't quite understand, things John Larson couldn't possibly know about. She must have a few facts, and they've emboldened her. They know nothing. My wife knows what I tell her, nothing more. I take a deep breath and remind myself to relax. Everything is fine. John Larson will not be able to turn my wife against me, no matter how much he dislikes me.

To be fair, John has every reason to hold a grudge. I'll admit it now. I set him up for his fall. He was once my mentor at the advertising agency, as I explained. He hired me during one of the most trying times of my life, when I'd just arrived back in town from Nashville. He believed in me, all those years ago. And I respected him, too. He was also the one who introduced me to Mia.

I smile at the memory of our first meeting, Mia Pilmer sitting at the glass-topped conference room table, her blond hair shining, her eyes bright and smart. Her long legs accentuated by a tight short black skirt. You could appreciate everything through that glass top, and there was a lot to appreciate with Mia back then. John had told me Mia was the best copywriter on the creative team, surprisingly one of the best he'd ever read, even though she was just out of college and so very young. Eventual creative director and perhaps even partner material, he had said. Thompson Payne and Pilmer it would be someday, John predicted. She was a product of New York University, at least a decade my junior, and from a wealthy New York City family. She was smart, beautiful, pure. The minute I took the chair next to hers, accidentally on purpose bumping my thigh against her leg under the conference table, I knew she was the one. I could feel the electricity zipping between us, drawing us together for all time.

Mia felt the physical attraction, too. I saw her blush as she shyly turned away from me at the conference table. Her mind, on the other hand, took some convincing. It was a sales job, one might say.

John, though, he and I hit it off right from the start. I guess the problem was simply this: at some point, we both knew I was the right man for his job. But he wasn't going anywhere. The partners weren't going to make him a partner, there would be no *& Larson* stenciled on the glass wall, they told him. So he was stuck, poor John. Eventually, I needed to help him move on. I was happy to be of service.

"Claudia says the credit card doesn't work," Mia says now, shaking her head at me and covering the phone. "What is she supposed to use to buy groceries? She had to leave the bags at the customer service desk at Kroger. Told them she'd be back to pay. This is embarrassing, Paul."

"Just tell her to use her credit card and I'll pay her when we get back," I say. I am a logical problem solver.

"Paul, she's a college student. We can't ask her to do that." The muscles on the side of her neck are taut, like rubber bands about to snap. I am wearing my calm, reasonable poker face again. Of course I knew the card wouldn't work, but Mia is understandably surprised. I hope she keeps her head on. I cannot stand it when Mia starts whining and worrying. It's beneath her, beneath us.

"When we get to the lake, I'll transfer money to the card. It will work by this afternoon. Okay?" It is my turn to pat her leg. She ignores the gesture and conveys the message to the overtired Claudia. I watch as she presses End on her phone with an overt display of melodramatic disgust. *Really?* She's acting like a child. It's only groceries. Big deal. It's not like the boys will starve. Our pantry is full of perfectly fine food. We have frozen organic macaroni and cheese lining the freezer. This is ridiculous. Neither the boys nor Mia understand what it feels like to be hungry, to be deprived: to open the door to an empty refrigerator, an empty pantry. So what if they don't have their first choice of snacks for the weekend?

"Paul, honestly. That's the only thing I asked you to do to get ready for the whole weekend. Leave enough cash, or enough credit at least, for the weekend. This is unacceptable," she says. She is rubbing the back of her neck, trying to loosen the rubber bands, I presume. I imagine her shoulders knotted with worry. It's sad, really, how the little things can get to her so easily. It's not uncommon lately. She's filled with anxiety these days, it seems. She's worried about the boys, about her health, the gutters getting cleaned, the recycling being taken out, about, well everything. Wouldn't it be ironic if all this worry is the cause of the weight loss? I've told her that's my theory.

Nothing I can say will make the situation better, so instead I turn up the music as Amy Winehouse belts out "You Know I'm No Good." I love this song, this whole playlist, and I know Mia does, too. Next up, Dinah Washington's "Cold, Cold Heart."

"Can we switch to the radio?" Mia asks. And then before I can answer, a static-ridden local station bursts into my ears, a country crooner hurting my psyche. No matter how often I explain to Mia that jazz is the highest musical form and country the lowest, still she tortures me.

The hairs on the back of my neck bristle as this stupid hick song fills the car. I'll bear it, though. We're in the middle of nowhere, about thirty minutes from the bakery where we'll stop and check for croissants. *It would be so wonderful if the universe leaves me some croissants today.* It doesn't seem that much to ask. I need Mia to relax and back off on the questioning. Perhaps baked goods will help. I'll suggest she eat a croissant or two rather than saving them all for breakfast. There's something to be said for instant gratification every once in a while. And then if she's happy, she'll turn my music back on.

I can't stop myself. I reach for the radio, punch some buttons; this whining country music is all I can tune in. This will please Mia as she is a country music fan. I had my fill of it when I lived in Nashville, thank you very much. Right about now I'm wondering why I discontinued the Sirius radio subscription in the Flex, a bad move when it comes to the middle of nowhere. Now I'm at the mercy of whatever station comes into range unless Mia switches back to my lovingly made playlist. A shame, really.

The country singer is the only one making a sound. The silence between us is thudding in my head. I didn't want today to be like this. It occurs to me that now would be a good time to apologize. The road is clear ahead, and I haven't had to pass anyone for miles.

"Hey, Mia. I'm sorry," I say. "That was my fault. I'll fix it, pay off the card as soon as we get to the cottage. Claudia will be able to use it this afternoon, pick up the groceries. All's well. In the meantime, relax. Enjoy the music. Everything is going to be fine."

Mia has pushed her sunglasses up on her head. She looks over at me with squinted eyes, probably a defense against the bright sunlight. She is staring at me like you would a spider making a web at your doorway, with both amazement and fear.

"What?" I say, not liking the look in her eyes. She usually gazes at me with such confidence, such love. Something has shattered that; someone or something has changed her opinion of me, I realize. *How did this happen and when?* I knew things were going to change, had to change as a matter of fact. I have a plan to handle it, of course.

Right at this moment I wonder what Mia sees in me. Does she still see the sophisticated older man of the world she pledged to love, honor and obey a decade ago? Does she still feel my experienced touch, does she remember everything I taught her about sex, about love? Does she still appreciate my encyclopedic knowledge of fine food and wine, does she dream of traveling with me to the exotic places I tell her I've visited? It's too bad we didn't make time to travel a bit, but the boys came along so quickly and, well, her place was in the home. I am no longer sure what she is thinking when she looks at me, not at all. But more than what she sees in me, it's what I see in her that I do not appreciate. I shake my head. This was supposed to be the best day, and it's deteriorating, decaying like the memories of childhood. You still have a sense of what it was like to be a kid, but the feeling of jumping into a swimming pool on a carefree summer day has faded. And you can never get that back.

Mia pulls her sunglasses back down and covers the squint. She folds her arms across her chest and says, "We're almost to the bakery. Do you have money for croissants?"

NOON

5

The bakery is closed. Croissants sold out. Even from far away, I can tell Mia is fuming, her hands in fists on her hips, but as she turns back toward the car she forces a smile on her face. She'll get over it, I remind myself. After I suffer through half an hour of hick country music for the remainder of the drive to the cottage, we'll be back to being cordial again as we drive through the gates of Lakeside. She is happy there. Once we have arrived, she'll forgive me for our late start. As we unpack, I will play some jazz, a far superior song structure than this simplistic insult to music blaring through the car radio at present. All will be well once we arrive. Marriage: it's a give-and-take. One day, I get my way, the next, I do something nice for my wife. It's how it goes. I reach deep into my patience well and find it's almost dry. Almost.

It's never ideal when I run totally dry, trust me. Plenty of people in my past found that out the hard way. But I'm more mature now, I don't let myself get that depleted. I know how to soothe myself, I know what, and who, I need. And I usually get what I want. I'm sure you've figured that out already.

The good news with the detour to this strip mall in the town of Port Clinton is that I am at last getting to stretch my legs. When I finally parked the car and we climbed out, I realized my back was seizing up on me. I ignore this old-man type of physical pain, just as I ignore cashiers and parking lot attendants. They are all a bother, beneath my wasting a breath or thought on.

The fresh air feels good, crisp and clean. Although you can't see the lake from here, you can feel the water's presence like you do when it's about to rain. There's just something in the air that's thicker, moist and heavy, like a humidifier on a dry winter's night. There are cars towing boat trailers parked near us. Bumper stickers proudly proclaim the town as the Walleye Capital of the World, although I read they lost that distinction lately. Life: it's transitory. And in life, there are always winners and losers. It's nice to be a winner.

"How about getting some ice cream, honey?" I say as Mia returns with a frown on her face. She wanted to make certain the bakery was closed by walking across the parking lot, even though we could plainly see from here that nobody was inside and there were chairs on the tables. I guess she likes torturing herself, pressing her nose against the front window of the darkened shop, like a puppy hoping to get adopted at the shelter. Just like most of those puppies, the odds weren't in her favor. She lost.

"We missed them by fifteen minutes. They close at 11:30," she says. I don't correct her and point out that it's actually already noon. "I don't feel like ice cream right now."

"Not even Toft's?" It's a famous ice cream parlor from Ohio's oldest dairy. I smile thinking about the bright blue Toft's sign, the ridiculous sculpture of a cow wearing sunglasses inside a white wooden pen in the parking lot, the smell of vanilla beans and strawberries when you step inside the door. We have spent many an afternoon on the outside patio with the boys, ice cream dripping onto the round blue tables while they tried to lick every drop before it melted. My mouth is watering just thinking about a scoop of Java Chip. In a bowl, not a cone. With bowls, you're always in control.

"Not even Toft's. Besides, dairy is bad for you, you know that. It's mucus. Perfect for baby cows but that's all," Mia says, opening the door to the Flex. If the car hadn't been between us, I know she would have shot a glance at my belly. I hate that. "I would like a salad or something, though. Do you think the restaurants are open in Lakeside?"

Our eyes meet across the top of the Flex. She looks small, and no longer as angry. I feel like a large disappointment. I hate that feeling. She is waiting for an answer. I am preparing for country music mush through the speakers as my penance.

"Yes, I checked. Everything is open. We can eat in Lakeside," I say with gusto. I'm suddenly very hungry, and I hope food will fix the hollow feeling forming in the pit of my stomach. "I'm sort of craving Sloopy's pepperoni pizza about now." I open the car door and slide back behind the steering wheel.

"Pizza is a terrible choice, Paul." Mia clicks her seat belt into place. I see her look at my stomach as she adds, "Processed meat, dairy—well, whatever. It's your life."

"They have salads, too," I say. I know I sound defensive. I just can't have her ruin my favorite pizza joint, too. I give her the freedom to eat as she pleases, so I deserve the same respect, don't I? She gets to eat and do whatever she wants all day long, and all I ask for is just that: respect. "You are ruining food for me."

"Maybe that's not such a bad thing," she says. She thinks it's funny. She finds another of her favorite country music stations and turns the sound up. I fight the urge to roll my eyes. Or punch the button to start the playlist, our playlist with the Police's "Every Breath You Take" up next. That is the music we should be listening to instead of this. I keep both hands on the wheel but it takes willpower. Marriage, I remind myself again, is a give or take. I'll give now, so I can take charge later. We're so close to Lakeside. I can handle this.

Now I know who this new Mia is reminding me of: working girl Mia. The woman I met at Thompson Payne in the conference room. Confident. Sharp. Later, once we'd begun dating, she told me she'd never been in love before me, not really. And I told her what I told you: I knew we were perfect for each other from the moment we met. As long as she could become the wife I was looking for, of course.

She was the most beautiful person I'd ever met back then. Physical perfection she's retained to this day, with the exception of the baby fat years, as I've noted. I poured on the Paul Strom charm, asking her to dinner that very afternoon. John had told me the company policy, of course. But no one paid any attention to policy like that, especially when it involved agency superstars like I knew I would become. I dropped by her office; it was a late afternoon in September and the sun was already making its way to the horizon. I knocked on her open door and she looked up. When a faint blush began circling her cheeks, I knew she was mine.

"Do you have plans for dinner tonight?" I said, leaning against the doorway. I was wearing a new designer suit, navy, with a crisp white shirt and a red power tie. I knew I looked good. Her office was messy, a typical creative desk, strewn with rough sketches and preliminary layouts for ads; storyboards for television spots were tacked to the cork-covered wall on her right. The only non-work-related item on her desk was a framed eight-by-ten photo of her parents, who were notable Manhattan movers and shakers I already knew from my research. The only surprise: her office had a window as big as mine. That meant the partners were wooing her, though not the way I was, of course.

Behind her desk, Mia blinked those big blue eyes.

"I was thinking Diamond's, the new restaurant in German Village. I haven't been yet, but I hear it's fabulous. I should be able to get us a great table." I managed to employ my smile-wink right then and I saw she was interested. It was the chemistry in the air, that zing of electricity rushing between us. And we had barely touched yet. I felt an attraction to Mia that was foundational, at some cellular level. I knew she sensed it, too.

"Sounds good," she said. "I hope to be finished with this ad by six, seven at the latest."

"I'll make the reservation for seven thirty. Shall we meet there or can I give you a ride?" I was hoping she would let me pick her up and drive her to the restaurant. I had a sporty two-seater black Audi back then, a convertible. She would look fabulous sitting beside me, I remember thinking. And then there was the anticipation of walking her to the door, of being asked inside. But it didn't happen.

"I'll meet you there. Thanks, Paul," she said, blinking again, the color still in her cheeks. She tapped a pencil on her desk. She needed to get back to work, I realized.

"See you tonight," I told her, disappointed I'd be arriving alone. I was hopeful I wouldn't be leaving by myself after dinner. I was officially smitten. I knew I would do everything in my power to make Mia realize what a catch I was, too. It was time for my best moves, my most charming seduction. Of course I would succeed, I always do. When you've got it, you've got it. I'm not bragging, really, I'm just telling you there are some things I'm really good at and this—women— is one of them.

At dinner, I continued my offensive. When the chocolate crème brûlée arrived, you should have seen her face.

"This is my favorite dessert," she said, clapping her hands as they slid the decadent custard in front of her at the table. "How did you know?"

It's funny the things you can learn on the internet, the little details that can betray so much about a person if only you know where to look. Like pictures on a society magazine's website—a lovely young woman at a banquet with her wealthy parents, dainty dishes of a certain decadent dessert on the tables in front of them. I've never been one to pass up the opportunity to glean information on the people in my life—colleagues, clients, business rivals. Women. You never know, do you, when a trivial bit of background might turn the tide in your favor. But I could hardly tell Mia any of that; it was our first date, after all. Instead I smiled, gave her the signature wink and said, "A lucky guess."

With the pleasant memory of a Mia who savored her desserts fresh in my mind, I have succeeded in tuning out the horrible country music bombarding my brain and focus instead on the happiness I feel driving into Lakeside without having to pay a fee. The gates don't drop until Memorial Day weekend. I smile as I drive the Flex, too quickly per the posted 15 Miles per Hour sign, into our blissful little retreat. Whenever I drive into this place, with its charming cottages, most with rocking chairs dotting their porches, this community with its vast stretches of green-grass parks and big blue sky and water views, I'm reminded that I've made it. I know everything will be fine, no matter what the future brings. I've always believed that. Mia still loves me. I take a deep breath, sucking in pure Americana.

Enjoy the drive, I tell myself, noticing the little cottages in pink and white and red and green lining the street, with their tulip flags flapping, their cement geese dressed for spring. Enjoy driving through this picturesque Eden, heading toward Lake Erie, a lake so shallow all of the water turns over every two and a half years. Bet you didn't know that.

Did you know if you didn't put your foot on the brake as you came to the end of this street, you'd drive across some bright green grass, over the dark sand beach and into the water, ending up at the bottom of the shallowest Great Lake in the United States?

It's still deep enough to kill you, of course.

12:30 P.M.

6

I turn right and, lucky us, find a parking spot, the universe making up for the croissants. This is the way this day is supposed to go, smoothly, joyously. Now that we are finally here in Lakeside all will be well. Except for the fact that it's crowded. This is unexpected. I imagined we would find Lakeside deserted, like an old Western town after the gold rush. But that isn't the case.

I can see from the street that Sloopy's Sports Café is bustling with midwestern vacationers, no doubt mostly from Ohio, enjoying the first sunny weekend in May. On the surprisingly busy main street of town I see men wearing sports shorts and T-shirts, T-shirts that will change to wifebeater tank tops when the weather heats up. Many of the guys who vacation here love the Cleveland Indians and the Ohio State Buckeyes. They'll tuck a football they carried to lunch onto the seat of the booth beside them, and play pass with their kids after lunch. They will be upset, very upset, if their sons don't throw a perfect spiral by age ten. I know from experience, trust me.

The women wear stretchy yoga pants or tennis clothes, although I don't agree with that look unless you are thin. If you aren't a thin woman, you should wear a dress. A loose-fitting dress that will cover all your excess, that will hide your sins. The kids are hyper, just like my boys are when they're here. They'll agree to sit with their parents only long enough to gobble a pizza slice and then they're off, enjoying the freedom of youth in a place where nothing bad ever happens. The smattering of youngsters I see on the sidewalk look sticky and sweaty, like they could use a long shower.

I cover my disdain for my fellow Ohioans behind my poker face and sunglasses. I shouldn't be surprised that Mia and I aren't the only ones hoping for a peaceful weekend getaway, but I am. I'd relied on my memory of last year's preseason visit, but perhaps it was in April. But it's fine. I'll adjust.

You have to be nimble if you want to get anywhere in life, that much I've learned. Take my early courtship of Mia, for instance. Sure, the first date had gone well, but I was aware that I needed to step up my game. Mia Pilmer was accustomed to the best money could buy and I knew she could smell a pretender deep in her soul. I waited a whole two days before I asked her out again, let her memory of our first date, our first chaste kiss, settle in her heart. And then, when we "just happened" to find ourselves on the elevator alone, I asked her to dinner at the finest restaurant in town for Friday night. Of course she said yes, and of course I surprised her by ordering foie gras. "My favorite. You are full of surprises, Mr. Strom."

I like to think I still am. It's a gift, this ability to anticipate people's needs. I can't say I didn't enjoy being one step ahead of my young wife-to-be. Soon enough, everything Mia enjoyed when she listened to my stories of foreign travel and television shoots in exotic locations, everything she liked that she thought she saw in me, I became. It's who I am now, with her. It's who we are together.

Sloopy's is located in downtown Lakeside, nestled on a corner of Second Street, part of a quaint block of storefronts in an old brick building. I pull open the forest green–framed screened door and usher Mia inside in front of me. There's a crowd standing in the doorway. She shrinks back into me, away from the large, muscle-shirt-wearing man in front of her. It's nice to feel her body against mine. My heart surges with love. I wrap my arm around her waist and hold her tight. As I inhale her familiar floral scent I can imagine us making love as soon as we get to the cottage.

We will hold hands as we walk up to the front door and I'll hurry to unlock the door, pulling her inside our second home behind me. It makes me hot just thinking about it. I'll slip my arms around her waist, pull her close to me as I lean in for a kiss. She'll press against me, opening her lips, as I feel her knees buckle. I'll swoop her up in my arms and carry her to the couch in the family room. It's new, we haven't even broken it in that way, the way we would have when we first met, when the attraction was stronger than common sense. The thought makes me smile.

A sweaty guy in a white tank top and green apron waves some plastic-coated menus in the air in our direction, and says, "Over here."

I squeeze Mia's waist and whisper in her ear, "Do I know how to wine and dine my wife in style, or what?"

Mia laughs, perhaps her first genuine laugh of the day, as I walk behind her to a corner booth, perfect for two. Perfect as long as you're both thin, I should say, trying to slide into my bright red seat, barely clearing my stomach under the Formica tabletop bolted to the wall and draped with a green-and-white-checkered plastic tablecloth. I'll breathe shallowly and be fine. I like this corner booth, even though it is sized for tweens, my back to the wall. I can see everyone coming and going. I might not be sporting a tank top revealing my guns, but don't worry. I can protect my wife from whatever could possibly come our way.

The walls and ceiling are painted green and someone has hammered a white lattice checkerboard pattern on the walls. The place is dripping with sports memorabilia. Ohio State football dominates, alongside mementos from any other Ohio sports team the Sloopy's staff deems worthy. They know their customer here, that's for sure. Ohio State and the rest of the pennants are a vibrant and colorful scarlet and gray contrast with the green-and-white decor. It's a look that couldn't be replicated but somehow works in this small restaurant. It comes across as quaint and, at this moment, extremely cozy—especially around my midsection. I should listen to Mia more when it comes to my diet.

"Good call," Mia says, seeming to relax. She smiles her big smile and looks at my belly. "Are you okay in this booth? You look a little snug."

I'm going to consider her comment a show of concern, not snark. "I'm fine. It was nice holding you. We should do that more often," I say. I almost believe I see the circle blush on her cheeks, almost.

"Mmm," she says as a specials menu is dropped on the table. The waitress who tossed it appears to be a student from an area high school. Charming hot-pink stripes streak through her long brown hair. She has a tattoo circling her right wrist and a shiny round nose ring in her left nostril. I wouldn't let her come home looking like this, not if she were my daughter. I wouldn't let her come over if she was a friend of one of my sons. It's a good thing I just had boys. Yes, I know boys can get tattoos, dye their hair and pierce various appendages. Mine won't.

"What can I bring you two to drink?" she asks. If she were chewing gum, the whole effect would be complete.

"An iced tea, please," Mia says. "No sugar. No sweetener."

"Same for me," I say, although what I really want is a Tito's Vodka on the rocks, no fruit. But alas, Lakeside is dry, so I must wait until I'm inside my cottage to have a drink. Yes, it's a dry community filled with drinkers. We just carry our roadies around in plastic cups and pretend it's Coke. The hypocrisy is amusing, and somehow, right. Unfortunately, it's only noon. Back in the heyday of advertising, long after *Mad Men*, but before the advent of more human resources–driven rules, hours-long liquid lunches were the name of the game. It was what you did to entertain clients, land accounts or just hang out with the other guys. Those were the days.

Of course, if you were trying to work your way up, as I was in the early days of Thompson Payne, you never actually drank as much as you seemed to be drinking. No, you made sure your boss's glass was never empty, you were quick to light the end of his cigar and you always told the funniest jokes. I kept John laughing up until the door swung closed on his face. It's just what you do in advertising.

"How old do you think she is?" Mia asks, clearly referring to the pink-striped creature fetching our tea.

"Likely only in high school, still living at home, terrifying her parents, who have lost all control of her. Scary, right?" I say. I'm finding it harder to breathe in this booth, the more I think about teenagers and tattoos and project both onto my little boys. My boys as teenagers is something I've imagined with an equal mix of hope and dread. They already know, even at six and eight, they would never be allowed to come home with a tattoo. They know my rules, at least as much as I can impart at these ages. No tattoos. No girlfriends who have tattoos. No swearing. No back-talking. Ever. Throw the football like a man, a perfect spiral. Always. They live in a dictatorship, not a democracy. End of story.

"I don't think she's scary, Paul. Just finding her identity. She's portraying her individualism through outward expressions, like tattoos and unique hair color. I wish I had been bold enough to do that in high school, or well, ever," she says. We are silent as the girl places the plastic cups of tea in front of us. Mia is lost in thought, thinking of all the small rebellions she should have taken part in during her youth. Hopefully, she is forgetting the ones she alluded to during the drive. She really should just let all of those ideas go. For both of us. For the best day ever. She tosses her sticky, plastic-coated menu on the table.

And adds, "I was such a good girl. Always trying to please. First my parents, then you. I never got to rebel."

"I just don't see you with a nose piercing," I say. I'm trying to sound breezy, carefree, but in my head a little bell of alarm is ringing again. *Of course you were the good girl, that's why we connected so strongly, at the cellular level. We were perfect for each other, still are in many ways.* My alarm bell is in overdrive; I'm overthinking everything because Mia spoke to John. I need to settle down, yet the prickle of pre-Lakeside unease remains. Why, I'm not certain. It doesn't matter, not really. It's just mildly disconcerting, this defiance Mia is verbalizing, has been demonstrating during our drive and continues now. Her little rebellion, stirred up by my former business associate, I suppose. How sweet. How frustrating.

Mia says, "It isn't about piercings or tattoos. It's about not being a reflection of what someone else wants you to be. You probably don't understand what I'm saying. You've always been so sure of who you are, what you want."

"I couldn't imagine living any other way, actually," I say. I wonder if she is asking me for something, for some understanding. Some type of compassion or empathy. I'm not good at those emotions, or, if we're being honest, any emotion except anger. Rage lurks deep inside me, ready to lash out whenever it's needed. But for those other, more feminine feelings, I have to fake my expressions. I taught myself how to imitate the look people have when they are feeling sad, for example. The corners of the mouth droop, the eyes fill with water. Back when we were first getting serious, when I'd convinced her I was the one, Mia told me I sometimes seemed to be on a five-second delay, like a live broadcast where the director thinks something censor-worthy might happen so they leave room for the bleep.

She was being funny, of course.

"Mia," I explained at the time. "There's a difference between not expressing things and not feeling them. Remember me, Poker-face Paul? It's a blessing and a curse. I'm a guy. It's how we are, genetically. You know, hard on the outside, soft on the inside. The delay, honey, is all in your pretty little head."

We were out to dinner, another rather fancy place that has since gone out of business, French I believe. Mia looked at me over the flickering white taper candle and said, apropos of nothing, "You don't seem to be listening, Paul."

I was stumped, of course. I had been listening, listening

closely, but what I hadn't been doing was showing her I was listening. A mistake. But I had no idea what had brought this up. Everything was wonderful. Sex, dinners, everything. What I'd been reflecting on, when she'd surprised me with her random observation, was the fabulous sex we'd had just that morning. It was amazing, once I'd unlocked the key to her sexuality, so to speak. The physical passion she'd been missing in her sterile, privileged upbringing, well, it was to be expected of the rich. They're nothing if not stiff. But now, behind closed doors, my Mia was free of all those silly inhibitions, at least most of them. But why this?

"What, is something wrong?" I'd grabbed my wineglass, taking a big gulp.

"Remember, I told you my mom's best friend died this morning? She was like a second mom to me." Yes, yes, I remembered, but mostly I remembered the sex. It had started out as my way of providing comfort, but it's safe to say I'd successfully distracted her from any focus but me. At least, I'd thought I had.

I noticed Mia's eyes filling with tears. She was sad. I hadn't remembered to carry that emotion with me all day at the office, on her behalf. I should have cradled her lovingly after sex and told her how sorry I was about that woman who died. I should have walked into the restaurant with a frown on my face, my head tilted down with sadness. "I'm sorry, Mia. I completely forgot." I reached across the table and patted her hand. On cue, my eyes glistened with sadness.

She seemed to consider me, tilting her head. The sadness had been replaced with something different, something I couldn't read. I needed to change the subject. "Hey, so when is the funeral? I'd like to go with you."

Mia snapped back to sadness, leaned forward, and reached

for my hand. I'd said the right thing. Of course I had. "I'd like that. It's this Friday. And you can meet my mom and dad, too."

Shit. I'd convinced her of my hidden emotional depths, but now I had agreed to fly home with her. I'd known I had to get that over with one way or another. Maybe a funeral would distract them all. I liked the focus to be anywhere but on me in these types of situations, when I was setting the bait but hadn't yet hooked my prize catch. The fewer people involved the better, I'd learned, but it was too late. I was headed to a funeral in New York, and an encounter with her parents. Remember, I am nimble, always in control. I played it to my best advantage, as always.

At home these days, I am king of our castle and my queen needs to fall back in line. It's a bit late for Mia to be contemplating finding herself. What could she possibly find that I don't already provide? She knows that I'm all about a traditional family and that I will take care of her and the boys. I'm all about action, like a superhero. I'm about planning, achieving and success. And protection. I protect her and the kids from any harm that could come their way. From grandparents and babysitters, from stray dogs and jealous neighbors. We're superior. They know that, Mia and the boys. Especially my boys. I've told them since they were tiny. They are my life, my future.

Across the table from me, my wife's hair looks almost white in the bright sunlight shining through the Sloopy's window. She's lovely. But something's wrong.

"All this talk of rebellion. Are you trying to tell me something, Mia?" I ask. I watch as she drops her eyes, suddenly fascinated with the menu. She's hiding something. Her eyes give her away. After a moment, she looks up at me.

"No, Paul. I was just having a friendly conversation, that's all. And speaking of friends, have you talked to Richard or Tony lately?" she asks. She has flipped over the shiny menu, no doubt on the hunt for the lowest calorie offering. *Why is she asking about old high school and college friends?* It's strange. These days, I don't have friends, per se. I'm a family man now.

Mia adds, "I mean, whenever I see Ohio State stuff, I think about them. You and Richard were tight back in high school, you told me. Same with Tony during college. I remember both of them being at our wedding. I don't think we've seen them since. My old friends and I manage a phone call now and then. I know it's hard, with kids, to keep really connected. Most of my friendships have suffered since we married. But do you guys talk, catch up? Does Richard still live in Grandville? Is Tony in Nashville?"

In high school and college, you're supposed to hang out with friends. Act like buddies, do guy things together. When you graduate, you get a job and get married. That's what you do. Until your bride-to-be tells you that you need groomsmen for the wedding and then you pull a couple out of the past like a pop-up retail store, only open for a small window of time.

"I'm not sure. I've lost track of them," I say. "Why could this possibly matter? That was the past. This is our perfect now." She is stirring the pot. It's not wise.

"Just wondering," she says as the scary waitress appears at our booth. She taps her pencil on her pad of paper, the noise an annoying beat on my temple.

Why hasn't my wife shown any interest in my so-called friends before now? Why do they matter? They never did. High school is something to get through, get past, to get on with life. College fraternities, like where I met good old Tony, well, let's be frank, they are a means to an end. Get into a good one, despite your lack of legacy, and you're set. At least I was. The "guys" all had some notion that I was a legacy Sigma Chi. Suddenly I was one of the top rushees—me, a guy from nowhere, from no one. Insane. I have no idea how they got that idea in the first place. Well, maybe I do. But it worked. I used it to my benefit for four years and when I graduated, I was more than happy to leave that whole drunken mess behind me. All except what I picked up in one of my favorite classes, Greek Mythology, that is. Some things in Nashville were very good, at least in the beginning.

"What'll you have?" asks our waitress, the Ghost of Teenagers Future. She terrifies me.

"The Cobb salad. Dressing on the side. No ham, no turkey, no bacon. Just the tomatoes and eggs and no cheese," Mia says.

Pink hair and I both roll our eyes. I discover I like her a little.

"I'll take a small pepperoni pizza, extra cheese," I say and my stomach growls appropriately. "Make it a medium."

I wonder again why Mia brought up my friends from another life. I'm concerned about all these questions. They are throwing me off. So far today, she's asked me about my former boss, John, a coworker, Caroline, and now Richard and Tony. Something is up.

"Why all the questions today, honey?" I ask. Best to address the elephant in the booth. And then I'll tackle this ridiculous notion of my wife getting a job and working for John, of all people.

"Oh, I didn't realize I was asking that many, actually," Mia says with a smile. Not the orange slice–smile of happiness, though. She's bothered, troubled. Is it the way my stomach is dented by the booth or is it something more, something deeper than my visceral fat? I'm not certain, but I know I'm once again on guard. Mia dabs her eye with a thin paper napkin. "Sorry. It just seems like it's been a while since we've talked."

Has it? I believe we talk frequently. It's hard, with the boys, but still, we talk. I try to hurry out the door in the morning, true. And then, when I'm home for dinner, it's more kid talk at the table. In bed, we both read, or watch TV. Maybe she's right. We speak in surface pleasantries, but there's nothing wrong with that. I feel her watching me.

"Honey, we talk more than a lot of couples," I say. But I wonder if that is true. I do know that lately I have been attempting to talk very little, to be helpful manually, physically with the boys, but to maintain distance emotionally. That is not hard for me. I would never share what is in my busy mind with anyone, most especially Mia. I don't enjoy reflecting on how much I do or don't communicate with anyone. The less said the better; the less that is repeated about you around town, the fewer things the gossips have to share. It's inevitable, though, that people will talk about me and my family. We're enviable: the successful businessman, his beautiful younger wife and their two cherubic sons, living on the best street in the best suburb. It's a shame, really, because when your life gets enviable it stirs up those gossips.

Mia looks like she's about to give her rebuttal when Teenage Nightmare appears and drops Mia's salad in front of her and my pizza, with a plunk of tin, in front of me. It smells heavenly. Pepperoni pizza is the scent of happiness and escape. It's what you get to eat when you're having fun, when you don't have worries about weight or money or anything more than what's on television tonight. Pizza is bliss in my book.

I take a big bite of bliss. I feel grease dripping down my chin. This pizza tastes so good I'm tempted to keep eating instead of using my napkin. Sloopy's chef won an international award, traveled to Italy to compete over this pizza. I savor the bite but I do wipe my face.

Mia picks up where we left off. "How would you know if we talk more than other couples? What friends of yours would you measure that against?" she says. She has a black olive stabbed on her fork, poised in the air like a miniature hammer. She puts the olive in her mouth and chews slowly. She is implying I don't have any friends. This is a theme she has been pushing all day for some reason. She knows I don't have time for friends. I am focused on family. This is my role right now. I am tired of this entire discussion. It's time for a pivot.

"Actually, I'd say it's the opposite—other couples measure themselves against us and come up lacking. We are blessed. Handsome, healthy children, the best home on the street." I set down my slice of pepperoni heaven and watch her eye it with distaste. Together we watch as the greasy cheese oozes onto my plate. "Anyway, I'm starting to think this is a silly conversation. We're in our favorite vacation place in the world. It's time to relax and enjoy ourselves. In fact, there's really only one issue I'd like to discuss before we officially commence our vacation and that's to talk about this so-called job you think you're starting on Monday. Isn't that what I heard you say, honey?" I'm smiling, tilting my head with sympathetic understanding, like when you discover your child has accidentally wet his pants. They're embarrassed it has even happened so you treat them with compassion, not anger. That's what I've learned to try to do. It's not easy, feigning care.

Mia's face gathers into a storm, blue eyes narrowed, chin pointed at me in anger. "Yes, Paul, that is what I said. I am starting my job Monday. I'm a virtual employee, and I am

excited about this new opportunity. You should say congratulations."

Lacking any other idea, I shove the remainder of the slice
of pizza into my mouth, cheese strings cling to my chin before I wipe them away. I chew slowly. My wife does not
work. That is not our situation. No matter what. She stays
at home and cares for the house and for the children. Opti-
mally, she learns to cook, but at the very least, she sets a nice
table. This is what we talked about, what we agreed to, even
on our very first date.

How different is the face looking at me across the table from
that night with the crème brûlée more than a decade ago.
That magical evening, we'd arrived at Diamond's restaurant
at almost the same time, and as I held the door open for Mia,
I fought the urge to lean forward and kiss her. I smelled the
fresh floral scent of her hair, I noted the way her black dress
hugged her body, and I saw her blue eyes sparkle in the dim
restaurant light as she looked over her shoulder, tucked her
hair behind her ear and smiled back at me.

We'd spent almost three hours at dinner, talking and laughing, getting to know each other. Her expressions were loving and warm, never challenging. She shared her dreams and
I followed suit. So of course she discovered we both wanted
kids, and how we both longed for the traditional American
family. She didn't exactly articulate the whole working dad,
stay-at-home mom part of the dream. But that was fine, it
would take time and gentle persuasion. I knew I'd fallen for
a working woman, but she didn't really need the job, not
with me providing for her. Not with the trust fund she came
with. It was so endearing, though. Many of the wealthy are
lazy; they don't even attempt to prove their worth. Not Mia.
She was a hard worker, a skilled copywriter. She was. The

job was valuable to her, for her, for that moment in time. It brought us together, because otherwise, our two worlds never would have collided.

"So, your goal is children and a white picket fence?" I asked over the flickering candlelight. My heart was beating with excitement. She was my perfect woman.

"Yes, of course. The whole suburban dream." She smiled. "I mean, after I work for a while. I love my job. I'm not in a hurry. And fortunately I'm young."

Yes, she was, but I was smart. Work was only fun if you were assigned good projects, if you were praised, learning. I could stop all her momentum at Thompson Payne with a few well-placed words to the partners. And once she was pregnant, she wouldn't need an office to make her feel important. She'd have me. And a baby.

"There's no more important job than being a mom," I said, leaning forward and fighting the urge to reach for her hand. It was too soon. There were certain steps one must take when reeling in the object of one's desire. It was time to listen, to continue to research her family, her past. But I did have a few more discoveries, like what she wrote in her high school yearbook as her "biggest wish."

"There's another dream, too, right? There must be a best-selling novel floating around in that pretty little head. You can write during naptime."

Her eyes twinkled in the candlelight. "You've thought of everything. How did you know I want to write a novel?"

How indeed. "Most copywriters are frustrated novelists, I've found."

We agreed, it seemed, on everything. I am not revising history. I'm not. She dreamed of a husband. Check. Traveling the world. (I told her we would, but we wouldn't.) She dreamed of a home in the suburbs and children. Check. She dreamed of being a working mom. (No way.) She dreamed of finding an older, more sophisticated man who could provide for her and teach her the meaning of love. Check.

It was all pretty easy, really. I didn't even have to charm her that much. And when I walked her to the valet line outside Diamond's that night, I'd slipped my hand around her waist, sending a bolt of electricity straight through me. She leaned against me slightly as we waited for her car.

"See you tomorrow. Thank you for a wonderful night," Mia said as she slid behind the wheel of her car, a VW Rabbit of all things, while I tipped the valet. I held the top of her car door and leaned forward, hoping for a kiss, my head literally dizzy with desire and the bottle of wine we had shared.

"I had the best time, thank you for coming," I said. Mia tilted her head and then lifted her face toward me as I leaned in and gently brushed my lips against hers. After a moment, I pulled away. I had confirmed we both wanted more, needed more.

"See you tomorrow, beautiful." I closed the door and waved as she pulled away, wheels bumping along the brick streets of this historical part of town. I didn't really need to sabotage her career at the agency. As soon as she found out she was pregnant just a few weeks after our honeymoon, she had one foot out the door. I mean, she had been complaining for months. Soon after our first date, she'd been assigned to the boring electronics account and as everyone knows, technical copywriting is the worst. She hated that account. I have no idea why she was assigned to it. Well, maybe I suggested it. But still, it helped her see where she belonged: at home. It all worked out, she agreed.

But now, right now, we aren't seeing eye to eye on anything. Not food, not the kids, not about her working outside the home. I know, you're thinking, given most couple's circumstances in general, and mine in particular—and you don't even know the whole story—I should be grateful she wants to bring in some extra money to the household. Perhaps I'll consider it. But not if it means she'll be working with John. No way. Together, they each know too many pieces of me.

"I can't congratulate you, Mia, because I forbid it," I tell her now. In my lap, my hands are clenched into fists. I'm furious. I know what happens at workplaces. I've shredded my napkin and white bits sprinkle the ground around my feet like snowflakes.

Mia's face cracks into a smile and then she begins to laugh. It is not a happy laugh. Our pink-striped waitress appears and refills our iced tea with a quick, sloppy pour from a plastic pitcher.

"Glad to see somebody is having a good time. What's so funny?" the girl asks. She's quite sure of herself. Millennials have no respect for private conversations. I'm about to swat away Teenage Mutant Ninja Turtle when Mia says, "Him."

Mia points her index finger at me. "My husband doesn't want me to go back to work. I'm trying to convince him I'm bored all day, with our boys in school. But he doesn't think women should work outside the home once they marry. He's so old-fashioned that way. It's charming, I suppose. I guess he wants me all to himself." Mia winks at me, smiling. I don't believe the smile is sincere, however.

Ghost of Teenage Future says, "That's sort of awesome. I mean, I guess if you want to work he should let you. Everybody should be able to do what they want but it sounds like you have a pretty sweet deal. Me, personally, I'm marrying a rich guy, staying home and having babies."

I've found an unlikely ally, one with a ring through her nose and black eyeliner soaring like bats from either eye. I guess you could say she has her own style. "Yes, my wife is living the dream, the perfect scenario, just like you will one day." I nod at Mia, who is staring at me and shaking her head back and forth in a slow, measured no. "Can we have the check, please? And a to-go box for my last slice."

"Sure," says the waitress, hurrying away. I wonder if we now scare her more than she scared me.

"You're one of a kind, Paul," Mia says. She slides out of our booth with ease. I feel as if she is running away from me but that's ridiculous. We arrived here together. She has no-where to go. "I'll meet you at the car. I need to make a call. To Claudia."

"Tell her the money will be in the account in half an hour," I say. Mia turns and walks to the exit, pushes with both hands and bangs her way out through the screen door. I watch her walk down the sidewalk until she disappears. I need to fix this tension, calm her down. My wife shouldn't be running away from me, she should be standing by my side. *I'm good at this*, I remind myself. I'm typically calm and in control, hiding the fire deep inside. The past six months have been tough, and I've lost a bit of my power around the home—it seems ap-parent by this display, by the car ride conversation, too, that Mia isn't pleased with me. But I'm not worried. I know Mia, my empathetic, sweet wife. And of course, I have my plan.

I briefly consider making a call, too. It would be nice to speak with someone kind and loving, someone still enamored with me. But I counsel myself against it.

There will be time later for that.

2:00 P.M.

7

I pay the bill and slide my last slice of bliss into the box for later. It's so cheap here compared to prices in the city, and I tip the pink-haired girl generously. I see that she's watching me, clearly attracted to an older, sophisticated and successful man. No doubt she'd like a father figure in her life. I smile and slip out of the booth. I need to focus. I need to find Mia.

I pull on my sunglasses as I step out into the sunshine and onto the busy sidewalk. Tourists are walking up and down this main shopping street, meandering three across like human roadblocks, mindlessly weaving and darting into the trinket stores and art shops. There should be a rule that adults cannot walk three abreast or even two across on crowded sidewalks. Everyone should walk single file, destination in their sights, briskly and with purpose. Unfortunately, humans are like sheep, most of the time. They need a shepherd or they are a milling-about mess.

Except children, I realize, as a gang of youngsters runs past me. They are purpose driven. Our kids are no different. They love this street. Down here they can buy candy and cheap new toys with quarters and, at the most, dollars. I see a couple of boys zip by on bicycles and think fondly of my sons. I miss them, just now. I picture their small hands waving goodbye as I dropped them at school this morning. So sweet, so trusting. I'll be with them again soon. Right now I need to find my wife and I'm anxious to get to the cottage.

I spot Mia and relief washes over me. She is leaning against the side of the Ford Flex, staring at me while she talks on her phone. I wave but she does not. She ends her phone call as I close the distance between us. I pull her into my arms, careful not to get pizza grease from the box on her lovely blue sweater.

"Honey, let's not fight anymore. Let's think about this job thing, not just jump at the first offer. If, after you've given it some thought, after we've weighed the pros and cons together, you're still interested in getting back into the advertising game, let's send your résumé out and get a number of offers." *Problem solved.* It's what I do.

She looks up into my eyes; her lips part, but she doesn't say a word. I release her and open the passenger door for her, and she slides into the car. I close the door behind her and walk to my side, chuckling at the memory of our first date, and the difference ten years can make.

"It's almost strawberry time," I say, changing the subject. "Almost time to see your little strawberry babies."

"Yes, you're right. I'm excited to see how they're doing," she says. She sounds genuine, happy. *We're back on track*, I think. I push the button to roll down our windows, enjoying the breeze from the lake to my left. Between the lake and this street lies the heart of Lakeside, the main park with a putt-putt golf course, children's playground, a performance gazebo and shuffleboard courts. Shuffleboard is serious business here. I hear the church bell clang twice. Two o'clock. This day is moving quickly.

Past the park, the bicycles thin out and I can drive a bit faster, fifteen miles per hour now. At Laurel Street, I turn right, forcing myself to ignore the Boones' huge cottage dominating the corner, hoping they aren't here for the weekend. Once on Laurel, our cottage is on my left, bright white against the lush green grass of our yard. I turn into our driveway and take a breath as I bring the car to a stop. Before I even turn off the ignition, Mia is out of the car without saying a word. I put the car in Park and reach for the to-go box I placed on the floor in the back behind me. It's holding the last slice of pizza from lunch and I'm tempted to gobble it down right now. But I should follow Mia. She's headed to check on her strawberry crop no doubt.

As I make my way to the backyard, following her, I'm startled. There's a man standing next to Mia, looking down at the garden. The man is fit, with broad shoulders and dark brown hair. It's Buck, I realize quickly. I would know him anywhere. They stand so close their shoulders are almost touching. Buck and Mia. How long has he been standing back here, awaiting Mia's arrival? Is she the highlight of his day, his week?

"Hey, Buck," I say, my voice ricocheting against the back fence, sounding loud and strong. *I'm protecting what's mine*, the voice says.

"Paul," Buck says, turning around and extending his hand. His chiseled face is shaved and wrinkle-free. I notice a dimple on his right cheek that I hadn't seen before. How cute. I shake his hand firmly, hoping it hurts.

"They've taken root, Paul. Buck has done me such a favor,

caring for them like he has," Mia says. Her voice drips with admiration and affection, the opposite tone from the tone I'd experienced most of today. She puts her hand on Buck's forearm and adds, "I better go help Paul unload the car. Come over for happy hour tonight?"

What? I'm stunned. This is our weekend together. What is she doing inviting Buck over for drinks without even asking me first? "Honey, we have plans," I say. "Sorry, Buck. It's our little getaway weekend. I'm sure you understand."

"No problem," Buck says, blinking but holding my gaze.

"Don't be ridiculous, Paul. Buck has been an invaluable help with the strawberries. Let's be neighborly, shall we? Come by at six," she says before walking past me back in the direction of our car. I turn and watch her, unable to face Buck. I've been humiliated but there is nothing more I want to say to this man right now. I walk away, heading back to the car, leaving Buck alone in our backyard. I imagine him standing there smugly, our neighbor the garden gnome, watching me follow my wife like a trained dog. Well, this dog isn't well trained, and he's a guard dog. This will not be the last on this topic.

I reach the Ford Flex as Mia is unloading the trunk, carrying the laundry basket from our house. I have no idea what she has filled it with but most likely it's stuff we don't need up here, and probably didn't need back in Grandville either. Creature comforts are coming out of our ears. We're so blessed.

"Mia, can we talk?" I say, standing between my wife and the house.

"Can you help carry things inside first? I'd like to get settled," she says, stepping around me. I notice she doesn't have the key to the cottage, but she turns the handle of the front door and walks inside. *Why was the cottage unlocked?* I wonder.

"Mia, wait," I say, hurrying to the door. "The door wasn't locked. I need to make sure no one has broken in."

"Paul, the cleaning crew came today. I told them to leave it unlocked," she says, pushing past me to carry her white plastic basket to the family room couch. "Can you go get a load?"

How different this scene is than what I'd fantasized. There will be no eager lovemaking to kick off our preseason excursion, not with the stupid neighbor lurking in plain sight in the backyard.

"Sure," I say, walking back to the front door. The cottage is small, maybe 2,000 square feet, but it's lovely. Hardwood floors make the space warm and inviting. The first floor boasts a screened-in porch, a comfortable kitchen and dining room, and a small family room. Upstairs, there are three small bedrooms. It was built in 1927 or so, after the first big building blitz of summer cabins right next to the lake. The second wave of building was more refined if you ask me. The second block back from the lake provides each home with more land. More land means bigger homes. I love the big oak tree in the front yard and I love that we have plenty of green grass all around the cottage. Quickly, I peek into the backyard and notice that Buck is gone. Certainly, he won't go against my wishes and come over for drinks. This is our special day and three is a crowd.

During my second and final trip out to the car, my phone buzzes in my back pocket. I pull it out and check the number. I smile, though I know I can't talk now. I'm spending a quality weekend with my wife. And quite obviously, this time together was needed. I wonder what other surprises she has for me besides her newfound desire to work and her new confidence in directly contradicting my wishes in front of strangers.

I close the trunk and roll our suitcases up the front walk.

It's simple here, peaceful, tucked away from the hustle of the main street, the stresses of life back home. The wind ruffles the new green leaves on the oak tree and I know everything will calm down. We just need to unpack, and get our rhythm back. It's going to be the best afternoon.

Inside I pull the suitcases to the bottom of the stairs. I hear Mia up in our bedroom. The walls and floors are thin, a product of the time and the belief that no insulation was needed for summer cottages, I suppose. I pick up Mia's suitcase and carry it up the stairs, placing it on the landing before I head back down to retrieve mine.

By the time I climb upstairs again, Mia has wheeled her suitcase into our bedroom—an oasis of white furnishings with light blue walls—and is diligently unpacking as I join her in the room. There is enough space for our king-size bed, a small table on each side. That's it. One dresser at the end of the bed is split down the middle, with each of us getting our half of each drawer. The small closet holds eight hanging items, tops. The entire room with its white furniture and bedding and curtains and cozy size typically feels very soothing. At the moment, it seems crowded. The air pulses as it did in the car. *Ping.*

I glance at Mia. My wife's face seems to have softened, the frown lines not so deep at the sides of her mouth. Maybe she is at peace with our decision, the end of the discussion. I could see that, read that feeling on her face. Or perhaps that's wishful thinking. I unzip my suitcase and unpack in silence. Instead of pursuing a conversation again, I have decided to let her be the first to speak, let her explain herself.

She will explain herself, I'm confident of that. Mia learned this lesson years ago. It was early in our marriage and Mia was delighted to receive a call from a high school friend who was in town on business. We didn't know we were pregnant, not yet, and so there was no reason she couldn't meet her friend for happy hour, at least no logical reason I could come up with at the time. So she went, promising to call me if she'd be gone more than two hours.

She forgot to call me. And she didn't pick up any of my calls, as they rolled to voice mail one after another. I was panicked. I phoned the dive bar on High Street where she said they were going, but the bubba who answered the phone said she wasn't there. I had been just about to call the police, something I would typically never do, when Mia waltzed through the door, eyes glistening, cheeks flushed with alcohol. She froze in the foyer, a deer in the headlights just before the truck hits.

"Paul, what's wrong?" I knew she could see the fire surging in my eyes.

"You never called. Where were you? I had all these thoughts racing through my head about what had happened to you, terrible thoughts. Newlywed disappears after night on the town. That kind of headline in the *Columbus Dispatch*."

Mia took a step back, a nervous smile crossed her face. "I was with Cathy, like I told you. We decided to go to dinner. Sorry. I was having fun. We hadn't seen each other in years."

My fists clenched at my sides. I took a deep breath, proud of how I had grown to handle these situations. "Mia, I'm not asking for much. Just communication. I was so worried. Come here."

She crossed the room and fell into my chest, smelling of beer and cigarettes, murmuring her apologies. "It won't happen again. When Cathy and I are together, we just lose track of time. It's always been that way. Do you understand?"

No. "It's selfish of you, now that you have a husband, but I understand, of course. I know it won't happen again."

"No, of course it won't," she agreed as I pulled her hair, tilting her face toward me and pushed my lips down hard onto hers. She never did see Cathy again, of course, and she spent that night making things up to me in bed, makeup sex at its finest. I smile at the memory and I'm about to call out to Mia, to remind her of that night, but then I remember, she will be the one to speak first.

4:00 P.M.

Mia isn't talking to me. That much is clear. She walked out of the all-white cloud of our bedroom without saying a word. But then again, I'm not speaking to her either. We are in some weird sort of truce, or a silent argument of sorts. I hope she is reflecting on her attitude and how she is ruining our best day together.

After all I've done for her and our family, you'd think she'd be more thankful, more appreciative and respectful about my stance on things, like working for my former boss for instance. It's sheer lunacy. It will lead to drama and I hate drama. Here's the thing, my coworkers all admire me, and my former manager John—well, he's afraid of me. Not afraid I'm going to hurt him physically, of course. He was just afraid that I was going to take his job. Turns out, he was right.

If he hadn't started supporting his son's sports team with company marketing dollars, he probably would have been able to hold on forever. But he made a critical mistake, and once I brought it to light with a few well-timed and confidential tips called into the CEO's ridiculously titled "talk to me" voice mail, well, of course he was asked to leave. That's all. I just don't see any reason for Mia to begin conversing with him, even if they once worked together at Thompson Payne. The past should always be left in the past. Almost always.

I miss Caroline. Well, actually, I miss everyone at work, but I miss her in particular. If you knew the circumstances, you'd probably tell me I'm crazy to still have these feelings, but I do. When I close my eyes, she's the woman who pops into my mind. It's a shame, really.

I close the drawer to the dresser and make my way slowly down the hall. I stop in front of a framed photo of the boys, both sitting on Mia's lap, smiles on their little-boy faces as the sun sparkles on the lake behind them. I took the photo, maybe five years ago, back when we were the guests of the Boones. But now we aren't anyone's guests. We are residents. Cottage owners. Second home people. The life my wife was accustomed to living—that's what I've re-created for her here.

Next to the photo of the boys and Mia is a framed picture of Mia's parents, Phyllis and Donald Pilmer Jr. of New York City and the Hamptons. It is the same photo that was on Mia's desk back at Thompson Payne. I pick it up to study it. Phyllis is an older version of my wife, with shorter hair and a rounder face. Donald has a large nose that Mia was fortunate not to have inherited, and round dark glasses that make him appear to be examining you closely at every encounter, as he did me on our first meeting more than a decade ago. He's also bald, no doubt the reason for some of his disdain toward me: my full head of hair must taunt him.

She's their only child, my wife. I know they believe she

married too young, too quickly and beneath her status. I've worked hard to try to win them over, of course. They're family. Our first meeting, when I accompanied a sobbing Mia across the country for the funeral, went fine. Her parents were grieving, and basically ignored me. They underestimated my staying power and Mia's dad in particular is probably kicking himself to this day.

He should have seen me coming, but he didn't. After the funeral encounter in New York, our next get-together was in Columbus. Mia invited her parents to fly in for dinner, to really get to know her new boyfriend, yours truly.

Of course, I poured on the charm. I wore my best suit, hosted them at the city's private dinner club on Broad Street, The Columbus Club. It was once the governor's mansion and until just a blink of an eye ago, women could only enter through the side door. I loved that tradition. Mia's dad seemed impressed by the history of the place as I showed him around while Mia and her mom sat gossiping in one of the front rooms.

"This photo is from the 1930s, a very old boys' camp in Maine. Exclusive. I was so lucky to go there," I said, pointing to the framed print of gangly white boys sitting on a dock on a pristine lake. "Followed in my old man's footsteps."

"Is that so," Donald remarked. "I went to a boys' camp in Maine. Made me who I am today." He clapped me on the back then and I thought I was in. "How many summers?"

Here's the thing with the whole summer camp, boarding school, fraternity-joining, privileged act. It's tough to fake. Whatever he was asking, it was code for something else. I pivoted. "Donald, what fraternity were you in?" By the time his answer was due, we had rejoined the ladies.

"We had final clubs, um, you wouldn't understand. Mia, you look beautiful," Donald said. Snooty shit.

The host showed us to our private room, a table for four in front of a roaring fireplace. I'd ordered a white rose centerpiece.

"Look at those. My favorite flowers," Phyllis cooed, leaning forward and smelling the roses. I looked up and Mia was smiling at me.

"How thoughtful, Paul," Mia said and squeezed my hand as I pulled out her chair for her.

"Paul, is this for me?" Phyllis was holding the gold-encrusted antique pillbox I'd had them place at her seat. I nodded, humbly. "Exquisite. Thank you."

I could feel Donald staring at me with a look that was the opposite of the one that Mia and Phyllis were sending my way. But it was too late. I proposed a few months later, calling to ask Donald for Mia's hand, giving the excuse that I couldn't pull away from work to fly across the country and ask in person. I found out later Mia's mother called her in tears, begging her to slow down, even though I'd already given the woman the first of what would become a sea of antique pillboxes meant to win her over, the traitor. But Phyllis was too late. The combination of chemistry and promises had set the hook; Mia was no longer under their control.

On the plus side, they treat me with deference; they must if they want to see their only grandchildren. Somehow they know this, perhaps because I may have implied it to Donald during our second phone call, shortly after we announced we were having a baby.

"Congratulations, Paul. Quick work." Donald's words were filled with distaste, like he'd eaten a rotten egg and didn't know where to spit it out.

"Thank you so much, Donald, or should I say, Grandpa," I said. I stood in my office, my corner office at the ad agency, feeling like the world was my oyster. And it was. "Now may be a good time to establish a trust, you know, for the grand-kids. I just read an article about that."

"Did you? How interesting. Let me give you a little advice, Paul. Do not presume to tell me how to invest my money. I will take care of my daughter and her children. But don't ex-pect anything from me, Paul. Not a dime. I see you for what you are." His words sounded like gravel. Too bad he wasn't warming up to his only son-in-law. His loss. We could have gone fishing together, or perhaps, joined an investment club together. I know from my research that he likes to take ex-pensive trips. Golfing in Scotland with his only son-in-law would have been swell.

"Listen, Donald. Can I speak freely here? I take good care of your daughter, and I will take good care of your only grandchildren. I'm not sure why you don't like me, but I wish you and I could build a relationship. It could benefit both of us, you see. I help you keep your relationship with Mia and your grandchildren—a relationship you know won't end well if you make her choose between us—and you get to take on the son you never had. Let's take a trip together, to Scotland or somewhere. How about it? You might just change your mind about me." I prowled to the corner of my office, wiped some dust off the ficus tree leaf. The cleaning service clearly needed to be changed again.

"We will not be friends, young man, and you are certainly not my son. You are my daughter's husband. That's it. Noth-ing more." This time his voice was quiet.

I dropped mine to match. "Well, your loss. But like you, I'm king of my castle and if you ever want to see your grand-kids, you better make sure the king is happy. Talk soon." After I hung up, I called my secretary. My plant was drowning in dust. It was embarrassing, really. What if a client noticed? "Change cleaning companies, immediately."

"Mr. Strom, we just changed services two months ago. Give them a chance." I know my secretary didn't want to go through the work of finding another cleaning service but too bad. I didn't like the way my secretary was looking at me lately, like she was sizing me up. Disrespect from the help isn't ever tolerated. I would need to make two changes, it appeared.

"This is not up for discussion. Just do it," I said. "And go ahead and take an extra half hour for lunch. You deserve it." I was a demanding boss, but I could be kind, too. Just ask anybody. Up to a point. This one had reached it. When my patience ran out, it was over. She'd find that out when she came back from her extra long lunch break.

But with Mia's parents, I must be subtle in my control. I allow the Pilmers to see the boys, of course, ever since Mia told me they'd set up large trust funds for them. So nice, and she gave me access to the accounts so I could monitor them. I was sure old Donald wouldn't like that, but too bad. Mia was in love and what was hers was mine.

And when they are granted a visit, my in-laws dote on Mikey and Sam just like grandparents are supposed to, bringing them age-appropriate presents as they should. I make sure that chance doesn't happen too often, stretching out time between visits—theirs to Ohio and ours to New York—to be certain absence makes their hearts grow fonder, or at least kinder, when it comes to their only son-in-law. I know Mia and her mom do video chats often, and the boys get to see their only living grandma then. Now that I've made Phyllis a grandmother she's gotten over any lingering reservations about our hasty marriage, so I keep sending the pillboxes. Easy trade.

It's nice that Mia came from a family of means, especially at year-end when they gift us serious cash. We often don't make it to New York for Christmas; usually I have a work commitment conveniently pop up. But the money still arrives, checks tucked inside crisp linen envelopes. Four checks, one made out to each of us. Arguably, this could have been a reason to have a third child. Had I known about these checks rolling in every year, or calculated the payment over the life of a third child, I probably would have said yes to another.

Helps out a lot, those gifts, but they won't arrive for another seven months. That is not in time. Mia's quarterly stock dividends don't hurt either, although that money already has been spent. I can't even imagine how many shares we will end up with in all of those blue chip companies, once Phyllis and Donald pass. They're younger than my parents were, but they live in a big, crazy city, so who knows what could happen to them. Her inheritance could appear any day, anytime now. Just like the letter that appeared from Mia's Texas uncle, Donald's brother Derrick, the family's black sheep. Wasn't expecting that at all. That's why there is no need to worry about money. Opportunities arise all the time. I've been waiting to share the Texas news with Mia and I will, when the time is right.

Of course, I knew Mia Pilmer was rich, was told that before I even met her. But I didn't even think about her money when I was courting her. I was an established advertising executive and she was a young beauty just out of college. Why would I ever have thought of such a thing as her future inheritance from her parents, or an uncle or otherwise? That would have been shallow.

I have heard the rumors that Mia's father is a corrupt businessman who learned everything from his father, Donald

Pilmer senior. I'm sure you've heard them, too, so I'm not being a gossip. It's just that whenever a certain family is that rich for generations, you can be sure they cheated somewhere along the line. Robber barons, investment bankers, bankers in general, you know the type. Especially when they're from New York. You may think I sound like I'm jealous, but far from it. I appreciate a good con job, and I'm benefiting from the corruption myself, so more power to the Pilmers. It's just that you have to be careful in families like this one. One day your luck runs out. You just don't want to be the generation that blows it, the end of the line so to speak. At least my boys will carry the Strom name on their passports, even as they carry the Pilmer cash in their pockets.

I hear the front door open and wonder if Mia is coming or going. I place the photo of her parents back down on the hall table, next to the photo of my family, minus me. I notice I've left fingerprints on both of the silver frames. I don't feel like wiping them off.

5:00 P.M.

9

I hurry down the stairs and discover Mia has gone outside; she's standing on our front lawn, the phone pressed to her ear. She is probably driving the babysitter crazy with her check-ins every few hours. I know I'd want to smack her. Maybe that's why Claudia is on drugs, to deal with Mia's incessant calls.

I walk into the kitchen and note the time on the round clock tacked to the wall above the back door. It's five o'clock. A perfectly acceptable time to enjoy a cocktail, I realize. I look around the simple kitchen, getting my bearings again after not being here since last summer. Everything is in place, thanks to Mia and the cleaning crew she called. I notice the bill on the counter.

Written in barely legible script are the instructions: "For spring opening and cleaning. Please send payment immediately. Thank you. Betsy." I pull an image of Betsy from my mind, and see a woman with missing teeth who smells like an ashtray. She and her crew do a good cleaning job, despite her personal toxic scent. I haven't opened the cottage before, but imagine it must be a messy job. The place has been closed up tight since the end of October. All kinds of bugs and grime and who knows what had accumulated, I'm sure. A distasteful job, far below anything I would ever consider doing for a living. How is it that some of us are housecleaners, and some are executives? There's the universe again, bestowing brains and looks and charm on a chosen few of us, the lucky ones.

I open the cupboard and pull out a cocktail glass and then another for Mia. I'm going to wave the white flag, so to speak, with a vodka tonic. I open the refrigerator. It's empty. We haven't been to the store for limes, or anything else. I realize I should offer to go. I pull open the back door and step onto the driveway, walking around the house to find Mia. Her back is to me, and she's still on the phone, her head tilted to the side, bending into the phone in her hand.

I quietly walk up behind her. She doesn't know I'm here.

"I'm so glad. That is perfect…Yes, Mom, I'm fine," she says, and as I wonder why she's speaking to Phyllis, she turns and screams, dropping her phone into the grass. "Paul! Why did you sneak up on me?"

I hold up my hands, shocked by her outburst, and the fear in her eyes. I have no idea why she is so jumpy, but attribute it to our earlier tense talks. I need to calm her down, get our best day ever back on track. She needs a drink. I watch as she bends down and picks up her phone.

"Mia—" I begin, but she holds her hand out to stop me.

"Mom, I'm fine. Paul just snuck up on me, that's all," my wife says into the phone. A moment passes. I wonder what

Phyllis is telling her daughter. "Good. Yes. I'll call you to-morrow. Thank you again."

She pushes the End button and then she looks at me. "What were you doing? Why were you sneaking up on me?" she says. I see panic in her eyes.

"Calm down, honey," I say, taking a step closer to her, wanting to pull her into my arms. She steps back, shoulders at her ears, eyes wide and unblinking.

"You scared me," she says. She has folded her arms across her chest, like a coat of armor.

"Obviously. I was just coming out to ask if you'd like a cocktail. And, if you'd like lime, I'd be happy to run to the grocery. I'd be glad to get anything you need," I say. I want to tell her to remember that I am her knight in shining armor, but I don't.

"Yes, that would be lovely. I have a whole list of things we're missing. And did you transfer the money? For the boys?" she asks. She seems to be calming down now. Her eyes aren't as wide or wild.

"Done," I assure her. This is a lie. But I will handle it as soon as I go back inside. "Where's the list? I'll just be gone for a little while. Unless you want to come with me?"

"No, I'll stay and finish getting the cottage in order. The list is on the table by the front door," she says.

"Okay, I'm on it," I say, turning to walk back toward the house. I pause and turn back to face my wife. I'm suddenly concerned. It is odd that she would be speaking to her mother on a Friday evening. Typically Phyllis and Donald's social life wouldn't allow for any type of evening chitchat. They appreciate cocktail hour more than most. I study my wife and I say, "Hey, is everything okay with your mom?"

"Yes, she's fine." Mia blinks, breaking eye contact, and

then bends at the waist, eager to pull what must be a weed out of the garden bed that edges our house. I know soon she will be planting pots of bright red geraniums to complement the bright red door of the cottage. The garden beds will be filled with white flowers: daisies, hydrangeas and other varieties that I cannot name. Some magically appear and some Mia plants, carefully digging holes and tucking in the flowers as if they were little kids ready for sleep. By midsummer, her gardens, our gardens, are always the talk of Columbus. I know that will be the case here, too. She still doesn't look at me, concentrating on her weeding. Her hands are covered in wet, smelly dirt. I sniff.

I haven't moved. She stops weeding, stands up straight and says, "My mom and I were just touching base, you know."

She tosses that refrain, "you know," onto the end of her sentences when she wants the conversation to end. Something she's clearly hoping for as she continues to ignore me while managing to yank out almost everything within reach. I wonder if she may be pulling out some perennials, but I hold my tongue. She knows gardening like I know sales. I decide to let the issue of this conversation with her mom go for now. I feel confident Phyllis is under my control and that she has been loosely under my spell since the first pillbox.

"Good. Glad to know Phyllis is well. I hope you gave her my best. I'm off to the store," I say and walk away. I'm not going to let Mia's strange behavior bother me anymore. We're going to have the best night ever together. That will smooth over any of the tension left over from the drive.

It's probably due to her new diet restrictions. Ever since she found the holistic doctor, she's been even crabbier. She started a few months ago with our general practitioner. He had diagnosed my wife as just a stressed-out mom, after ruling out lupus, and then ulcers. Maybe it was general fatigue, he'd told us. So many busy moms suffer from it. He sent us home, telling Mia to get more sleep each night. Brilliant diagnosis. On her own, Mia found some quasi-medical practice that believes in "holistic" medicine. She's been getting IV drips of vitamins once a week, eating vegetarian, drinking water out of glass bottles, but still, she doesn't feel well. Poor Mia. Nothing seems to help her constant stomachache and general nausea. I'll make sure she has a very nice meal tonight.

Back in the kitchen, I pour myself a shot of Tito's vodka, tipping it back quickly. A small shudder runs through my body as the alcohol hits my system. I walk through the house and find the list on the table next to the front door, as Mia had instructed. There's a lot more than limes written in her precise and elegant penmanship: cheese, crackers and grapes. Coffee for the morning. Bread and peanut butter. Water in glass bottles. Lettuce and apples, organic. Mia's favorite cereal and milk. Jam for the croissants. Well, she won't need that. It's not that long a list, I suppose. Nothing compared to what she fetches from the grocery store for the boys and me each week. I will handle gathering these items with pleasure, I tell myself and put a smile on my face.

As I back out of the driveway, I realize the car still holds the aromas of our drive. It smells of Mia's new organic body lotion, lime-and-coconut scented, and my spicy aftershave. There is a hint of sweat in the air, and the smell of pepperoni pizza grease, from the slice I couldn't finish and took to go, now waiting for me in the refrigerator. And there is one other scent I register as I wave to Mia and turn the corner, watching her and our cottage disappear in my rearview mirror. It's the smell of my boys, the distinct blend of stinky sweaty soccer gear and after-bath freshness.

Briefly, I wonder if I should have included them this weekend, made them part of the plans. No, it's fine. They're the
future, the symbols of my immortality. They're fine back
home with Claudia.

5:30 P.M.

10

Frank's Market, the small grocery store just outside the main gate of Lakeside, does a booming business in the summers, though I'm not certain how it survives in the winter. The cramped parking lot is crowded with cars tonight. I squeeze the Flex in beside the metal chest filled with self-serve bags of ice for one dollar.

There are barely any people in Lakeside year-round, as I mentioned. Certainly no one would be buying ice during the brutal winters. Buck is one of the few exceptions if he actually does live here full-time. It's weird to stay here year-round. It's not a place conducive to that. It's cold and isolated and void of creature comforts. Maybe Frank's closes in the winter months. It should.

I walk into the place and push my mini shopping cart down the first aisle, almost running over the tennis shoe of a woman standing in my way. I give her a look and she steps back as she should. The shelves are crowded too close for regular-sized carts, and there are far too many people in the store for shopping to be anything but a chore. I will hurry.

I shake my head, looking at the selection—you can't be picky here. The produce looks like it has endured being at a large grocery store first; I imagine that after it was not selected by shoppers in a big city, it was shipped here for its final chance. The lettuce is strictly iceberg, wrapped in plastic, and more white than green. The apples are bruised, and the grapes, well, they're simply unacceptable. "Sorry, honey," I mumble. Turning the corner, I find crackers and Mia's cereal, both looking as if they may be undamaged. But looks can be deceiving. I find the cheese selection. Three offerings: Cracker Barrel cheddar, string cheese for kids, and Velveeta slices. The cheddar it is.

Typically, Mia will go to the gourmet market near our home for provisions for the lake, but this trip, she said, she ran out of time. I'm not sure what she was so busy doing, but it's not like we'll starve. We'll just eat more simply. Up here, they haven't heard about organic foods, and as far as vegetables, well, it's mostly in cans unless it's corn, iceberg lettuce or potatoes. The limes look passable, thank goodness.

There is a sushi place we like just a short drive down the coast, but these days, we don't go there much. The kids like it because they have hibachi grills and chefs who flip shrimp tails at them, make volcanoes out of onion slices and basically entertain them through the entire meal. Before Mia stopped eating "animal protein," we liked it because they have sushi-grade fish and a full bar, and the kids are happy. Their vegetarian options, however, aren't "optimal," according to my wife. Since she has changed we haven't been. It's a shame.

This grocery store is not optimal, according to me. It reminds me of a gas station, but with some attempts at fresh food tossed in. I think they should stick to packaged stuff and alcohol. Oh, and yes, that is the primary reason Frank's Market survives, I assure you. Ten feet away, you drive through the gates of a dry little town. All of us heathens stock up before we enter, and pop over here to replenish.

As I wait in line to check out, I wonder if Buck will have the nerve to show up at my house for happy hour. It's a disturbing thought, nagging at the back of my mind: he actually might. I check my watch, and note the time is 5:45 p.m. My ideal scenario would be to arrive back at the cottage before him, if he were to appear. Then I would be the one answering the door, there to discourage his presence at my home at all. If he or Mia insisted, I would find a way to tell him man-to-man why lingering would not be prudent. I need to hurry.

There is a line of five other customers in front of me and one cashier, a local or Frank himself perhaps, a thin man with a circular bald spot on top of his head and stringy gray hair pulled into a strange-looking ponytail. His nails are yellowed, presumably from smoking.

Those fingernails resemble my late father's, yellow and cracked. They bring me back to my childhood, sitting at our dining room table, a dinner plate in front of me with an untouched portion of green beans. My father was tapping his yellowed fingernails on the table. I must have been Sam's age, maybe younger. I had finished eating the meat loaf and the mashed potatoes, but I was not able to get myself to ingest any of the beans. My mother had kindly suggested that I be allowed to leave the table but my father stood up, shoving his chair back into the dining room wall.

"He will sit at this table until that plate is clean," he said. He was the king, and we were all his subjects. My little brother gave me a sympathetic look before pushing his chair back and hurrying to carry his plate into the kitchen. He knew the storm was brewing; the air was thick with tension. My stomach threatened me with bile. My mother touched my shoulder on her way to the kitchen, but said nothing. I heard her murmuring to my father in the other room, smelled the sulfur from the match he'd blown out after lighting his cigarette.

"I told you he will finish it all. That's final," he yelled at my mother. I could hear the sliding glass door to the back patio open as he stepped outside, closing it with a solid thud.

I remember I wished then that we could lock him out there forever. I remember that feeling of hope and escape if it were possible. But I knew in my heart, from my earliest childhood forward, there was no escape from a dictator. He was bigger than me, larger than life. I had to learn to outsmart him, to play his game better than he could. Until we were teenagers, he beat us. He had a fondness for yanking his belt out of his pants loops and slashing our thighs and bottoms with it for the smallest offenses.

I don't want you to feel sorry for me, of course. Everybody has to go through things in this life. Sure, I sugarcoat my childhood when I'm talking to strangers, when I'm talking to anyone, including Mia, about it. I tell them about cozy family dinners, at the house and out at the fancy restaurant. But that's a survival trick I learned from my mother, I suppose. You don't discuss family dirty laundry, not at all. You smile and quietly accept what comes your way. Don't make waves, not until you're the one in control. Then you get your revenge.

My six-year-old self finally gave in after a couple of hours sitting alone at the table in the dark. I picked up one of the green beans, grown limp and cold and slimy, and placed it on my tongue and then slid it to the back of my throat. Of course, I vomited my dinner all over the table, and myself. I knew I would, I suppose, somewhere down inside. I won that battle. Never had to eat a green bean at my house again. They're symbolic of victory for me now. I made a point to eat them whenever we were someplace else, like the nice restaurant in town. I pretended to love all green beans except the ones he wanted me to eat. Each green bean I ate in his presence, say at a restaurant, slowly and with a smile, reminded my father of the night I won. It was a green-coated foreshadowing of my ultimate victory.

By now you're probably wondering why my wife and I were comfortable living in a home next to my parents, the same dictator and his accomplice who were the villains of my childhood. Well, the simple answer is we needed help with childcare, for starters. Plus I am too old to beat with a belt, and I didn't need his money to live. He couldn't hurt me anymore and he wouldn't dare touch my boys.

Perhaps I also wanted to allow my parents a glimpse at how great my life is compared to theirs, how beautiful my wife is, how rich we are. Our house is bigger, of course, twice the size of theirs and we have double the backyard. It was almost as if they lived in the outhouse of my large mansion, or at least I liked to think of it that way. My life has more of everything. I proved to them that I could move into this upscale suburb now, when it was the place to be. When they moved here, it wasn't. They were just lucky. Me, I'm übersuccessful. I wanted them to see that, to see each of my boys and how happy they are. Watch as they eat whatever they'd like, as much or as little as they wish. Yes, living well is the best revenge.

I'm the opposite of my father in many ways. I fight to be like that, to be his opposite, every day, tamping down the anger that's there, the fire-filled rage he instilled inside me from an early age. It's like a wildfire that is 80 percent contained. It flares up sometimes, but it's mostly under control. In fact, most people who meet me in the business world think I'm easygoing, friendly, the life of the party. And I am, because I work hard to be those things.

Living next door to the person you despise gives you a constant reminder to be better, to do better. My little brother, Tom, moved away years ago, and none of us have heard from him since he graduated college. Well, he did "call in" to the private funeral, but that hardly counts. His absence all these years was a strain on my mom, I'm sure, no doubt contributing to her early onset Alzheimer's, even though he would never take responsibility for that, I'm sure. He'd rather hide in California, pretend none of us existed until there was a chance for an inheritance. Too bad, Tommy, too bad.

Who knows, maybe it wasn't Tom's fault. Maybe my mom just wanted to fade away from the ogre she had married and allowed to rule her roost. That could be the case. My hope back then was that it was contagious, the Alzheimer's, that soon I'd see my father decline into a babbling, drooling mess. I dreamed about that too often, imagining his slip into helplessness as a just punishment for his crimes. It never happened, but that's fine because the gas took care of it. It doesn't bother me that I now live next to the house where my parents died, though as I mentioned, Mia thinks it ought to. Why should it? We all go sometime. It was their time.

As for my long-lost brother calling in to the funeral, that really happened. Mia and the boys and I walk into the funeral parlor, both caskets closed up in front, the rent-a-pastor standing stoically, awaiting our arrival.

"I'm sorry for your loss," the preacher said, nodding at us.

"I'm sure you won't mind that we have one more person here who wishes to pay his respects. Your brother, Tom, couldn't be with us today in person, but he did want to participate in the service remotely."

That's when the preacher pointed to a cell phone propped on top of my dad's casket.

"Are you kidding me? Tommy?" I managed before Mia grabbed my arm.

"Hey, big brother. How's it going?" the cell phone said.

I tilted my head, the shock clearing at the sound of his voice. I knew why he'd made contact, but there was nothing left. I'd made sure of it. "I've been better, Tommy. Where are you?"

The cell phone voice laughed. "Same place as always, big brother. But now's not quite time for small talk. Shall we get on with the service, then?"

I swallowed and shrugged as Mia guided me into the seat next to hers. The preacher spoke for what seemed to be no more than a minute and then it was all over. We said amen and I leaped up, grabbing the phone, pushing the button to get it off speaker.

"Tom, listen, I need to talk to you," I said. I cupped my hand over the phone, my back to my family, my waist pressing against my dad's coffin.

"There's nothing left to say. I'm assuming you'll split any inheritance that is left, as that's customary and fair, but I suspect I'm not going to get anything. The pastor has my attorney's information, if you do find it in your heart to share any proceeds of their estate with me."

I kept my voice low, in control, and said, "They were totally leveraged. There won't be a penny left after funeral costs. But why don't we meet, talk about this in person?"

"Right. I figured you'd say that. Have a nice life, Paul."

And the phone went dead. He's a piece of work, that brother of mine. Crazy, too. I just wish I could get my hands on him, you know, to talk, brother to brother. I've tried to find him, but I have no idea where he is hiding. California is a frustratingly big state. I'm sure he's having a happy little life. He sounded good. I'll find him if and when I need to. He and I are survivors; we both escaped our parents, we just did it in different ways.

I know what you're thinking. I'm being too dark on this special day, thinking about dreary memories instead of focusing on the moment here at this wonderful little community hugging the lake. Instead of thinking about my deceased father, who died before any cognitive slip could happen, unfortunately, I should focus on the bright orange sky proclaiming the sunset. Or smile about the fact that I'm up next to be checked out by the man with the yellow fingernails. Or I could congratulate myself again, for outsmarting the yellow-taloned dictator, for rising so far past him and his pungent reach.

Fingernails just like my dear old dad's drum on the counter. "How you doing?" the man behind the cash register, Frank or not-Frank, asks. "Find everything you need?"

He is smiling at me, revealing teeth also yellowed from tobacco, like corn kernels dangling from his gums. Did I find everything I need? Well, no, of course not. Do we ever?

"Yes, just enough," I say, flashing my pearly white teeth and cutting myself off before adding: *considering I didn't go to a real grocery store.* Because even though that is the honest answer, I've learned people don't often want to hear the truth. Some get their "feelings" hurt. As if a feeling could be hurt. Strange, us humans, stranger still. I've told you I'm a student of emotional reactions. And I'm an actor. I've studied how to imitate the reactions one is supposed to have: tears for sadness, or at least droopy eyes. Smile and twinkling eyes for joy. You know the rest. You've probably learned how to fake some yourself. I mean, are you actually as heartbroken about a friend's dog dying as you say you are on Facebook? Come on. *It's a dog.* Though I'm sure you probably feel more emotions than I do. I feel anger and lust, mostly. Sometimes, I must admit, I feel proud of myself.

"That's it, then?" the man asks, as if the empty counter in front of him couldn't answer the question.

"I'll take a pack of Marlboros, red," I say, surprising myself. I don't smoke, never have. "Matches, too, if you've got them." That was a gut reaction, an impulse purchase they call it. I wanted to feel a pack of cigarettes, his brand, in my hand again, to feel the power of crumpling the pack beyond smoke-ability. One of the tiny acts of defiance of my childhood. Oh, and I need matches. Always have a pack of matches on you, dear old dad told us, in case he needed to bum a light. We were his servants, Tommy and I. But in his defense, I've found it a good practice to have quick access to a flame.

"Sure," the man says, reaching behind him to the locked cabinet, turning the key and pulling out the pack. He seems to look at me with renewed appreciation. We're kindred spirits now, us smokers.

I slide my credit card across the counter, noticing the dirt and grime that years of packaged goods, plastic bags of vegetables, hands and sweat have ground deep into the countertop surface. I wonder how many different people's DNA is represented here. The man swipes my card and hands it back. I wipe it on my jeans before putting it back in my wallet.

"Got another? This one's been declined," he says.

I feel that emotion, the fire spark. "Run it again. It's an American Express. It has no limit," I say. I swallow to keep my voice in check. There are two people behind me, soon to be more. I don't look at their faces, just down at their shoes. The man behind me is a worker of some sort; he wears thick-soled tan boots and loose, stained khaki pants. Behind him is a woman with Nike tennis shoes and tight yoga pants. She's a weekender, a vacationer. I know they see me as a success-ful business executive.

"Still no go," the man says. "Just give me a different one—you're holding up the line."

We are no longer smoker comrades. "You're probably doing it wrong, but fine, here," I say. My voice is deep, angry. My jaw is tense. If I could see myself in a mirror, I know I'd see my father's dark, angry eyes. I've given him the credit card I save for emergencies, as I must get out of here and back to my cottage. The emergency card is one I applied for six months ago; it's just mine, not joint, but it's almost tapped out. The offer came in the mail at the perfect time. This card has been fueling most of my life.

"Receipt with you or in the bag?" he asks, sliding the mer-chant copy across the counter for me to sign.

"The bag," I say, signing with a jagged line, more of a *P* squiggle *S* squiggle than anything. My monogram is some-thing I'm proud of, come to think of it: Paul Randolph Strom. *PRS: almost a person. Just missing a couple things.* I smile; the fire is dying and something like relief is washing over me. "Have a nice night."

"Whatever, dickhead," I hear a male voice say to my back. I know it's the man in the work boots, because it isn't the man at the cash register's voice. I know working-man is jeal-ous of me and my life: my closet full of designer clothes, my grand home on a treelined, sidewalked street, my beautiful wife who he is imagining in tight yoga pants. Probably, he's tired of all of us, the wealthy city folk already clogging the streets and shops of his small town, and it's not even Memorial Day weekend yet.

The fire is almost out, and I want to keep it there. So instead of turning around, I chuckle and shake my head back and forth. *Poor working-man*, that's what I'm saying with my body language. I know he'll get the drift so I hurry to my car and load the three brown bags of groceries quickly. I don't have time to fight this man. I shove the cart up against the ice bag machine and jump into the car.

As I back out of the parking space, working-man appears in the red glow of my taillights. If I push on the gas, I'd run him over. It would be ruled an accident. He's barely visible in the fading light. He pauses, hands on hips, weighing his options, his chances. And then he flips me the middle finger of his right hand and I smile. He moves out of the way as I reverse, just like I knew he would. This life is about one thing, winning and losing. He knows he lost.

As I pull back through the open gate into the perfect little community, I check to be sure working-man isn't following me. I doubt he would brave the gates—we do have security even when it's not high season. Still, it is rather easy to follow someone, tail them in your car, if you're skillful and careful. I've done it before, not lately, but enough times to know how. It's sort of like in the movies. You wear a black shirt, make sure it's a dark, moonless night if you can. Most of the time, people don't notice their surroundings. They wouldn't even realize if the same car was following them for miles.

It's the same following someone on foot, or, say, sneaking into someone's home. It's easy if you're quiet and methodical.

Take my father, for example. It's as if he was blind, not deaf. It was the middle of the day. He should have seen me sitting in the corner of their cramped living room, suit coat tossed on the couch and my tie loosened, waiting for my mom to come home from running errands. He walked right past me on his way to the bedroom, but he didn't notice. He never did see me for who I am, always underestimating me.

It wouldn't have changed anything, but he should have seen me coming.

6:15 P.M.

"

I drive slowly down Second Street, and note the line of twenty or so people waiting to get into Sloopy's. That spot is going to be packed all weekend and my favorite pink-haired waitress will be making some good tips. I'm glad I made a reservation for us tonight at a new Italian restaurant in Port Clinton. It actually has its own herb garden, which will make my wife happy. I hope it's not as crowded there as it is here. I'm still surprised so many people had the same idea to head to the lake this weekend. The economy is back on track, I guess, for most people.

I pass the park, lit by streetlamps in the growing dusk, and see a young mother pushing her child on a swing. I have so many images in my mind of Mia doing just that with our boys, their squeals of delight floating through the air, reaching me as I sit on the park bench watching over them all. Neither of my boys inherited my rage, I am almost certain. I've seen no hints. No rock throwing, no toys mangled and destroyed. Instead, they play together nicely, are polite and happy, I think. The generational darkness of rage has skipped over them, though most likely it will appear in their children. It's a strong gene, anger. But for now, I will continue to nurture their happiness. They are my gift to the world, my sons are.

I stop in front of the Boones' cottage. All of the lights are on, it seems, in every room of the place. They are entertaining people from our neighborhood, no doubt, wining and dining them at their grand historic cottage. I try to look in the windows, to get a glimpse of who else may be seated at their long table for twelve. But all I can distinguish are shapes of people, some overall characteristics maybe, but not enough to identify who they are. Most of the neighbors don't know me, or care to, and the feeling is mutual. There's another feeling I can name: disdain. But they do know Mia, many of them, and are friends with her, too. Mia is a person many want to befriend.

Take Buck, for example. I turn the corner onto Laurel Street and our cottage is glowing with light, too. There are two people on the screened-in porch. They sit in the two chairs that face the sofa. The furniture is old and rather embarrassing. The ancient outdoor wicker set itself is valuable—they just don't make them like this anymore—but the fabric covering the cushions is obnoxious, a gaudy green-and-pink-floral design that reminds me of my mother's favorite teacup pattern, blown up. I know this set came with the place and we haven't invested in new cushions. Perhaps that is an expense for this summer. Because no matter how often the slipcovers are laundered, there is always the smell of dust, lingering and thick. It climbs onto your clothes when you sit too long, seeps into your pores like a small dose of poison. Sneaks up on you, I guess. I start sneezing if I spend more than ten minutes out there.

Mia knows this, and yet, there they sit. The two of them. In my cottage. On my porch during my romantic weekend. I dig my fingernails into my palm, enjoying the sting.

I pull into the driveway and stop the car in front of the back door. I realize Mia does not like it when I park here, considers it lazy, and would prefer it if I pulled into the garage. It is more civilized, she explains. That may be the case, but I'm late and I have three grocery bags. I am anxious to question Mia about the credit card, our credit card being declined, but will wait until Buck is gone. Which will be soon. We have dinner plans.

I pop open the trunk and gather the bags in my arms. I'm trying to figure out how to turn the knob to open the back door when Mia opens it for me.

"What took you so long? I thought you got lost," Mia says. Her face is flushed, either from laughing or from alcohol. Or both. She wrestles one of the bags out of my arms as Buck appears behind her.

"Can I help?" Buck says. "Must have been a big line at the grocery."

"There was a line, yes," I say. My tone is calm, measured. I am fighting fire. I place the two bags on the counter next to the one my wife plunked down. I look in the third bag and notice the pack of cigarettes. I had meant to leave them in the car. I reach into the bag and slide the pack up my palm and into my shirtsleeve. I will hide them in my briefcase upstairs.

"We'll unload these, Paul. Why don't I make you a drink? Tito's with a squeeze of lime coming right up," Mia says. "Go sit and relax."

I don't want to leave the kitchen, but I need to dispose of the cigarettes.

"Great, sounds good. And, honey, we need to leave in about ten minutes, for our dinner reservation," I say. I think I notice my wife and Buck exchanging looks, a silent communication of sorts. But I could be imagining things. My mind has been busy today. I don't say anything, just walk out of the room. I still need to remove the surprise from the glove box, but every time I remember to do so, our neighbor is around it seems. I will bring it out tonight, after dinner, once good old Buck has gone away for good.

I climb the stairs two at a time, hurry to our bedroom, and push the cigarettes into the pocket inside my briefcase and zip it closed. I take a moment in the bathroom, quickly brushing my teeth and splashing water on my face, adding a little aftershave. I examine my shirt in the mirror and decide I should change. This is our special day. I hurry back into our bedroom and pull out my favorite thin navy cashmere sweater. I tug on a crisp white T-shirt and then the sweater. My eyes are still dark, but brightened a bit by the sweater. My jeans look fine, and my leather loafers are a statement by themselves. A present from Mia a couple years ago, they're Gucci. Classic.

I turn off the lights to the bedroom and head back down. "Buck and I moved inside," Mia says as I reach the bottom of the stairs. "I know how you hate that musty old porch. Here's your drink."

I just now realize Mia has changed into a dress. It's midthigh, a shiny champagne-colored silk. She's wearing heels, and her legs look fantastic. I should have told her so. I am positive Buck has beaten me to the punch. Buck is sitting in my favorite chair. I glare at the back of his head as I walk to the seating area.

Mia has placed my drink on the coffee table next to hers. She pats the couch cushion. This couch is new; we had a decorator help select this entire seating area. The couch is a light tan, firm but still fluffy. The two club chairs are upholstered in a pale blue cotton. They are the most comfortable chairs I've ever owned. Buck is seated across the coffee table from Mia, in one of my comfortable club chairs. Those are much more comfortable than the couch, but I choose to sit down next to my wife, squeezing her knee with my hand as I do.

"Ouch," she says, pulling her leg away from me. I must have grabbed a bit too hard.

"Sorry, honey, just wanted to tell you how great you look in that dress," I say. "Got carried away. Cheers!"

"How thoughtful, Paul," Mia says. Her tone makes me think she doesn't believe I'm thoughtful at all. "Cheers."

"Cheers," Buck says, raising his glass in my direction. His handsome news anchor face is not cheerful. I don't think he liked me touching my own wife. His eyes narrow as he says, "What restaurant are you dining at tonight?"

"Oh, some new Italian place in Port Clinton," I say. "They have their own herb garden, so I knew Mia would enjoy it." I turn to smile at my wife and she offers a mild close-lipped smile back. I may put my arm around her shoulders and pull her in to me, just to see his reaction, and hers. Perhaps a romantic kiss on the cheek is in order?

"Ciao Bella," Buck says. "Nice place. Good atmosphere for up here."

"Glad you approve," I say. "Well, look at the time. We should get going." I smile at Mia and fight the urge to yank her up from the couch by the arm. I'm also resisting the urge to kick Buck out of my house. Best thing for me to do is to stand. So I do.

"Since you were running late, I moved the reservation back a half hour," Mia says. "So sit down, relax. We have time to finish our drinks."

Well played, Mia, I think. My mind is busy tonight, as I mentioned, and it flashes to another time, another home, another happy hour, this one in Nashville, Tennessee, with a different blonde woman. She was a Mia knockoff, really. Her name was Lois and she was captivating. She said those exact words to me: *sit down, relax, we have time to finish our drinks.* No doubt you realize by now I don't like being told what to do. I didn't back then either.

I was young. I couldn't control my fire. I didn't know that I could just stand up, for example, and walk into the kitchen pretending to be in search of ice and a snack. Lois had opened the door in her bathrobe, not even close to being ready. She told me to sit down and wait, like a dog. I stepped inside the door, pulling it shut behind me. Back then, my temper would explode immediately: a fistful of rage to a beautiful face, for example. We'd been together, Lois and I, for more than a year by then. She had no way of seeing this coming, as up until then our relationship had been all fun and great sex. But on that fateful night, we were to attend a cocktail party held in my honor by the professor I'd been working with. It was a very important event, a thank-you and a congratulations, an introduction to society so to speak. Lois wasn't ready when she said she would be. She completely disrespected me, and the importance of the night. It wasn't my fault, not really.

Blood was flowing from her nose as she looked at me in shock, the front of her bathrobe turning reddish brown, her bright blue eyes shiny with fear and tears. I looked down at my fist, rubbed my knuckles where her flesh had stung, and shook my head.

"Lois, please, never tell me what to do," I said. We were in her tiny apartment, now ours, a place I knew intimately since we'd made love on just about every counter and piece of furniture. I walked quickly to the kitchen, turning on the faucet and soaking a dish towel before wrapping it around several cubes of ice. I pulled the paper towel roll from the holder and presented everything to her. I shook my head in disgust. Now we wouldn't make the reception. She'd ruined everything.

"You need to put ice on your face. Lie back and the bleeding will stop," I said. I wasn't at all sure this was the case, of course. The few times I'd been in fights before with boys my own age, neither had sustained serious injuries. My father always was careful his blows fell in places easily disguised by clothing. Unfortunately, Lois's injury seemed serious and quite visible.

"Leave," she whispered. She refused to take the ice or the paper towels so I dropped them onto the couch next to her. She was shaking, violently, and I wondered if I should hold her, squeeze her tight. I was afraid, somehow, that maybe I would hurt her more. Could hurt her more. I stood there, immobilized, my feet weighed down by cement. The times I'd seen my father strike my mother flashed through my mind. Her screams, his empty promises. These memories were loud, thudding through my brain.

But between Lois and me, at that moment, there was only silence. I remembered checking my watch. There was blood decorating its face.

We'd met in Greek Mythology class my senior year in college, when I was goofing off during the last semester of my undergraduate career, and she was a young, adorable freshman. She called me Zeus when we were in bed, when I'd make her orgasm like no one had before. She was a studious sophomore now, and I was doing consumer research for the professor, the one whose invite-only party we were going to miss that night, while I interviewed for jobs at advertising agencies in town. I'd finally accepted an account executive position at a prestigious local firm. This cocktail reception was my goodbye party, and my introduction to important people in Nashville. This night was to be my launch into the ad agency world. Why didn't she understand how important it was?

"Lois, no one can know about what happened here, do you understand? I'm starting my job tomorrow," I said. My voice was calm. Fatherly. It was logical that she would want my new career to start out well, unimpeded by innuendo and the like.

Her trembling was becoming more violent, but her eyes were focused on me intently, as if seeing inside me to my organs, my small beating heart. The blood flow from her nose had slowed, but her robe was now covered. Blood splattered in her lap, in the white cotton folds.

"If you leave and never call me again, no one will know. If I see you, or hear from you, I will press charges," she said. Her voice was quivering with fear.

Press charges, why don't you? I wanted to say. I would explain that she was delusional, that she fell into the kitchen counter but wanted to blame me. Sure, I could get out of any charges as quickly as she could press them. My father, I learned all the tricks from him. But I didn't really need her anymore. It was time to move on, establish my career. I didn't need this college baggage situation any longer.

"As you wish," I said, bowing at the waist before leaving. It was a reference to her favorite movie, *The Princess Bride*, and her reaction wasn't her typical reply. As I opened the door and stepped into the humid Nashville night, her scream followed me out. But I know there was still love for me in her heart. I'm unforgettable. Oh, and the cocktail reception was fabulous. Poor Lois sent her regards as she was under the weather.

Now, standing in the kitchen, I hear my wife laughing in the living room. Unwittingly, she is stoking the fire with her words, her actions and her joy. But it is fine. I've learned to control myself since that night in Nashville. I'm telling myself to relax: *Mia doesn't mean to upset you tonight.* I know she doesn't. We've been together a long time, we've worked out the relationship just fine. She's simply entertaining our unnecessary guest, our lonely loser of a neighbor. But soon we'll be on our way to dinner and everything will be back in control. We need to discuss the job, Buck, the credit card situation tonight during the meal. It might be uncomfortable, but once she understands my priorities, we will have the best night ever. It's certainly salvageable. And just like that, I have calmed myself down.

I wipe my sweaty palms on my pants legs before I walk back into the family room, carrying the bag of cashews I'd picked up at the grocery store.

"Nuts, anyone?" I ask. Both Mia and Buck shake their heads. I shrug and carry the bag over to the couch and take my seat next to my wife. "So, Buck, did you really spend the winter up here? Is it true you really live here full-time, year-round?"

"I did and I do. For now. It's a great place to find peace and think. It works for me," he says. His dimple appears as he smiles at us, the happy couple on the couch. He must be so jealous. He's so alone.

"And is it true your wife died?" I say. I mean, we've never discussed his lack of a spouse, man-to-man. At least I hadn't discussed it with him. Who knows what Mia knows. All I've heard through the grapevine was that his wife was dead. I thought it best to seem interested in our guest.

"Paul. Really?" Mia says. I note her cheeks are flushed and she shakes her head back and forth. Embarrassed, that's the emotion. Too bad, Mia.

"Yes. It's true. Stage four lung cancer, inoperable. She was a nonsmoker. Woke up in the middle of the night, short of breath. Five months later, I buried her." Buck says these things without emotion. The way I might say them if I hadn't practiced emotional responses. It makes me wonder about Buck. He adds, "It was the hardest five months of my life."

"Worse for her," I say. From the looks of it, my joke was not well received by my wife or our guest.

"Buck, I'm sorry," Mia says. "Paul's emotional intelligence is a bit lacking, I've come to realize. He tries but, well, Paul, you understand that was insensitive, right?"

I've slipped the matches that were left on the counter when they unloaded the grocery bags into my pocket. Right now I imagine pulling them out, lighting them all and throwing them at my wife. The fire. My left hand slides into my front pocket, but I can't reach the matches while seated. I take a deep breath and flash a smile at my wife. She's so cute.

I turn my attention back to the interloper. "I'm sorry for your loss, Buck. Is that why you quit your job and moved here, the middle of nowhere?" I ask. The neighborhood snoop's job may be in jeopardy, I tell myself. I know I can run circles around her anyway, if I liked gossip that is. Which I don't.

"Yes. I sold everything we'd built together. Our house, our apartment in the city, our cars except one. I sold my business and just started driving. Somehow, I took the right exit from the highway and found myself here," he says. He wipes his palms on his pants as if signaling that is the end of his explanation.

I turn to look at my wife. She is beaming, her face covered with a smile so big and so fake it must hurt her cheeks. Or maybe it's a genuine smile. One I never see. One that is reserved for Buck, the garden gnome.

"This is a perfect place to heal," Mia says.

Whatever. My mind flashes back to Lois. I did see her again, of course, on campus, but she didn't see me. I knew her class schedule, and I also needed to be sure she wouldn't ruin anything for me and my new job at the hippest advertising agency in Nashville. So I kept tabs on her. I'm a good follower, like I noted. She healed well. I heard through the grapevine that she told her friends she blacked out and fell. Had low blood sugar or something?

Found out she did undergo surgery to straighten things out. And I think she may have had a little something taken off the tip of her nose, a cosmetic enhancement. She looked good, last time I saw her. Better even than she looked before the little incident. Making lemonade out of lemons, that's my little Lois. She honored her end of our agreement, and so did I. I'm a man of my word. After launching my successful advertising career in Nashville, I moved back to Columbus. As for Lois, she's married, with a bunch of kids now. Everything works out.

"You two better get going if you want to make your reservation," Buck says. He stands up. How helpful. At his command, my wife finally rises.

"Yes, I'm ready," she says. "I'll just grab my purse."

"I'll show myself out," Buck says. "Have a good time." He waves his hand at me awkwardly, no doubt afraid to shake it. I still didn't get an answer on what he did before he dropped into our lives, but I don't think he was an actual anchorman. Business of some kind is what he said. I guess I will believe him. For now, I just want him out of here.

"Right, well, enjoy your evening." As I walk him to the door, I ask, "Any special ladies in your life, Buck?" It has been a year since his wife died, after all, and men have needs. I think that is a thing a guy would say to another guy.

Mia appears beside me. She must have overheard me because she says, "Really, Paul?"

Buck chuckles. "It's okay, Mia," he says. "I'm sure Paul just wishes me the best, don't you, Paul?" Buck slaps me on the back, firmly. A brotherly pat, that's what I'll consider it. I slip my hand into my pocket, rubbing the matches between my fingers.

7:30 P.M.

12

We are still late for our reservation even though Mia moved it back. I knew we would be. It's Friday night, and tourists like us have arrived at the lake. We are stuck in traffic. I take a deep breath. There is nothing I can do but try to relax. I've called the restaurant, and they will hold our table. It's a special table, for a special night. I'm thankful for their understanding and will tip the host. I hope Mia brought cash.

"Let's call Claudia and check on the boys," I say. I know Mia is tense beside me, clasping her hands tightly in her lap. She probably is worried I am upset with her for our late arrival at the restaurant, but I will show her I'm fine. Calling the boys is a peace offering. I am a normal, loving husband and father.

"They aren't home. They're getting pizza," she says.

"Well, Claudia can answer her cell phone at a pizza joint, can't she?" I ask. Logical question, I think.

"Let's not bother them during dinner," Mia says. *That's odd.* She is the person who has called Claudia at least four times since we left home this morning. "I mean, they're getting pizza at the movies. There's a new animated superhero movie out today. I told her to take them. I planned ahead and bought tickets for them online."

The hairs on the back of my neck are standing up. Is my wife lying to me? I wonder. This does not make sense, not at all. I refuse to believe that is the case. I know my wife. My wife loves me, and logically, I know I should trust her as much as she should trust me. We have two sons and a life together. She thought ahead and bought them all tickets to the movie. That is thoughtful, she is kind. I need to relax.

Love is such a complicated thing to us humans. We overanalyze, we fret, we try to understand it. It's easier to understand if you think of us all as animals, with needs and desires. That's what we are, all of us. Here, consider this: my wife loves me almost as much as Gretchen does. Gretchen benefits from the carefree Paul, the Paul without obligations. Mia, well, she gets a slightly less shiny version of the Paul who Gretchen sees, the version of me that Gretchen loves. Mia had that once, at the beginning of our relationship, but now she has two kids and, well, a history with me. The good and the bad. Hopefully, she still remembers the early, shiny years.

Ah, Gretchen. She's the one I've been fighting the urge to call since we left home this morning. She's the one who has called me a few times since we left. Sweet girl. I know she misses me. She tells me it's our six-month anniversary this weekend. But it isn't appropriate for me to talk to her on this day. I have rules. I don't want you to think less of me because of Gretchen's existence, so please don't. Our relationship doesn't harm anyone; it simply brings more joy to the world as a whole.

We are together almost every day now, and the fact I haven't touched her or talked to her today stings. Don't get me wrong, she isn't above Mia in my mind, she's distinct. Gretchen is fun, while Mia is family. Gretchen is youth and fucking—pardon, great sex. Mia is family dinners and strawberry patches and Scrabble. Am I explaining things well enough for you? They don't have anything to do with each other, and they'll never meet. I am the only overlap, the circle in the middle of the Venn diagram that depicts Gretchen's circle on one side, Mia's on the other. Their lives will never converge; they never will meet even though Gretchen lives in the next suburb over, a five-minute drive away. That is the way my world works. It is neat and orderly. Defined. I'm in control.

Nevertheless, Gretchen is angry that I'm away this weekend and have told her we will not speak on the phone. I am surprised she has called me since she knows the rules. She understands the way things are. I told her going in that I love my wife, and that I'd never leave her, although between you and me, there are no real absolutes in life, are there? Gretchen and I have something special, but not as special as what I have with Mia. I know this is confusing to you perhaps, but my relationship with my mistress doesn't have anything to do with my relationship with my wife. They are wholly separate, but both valued. Tonight's not the night for me to be thinking about Gretchen, but my mind is busy for some reason.

Yesterday, we ate lunch in bed, and Gretchen wore a navy silk nightgown that hugged her thin frame, accentuating her generous breasts. She's a gorgeous brunette, in her late twenties, who works at a lingerie store at the mall called I See London. We met six months ago, when I went to the mall to kill time, maybe buy a gift for Mia. I had suddenly found myself with too much time on my hands during the day, and going shopping seemed as good a pursuit as any. I told myself if I saw anyone I would explain it was client research for a new account. I mean, only women go to malls in the daytime, everyone knows that. But I had a business reason.

I wandered into the store bursting with silk finery in all shades of the rainbow. As soon as I saw Gretchen, I felt that familiar attraction—the buzz, the electricity—and I knew she and I were meant to be. I started by asking her to help me pick a lingerie set. We moved on to a discussion of the quality of the silk—given my extensive travels to Asia, I wanted only the finest and I knew how to spot it, I told her.

Her eyes glistened the moment I mentioned travel, and I knew she was nibbling the bait.

"Let me take you to the high-end lingerie area," Gretchen said, turning and tossing her long dark hair over her shoulder.

"I'll follow you anywhere, my dear," I said, adding my signature smile and wink.

It's as if no one else was in the store, no one else was in the entire mall. Gretchen and I flirted for at least an hour, as she held up options for me to consider, as our fingertips lightly brushed over the silk goodies, as we talked about our shared love of jazz music (yes!), our shared dream of moving to the beach (why not?) and spending a New Year's Eve in Paris (let's do it). She was captivating, young, enthusiastic, and the attraction was intense, instant. I wasn't looking, promise. I may have left my wedding ring in the car, but that was just an accident.

"So who is the lucky lady who will be wearing this?" she asked as she finished wrapping my purchase in a thick white gift paper, tying it with a red silk bow. She handed the pack-

age to me. Her fingers were blissfully unadorned, I had noticed early on.

I smiled then, waiting a beat. "I hope you like it. It's for
you."

Her lovely heart-shaped face flushed with color as I handed
the gift to her. "I couldn't."

"You can. I insist. I'm sure it will look wonderful on you."
I checked my watch. "I have to run. Meeting at work. It's
been nice talking to you, Gretchen."

I turned to leave, wondering if my hook had set. I'd reached
the door of the retail boutique and was about to enter the mall
when I felt a hand on my shoulder.

"Paul, wait. Can I see you again?" Gretchen asked. Her
flush deepened. "I really enjoyed talking to you, too."

I pulled a business card out of my wallet, a new card, with
my cell phone a substitute for where my work number had
been. But for that minor distinction it was an exact copy of
my actual Thompson Payne card, complete with my title,
Director of Account Services. Women love *Mad Men*. "Call
me. I've got to run."

It's hard to walk away when the currents of attraction are
so strong, but that's what I did that afternoon, fortunately. It
makes the eventual first kiss that much more intense, trust
me. I know about these things. As I left the store I saw Doris
Boone standing next to a potted plant in the mall. She was
staring at me like I'd committed a crime. "It isn't illegal to
shop during the day in a mall, is it, Doris?" I felt like saying. Instead I gave her a weak wave and hurried out to the
parking lot. Doris saw nothing, I told myself then. I was only
doing research.

Gretchen smells of strong perfume whenever she comes
home from working at I See London. She says French per-

fume is pumped through the air vents, a colorless scented gas. The smell is awful and makes me sneeze, like trying to sit on my outdoor porch in Lakeside. She tries to shower before we meet, before I arrive at her door, but sometimes she hasn't had time and I can never wait. I don't have a choice. Her skin is flawless, her lips full and pink. Just thinking about her now I feel myself stirring.

But I need to focus on my wife. Just tonight, moments earlier, Mia told a stranger that I don't have a high emotional intelligence, which is ridiculous, and now she's lying to me about my children.

"What's the name of the movie, Mia?" I ask. We're at another stoplight. The red glow fills the car as I turn to face her. She looks frightened, or maybe it's just the crimson glow.

"Super Dog," she says. "It's new. The boys are super excited. We can call them tomorrow morning. They'll be in bed before our dinner is finished, no doubt."

"Let's call them now. Maybe the movie hasn't started yet."

If I expected an argument, I'd have been mistaken. "Sure," she says. "Call from your phone so it will go over Bluetooth. We can both talk that way."

I pull out my phone and push Claudia's number. The light turns green as the phone continues to ring and then goes to her voice mail. "This is Claudia. Leave a message." Her voice-mail recording sounds as devoid of energy as the actual person. Definitely a druggie.

"Claudia, Paul Strom, and Mia, calling to say goodnight to the boys. If you aren't at the movies, please give us a call back. Hope all is well. Thanks," I say into the air. I never did put the money on the credit card. She must be paying for the popcorn and pizza out of her own account. Fortunately, Mia already took care of the tickets. If that is where they are, I remind myself. But really, where else would they be? My wife doesn't lie to me. I relax my shoulders and put a smile on my face.

"Oh, well, I guess you were right," I say. I glance in her direction.

Mia nods next to me. I turn on the blinker and we ease into the parking lot of the restaurant. We are here.

"This looks nice, Paul," she says as we stop in front of the valet. Not many restaurants at the lake have valet parking. I'm glad she is impressed, as am I. The young man opens Mia's door and I watch his face as he checks her out. *Not bad*, his face registers.

"Welcome to Ciao Bella," says a second boy who is opening my door.

"Thank you," I say, taking the ticket from him and hurrying to my wife's side. I slide my arm around Mia's waist and look down at my wife, feel her in my grip. She's so sweet and kind. Why does my mind imagine her doing anything devious? We walk up the steps of the restaurant and into a sanctuary of dim lighting, attentive service and dark paneling. I'm instantly pleased with my selection, my fine taste.

"This is lovely, Paul," Mia says. A hostess escorts us to the promised window table, a corner table with views of the lake. I need to slip this young lady some money. All I have left in my wallet is a ten-dollar bill. I hope that suffices. As I hand it to her, she nods and smiles. Suddenly, I wonder if my wife has brought her credit card. I watch as she hangs her purse on the back of her chair, and I feel relieved.

"Welcome," says a man who appears to be about my age and also appears to be our waiter. He has white hair and frosty blue eyes and a complexion almost as pale as the white linen tablecloth. He wears a black tuxedo jacket, black pants. Quite formal. I like it. "I understand this is a special evening. May I ask: anniversary, birthday?"

"No, just the best day ever," I say. Mia laughs with me. I like that sound.

"Well, that calls for some champagne, I'd say," the waiter says.

I look at Mia. It is polite to allow your date to answer.

"Sure, that sounds good," she says. "Is that okay with you, Paul, or would you like a cocktail?"

My wife also is so polite, so lovely.

"I'd love to drink some champagne with you, honey," I say.

"Wonderful," the waiter says and scurries away.

We both stare out the window. I notice a lighthouse perched on the rocks at the end of my line of sight, its bright spotlight warning boaters of the dangers there. As the spotlight turns, it leaves a darker blackness in its wake.

8:00 P.M.

13

"So how was your afternoon, Mia?" I ask. I feel as if I haven't really talked to my wife since our drive up. It is time to be polite and friendly, to enjoy a lovely dinner sitting at our special lakefront table.

"Wonderful, really," she says. The waiter appears, goes through the usual champagne ritual of popping and all. Once our glasses are finally evenly filled, he departs. Mia raises her glass. "Cheers."

"Yes, cheers, honey," I say. "And, listen. I'm sorry about lunch today. I feel like it left us unsettled. The notion of you working for John is causing so much stress between us. Let's get past that, okay?"

"Sure." Mia smiles, looks around the room at our fellow diners. "Pretty swanky place for up here. I'm glad I dressed up."

"You look gorgeous, almost as young as the first time I saw you in the conference room of Thompson Payne."

"Must be the lighting. Good old Thompson Payne. I can't even believe you brought that place up." Mia is still smiling but her eyes aren't.

My heart thuds in my chest. "Why wouldn't I bring up the agency? It's been a part of our lives since we've been together."

"Oh, Paul. I know you must be embarrassed, but isn't it time you told me?" Mia asks. What is she referring to?

"What are you talking about, Mia?" I ask. I take a sip of my champagne. I don't really enjoy champagne, I remember now, but the alcohol is welcome. "Are you not feeling well? Is something wrong?"

"That's what I'd like to know."

"Then no, of course nothing's wrong. And I'm never embarrassed, honey."

"Ha. Well, I guess that will make this conversation easier. Do you want to know what I'm talking about, Paul?" she says. "Okay, then. For starters, when were you going to tell me you don't have a job?"

Boom. There it is. I wonder how long she has known. I suspect John told her, but it doesn't matter. I have been ready for this. "It's a temporary situation, easily fixed. I didn't want to worry you for no reason. I've been interviewing and expect an offer any day," I say. See, easy question, perfect answer.

"That's not the point. You didn't even tell me you'd been fired," Mia says. She dropped her voice at the word *fired*, thankfully. Such lies.

"For your information, honey, I wasn't fired, I left," I say. I focus on exuding an air of superiority. No one would fire me.

"They let you resign, but they fired you. I know all about it, Paul. And about your real issue with Caroline."

The waiter appears and hands a menu to my wife before offering me one. He refills our champagne flutes, both somehow empty in such a short amount of time. They must hold hardly anything. The menu is impressive, heavy, perhaps the weight of a hammer in my hand. He bows and leaves the table. I take a long sip of my champagne.

"What issue might that be?" I say. She is stirring up things she shouldn't. Mia is not part of Thompson Payne anymore, hasn't been for almost a decade. Mia doesn't know what did or didn't happen with Caroline or anything else. Whatever she's heard, it's gossip. I hate gossip. Mia was just a lowly copywriter assigned to technical manuals. She knows nothing about the advertising world anymore. Nothing.

"Paul, you're going to make your wife discuss your obsession with a young woman at work? Really? Maybe we should just go," Mia says. She closes her menu and puts it on the table.

I close my eyes and take a deep breath. No matter what Mia has heard, Caroline is not an obsession. Not at all. She's a problem, was a problem, but now everything is fine.

"This romantic dinner is part of our best day ever. Of course we aren't leaving. I'll overlook the fact that you, for some reason, have automatically taken the side of someone you've never met over your husband? And you believe what John says, someone who's jealous of me and my success, over what I'm telling you? I see where I stand," I say. I am exuding righteous indignation as I take another big sip of champagne.

I stare at Mia and she meets my gaze, our eyes locked across the table. Who will blink first? My menu is flat on the table now, too. I feel my hands become fists on top of the menu. "This is ridiculous. I will not sit here while my wife spews out baseless accusations. There is nothing further to discuss about my situation. Let's talk about John, his big mouth and his ridiculous job offer that you will not be taking!"

Mia's eyes flash at me, defiant. I look away, turning my

head to scan the restaurant. I see the waiter hovering, watching, his pale blue eyes accusing me of being a jerk. And so I am. I flick my hand and shoo him away. He disappears.

"This isn't about John. He's not even the one who told me. You know who did? Doris, Doris Boone, of all people," she says. Her hands are folded together now on top of the menu, as if in prayer.

Doris Boone? How did Doris know anything about my life? And if she knows, who else does? My mind flashes to Doris hiding behind the plant in the mall; I see Doris gossiping on her Lakeside front porch, I see her coming to my house to talk to Mia after I've left for work. Doris Boone was in my brother Tommy's class growing up. She knows the Strom family, it seems. She's always been a problem. Fortunately I excel at solving problems.

"They say the wife is always the last to know about these things," Mia adds. She says this quietly, without anger. I watch as a tear slides down her cheek. That single tear softens my heart, douses the flame. I'm not a monster. She wipes the droplet away with her fingertips and takes a drink of her champagne.

Poor girl. "Oh, honey, Caroline was obsessed with me and it got out of hand. It was embarrassing for everyone involved, especially me. If anything, I was the victim here. She needs help. And as for the job, it was time to go. I'd been there forever. I didn't tell you because I was just trying to protect you and the boys until I made my next move. It will be a great job, better than anything at old Thompson Payne. Probably one of the greatest jobs in Columbus, actually. And I promise, I'm about to announce great things," I say. Slowly, I reach across the table and cover her hands with mine. She doesn't pull away. "Everything is going to be fine. Haven't I always taken care of you? I have several job offers I'm weighing. I just want it to be perfect and great. The best. And we have your trust fund."

Mia's eyes burn into mine. I see fire there. That worries me, and I try to take a breath. I tense my hands, push down against hers on the table. But I can't stop what she has started. Why is she bringing all these topics to light? Tonight, of all nights. She may have fire in her eyes, but she has now reignited my flame.

But why is she crying? Her tears seem real. Mia looks directly at me. She doesn't blink. I don't like what she sees, I don't like how she looks.

She is making a big mistake. Challenging our very foundation, our fabulous life. It's a shame, really. Now more than ever, she should focus on everything that is good between us.

Next to us a four-top is seated. The women are laughing in loud staccato bursts. The men give each other a high five. Don't they know this is a romantic place, a quiet place? I want nothing more than to silence them.

8:15 P.M.

14

It takes more effort than I care to admit to ignore the bois-terous group and refocus on my wife. Mia looks down at the table and pulls her hands from mine. She wipes a second tear away and studies me as if she's never seen me before. "That trust is for the boys, not us. We will not be touching it," she says.

"Of course. No problem," I say. Why not just agree with her for the time being? I need to calm down, I must calm down. It's time to order. We need to talk about food, and enjoy ourselves. I open my menu and read intently. "Are you hungry? I'm starving. They have fabulous veal parmesan, I hear. Oh, and for you, look at all of the entrée salads. So much to choose from." That's the gift of life. Choices. So many. You make a mistake, and you pivot. You move on. Like Lois, just a mistake, and now I'm with the woman I was meant to have children with. Everything else is just background noise.

The waiter glides up to our table, carefully avoiding making eye contact with me and instead, focuses his attention on Mia. He should. She's beautiful, my wife.

"Ready to order?" the waiter asks.

"I'll have the salmon salad, no salmon, please," she says to the waiter.

"Yes, of course, madam. Some risotto perhaps? Vegetarian?" he says. If the waiter finds this order as ridiculous as I do, it doesn't show on his face. This guy just doesn't have a sense of humor, not at all.

"Please, and thank you," Mia says.

"May I be of any other assistance?" he asks. What's with this loaded question? I mean, he's a waiter. Assistance?

"No, I'm fine. That's all," she assures him. Her eyes are shiny but there are no tears rolling down her cheeks.

Asshole. Who does he think he is? "I'll have the veal, and a house salad to start," I say, holding my menu in the air. He takes it, without looking at me, and walks away. I hope he understands he is losing all possibility of a tip.

I look around the elegant restaurant, white-linen-draped tables now filled with sparkly diners, women wearing their finest dresses and jewelry, men looking the way men look at all restaurants of this nature: the same from a distance. Up close, that's when you can tell the thread count of the fabric, the cut of the jacket. Waves of polite conversation and bursts of laughter wash over us as we sit in silence in our corner.

How do you get backed into a corner in your relationship, you ask? I'm sure you've never been here before. Ha! Typically, it begins with small misunderstandings, insults not forgiven, if you will. And then the negative feelings build like a child's block tower. One block placed a little too far over, and the whole thing comes tumbling down. For my part, I believe I've been fair and forgiving. I try not to hold on to things, I place my blocks quickly, to complete the metaphor. But frankly, it's easy for me. I always know what's coming in the chess game of life. You need to be thinking several moves ahead. Always.

Take, for instance, when the boys were younger, Sam a newborn and Mikey a little over two. Both still in diapers. Now, those were the crazy days, harried times. I'd stroll in from work—coming home straight from the office on most days, missing important client happy hours—to help out. Mia would just glare at me, dark circles under her eyes, and hand me one kid or the other. She looked horrible, really horrible. I was tempted to have my mom come help, but I knew that would mean I'd opened the door for Mia's mother to come, too, with her nosy disapproval, and we couldn't have that. I needed them to stay in New York, continuing to build their empire. So, instead, I was there for Mia as much as possible. Did she ever thank me? Nope. Did I hold it against her? Of course not. But there was no way we were going to add a third kid to the mess we'd created. I was helping us both out with that by saying no to another baby. She had gone crazy or something.

Now, I could hold that time against her, you see. But I don't. I have let go of all those messy, annoying years. But she is holding something against me right now. It's uncharacteristic. It's un-Mia-like, and I don't deserve this, not at all. She sits across from me now, not as a woman who is backing me into a corner. Her demeanor doesn't fit her words. Instead of looking angry, she simply looks sad. As if it were I, not her, who precipitated this turn in our evening, which of course is ridiculous. This is all her fault.

She turns away from me and faces the window, looking out

toward the water, her back to the rest of the busy room, her lovely face in profile to me. She appears to be wiping a tear, but I cannot be certain. She focuses her attention on whatever is just outside the window of the restaurant. I know, of course, the lake is out there, dark and brooding, and the lighthouse with its ever-bright warnings.

But as I look more closely, my face almost touching the glass, I see an outside deck, a terrace of sorts, with tables and chairs. I suppose during nice weather and certainly during the day, the restaurant expands with outdoor seating. A deck the restaurant must use once the summer season is in full swing. Tonight, there is nobody out there.

I look back at my wife. Mia is smiling now; I see her face fully reflected in the glass, the candlelight illuminating her white teeth, her small nose, her glistening eyes. But why is she smiling? Does she see someone or something that I don't out there?

"Something funny?" I ask. Her mood, if I am reading things correctly, was angry and now sad. Smiling does not fit. My wife twitches in her seat, and then turns and faces me. Did she jump in her chair? Did she forget I was here?

"No, nothing," she says, and she is no longer smiling. "Paul. What are your plans? If you haven't been offered a job at any advertising agencies around town, which I suspect you won't be, then have you branched out? Looked for other opportunities?"

Apparently she wasn't listening when I told her I have many options. I don't like that the conversation has shifted to me not working in advertising—the industry we both love—away from me forbidding her from working in advertising. My headhunter informs me I do have an offer on the table, from *Columbus City* magazine of all places. That was the call this morning, the one that meant we got a later-than-hoped-for start to our day. My headhunter is excited and believes this is the "perfect fit." But my headhunter is an idiot if he thinks this is remotely the right kind of job for a man of my business stature.

The magazine would give me the title of Chief Revenue Officer, which sounds made up and probably is. The sales force—all ten people—would report to me. Yes, you can call it what it is. I'd be a sales manager for a city magazine. This is not what I want to do. It is far beneath my skill set. If I must, I will take this job. Put a huge spin on it to anyone who asks and then find something suitable. I don't want to do this, put this lowly job on my résumé. But I can take it, if I must. It's just that there is so much money sitting across from me, why should I have to stoop so low?

"I have looked, and interviewed. As I said, I have several offers I'm weighing. I will negotiate them all and select the best package. I'll announce something soon," I answer. My champagne glass is long empty, and I need a drink. With the waiter both ignoring and hating me, I will most likely be devoid of a beverage for the remainder of this miserable meal. I scan the restaurant, the tables nearest to us and make eye contact with a young, stout woman who is the waitress for the next table over. She nods in acknowledgment of my wave, as if she'll be right over. Hopefully, our waiter hasn't warned her off.

"So that's your plan, then?" Mia says. Her arms are folded across her chest, and she's leaning forward, like a principal at school who has called you into her office so you can create your own punishment. Who would comply with that? I wouldn't. "Your severance, if you received any, has been gone for a while. Our accounts are all almost empty. You don't feel any sense of urgency?"

This meal will go on record as the longest dinner ever. I fight the urge to check my wristwatch—it's a sleek Apple Watch but if I don't turn my wrist exactly the correct way the display remains black and I must quite obviously push a button on its side to illuminate the damn time. I long for the olden days of watches that simply told you the time. I wonder where my old Nashville watch is. Unfortunately, I never did get the bloodstain off the band.

It's fine. I already know time is moving as slowly as my youngest son when you are waiting for him to complete a task. I appreciate patience is a virtue and applaud those who have it, as long as they stay out of my way. Here we are, though, the money/job question. But it's fine. As noted, I have been expecting this.

"I did receive some severance, as a matter of fact," I say. That is a lie. When you're fired, you don't receive much. They gave me two months' pay as a token gesture. Whatever. You just get called into the idiot HR woman's office and told you are fired. Your things are packed up into boxes by strangers. Security guards escort you out of the building as if you were going to go postal or something. As if you knew you were to be fired and had brought a gun with you. But you didn't, because these people are sneaky. No, they don't give you warnings, I suppose, so you can't bring a gun and blow off the head of the droopy-eyed, twelve-year-old-looking head of HR. I hate HR people. I never really had closure with mine, come to think of it.

She sat behind her desk, pointing to the chair in front of her. Her name was Rebecca More. The entire space behind her was filled with potted plants, like an untamed nursery, and smelled like fertilizer. The plants blocked the window so the effect was a perpetual cloudy day. This was not, of course, our first meeting. She had called me in almost three months earlier to inform me that a coworker had filed a harassment claim against me. I had been stunned. Two reasons. First, her outfit. I mean, we were supposed to be the top advertising agency in the region and this woman was wearing, I kid you not, something straight from Kmart. Black polyester pants, a light pink blouse that barely stayed closed over her gigantic breasts. Her droopy eyes were accented by black cat-eye shaped glasses. I almost started to laugh, thinking the creative team had tricked me into a television commercial shoot right here in our offices. Rebecca More could not work at Thompson Payne. She wasn't cool enough.

"Sit down, Mr. Strom," she said, motioning toward the white leather chair. I sat, playing my role.

"Call me Paul," I said, pouring on the charm. I looked around her office, trying to find the creative team's hidden cameras behind one of the potted palms. Any moment one of the young guys from that department would appear, his hair pulled back in a ponytail, and say, "We got you, man."

"Is something funny, Mr. Strom?" Rebecca asked. I bit my bottom lip to keep the grin off my face. Perhaps this wasn't a commercial shoot. No problem. She would be putty in my hands by the end of the meeting, that's what I had thought.

"How long have you worked at the agency, Rebecca? Welcome," I said.

I could tell by her head-tilted snarky look that was the wrong thing to say.

"I've been with the agency as director of HR for two years, Mr. Strom. We have been in meetings together. But that isn't important. This is a formal warning. You are to have no unnecessary contact at work with Ms. Caroline Fisher. You are to cease inviting her on to your account pitches. She was given the option to take this a step further, but she is giving you a chance here, Mr. Strom."

Rebecca closed the file on her desk, my file I supposed, and placed her glasses on top of it.

I sat across from her and blinked. I wasn't so much shocked as angry. *How dare Caroline, someone I've helped grow and prosper at the agency, turn on me?* We had something special at first. Something rivaling the connection Mia and I had. I know she felt it, too. Caroline had been new to the agency, new to town. I'd noticed her the day old Mr. Thompson was showing her around. But her second day, she was on her own. She needed a mentor, someone to show her the ropes and I would gladly apply for the job. When I saw her walking across the parking lot, I headed for the elevator and wouldn't you know it, we ended up sharing a ride up together. Just the two of us.

You know by now I have a type. Thin, young, long hair. Caroline is no different. She has long, dirty-blond hair that swings past her shoulders, green eyes and she wears tight jeans, high heels and blazers to work. She takes my breath away.

"You're head of account services?" she asked once I'd introduced myself in the elevator. "That's my dream job. I mean, someday."

She blushed, uncertain if I'd take her gunning for my job the right way. I didn't feel threatened, of course. Just turned on. Really turned on.

"Well, to prep for your eventual takeover of my position, how about if I assign you to the essential oil account? It's our most fun consumer-facing account at the moment." I offered the position as I imagined rubbing Caroline with lavender oil, her shoulders, her thighs.

"That would be amazing, thank you, Mr. Strom," she said.

"Call me Paul." I shook her hand as the elevator doors

opened, holding it a bit longer than usual. The sexual energy was there. It had been a promising start.

And then, boom. Once she found out I was married, suddenly I was a stalker. We had been working long hours on the essential oil account, preparing for the big pitch when my secretary interrupted, explaining my wife was on the line and it was urgent. It wasn't. Mikey had a fever, that was it. But it was enough. After I took the call, Caroline had changed.

I tried to joke around with her, put my hand on her shoulder like I had before the call. She shook it off.

"Paul, I didn't know you were married." She crossed her arms in front of her chest.

"Yes, so?" I said, focusing on the presentation scattered on the conference room table.

"Kids, too?" she asked. She blinked her big eyes at me and shook her head.

Of course she was surprised. I'd never met with her in my office, where the photos of my perfect family are displayed. And recently, I'd gotten into the habit of forgetting to wear my wedding ring. I'd been keeping her busy on the essential oil pitch, so busy she hadn't had a chance to bond with anyone else at the agency, hadn't had an opportunity to get the real scoop on me. But so what? So she didn't know about my family, but they didn't have anything to do with us, with Caroline and me.

We hadn't even made out yet, I hadn't kissed her full lips. I had been just about to make my first move. Such a missed opportunity. She didn't seem to be as sad about this development as I was. She seemed mad, come to think of it. Ah, the folly of youth. I knew she'd come around, welcome me into her life once she got over the little shock of my wife, and kids. Of course she would. She could feel the electricity between us.

Back in the Little Shop of Horrors I said, "There are two sides to every story, Rebecca." I sat up straight in my chair and leaned a little forward, full of power and anger at being wrongfully accused of something by this woman. She was a rank below me, Rebecca was, and should call me Mr. Strom. Caroline was several rungs below me—I thought of that and an image of Caroline's young, beautiful body, naked and below me, sent shivers down my spine. I composed myself and added, "Caroline is a young, impressionable junior account executive, barely out of college, and fully delusional."

Rebecca did that annoying, snarky head tilt again and said, "So you're denying the harassment?"

"Yes," I said.

"Do you know what harassment is, Mr. Strom?" Rebecca asked.

"Of course I do. That's why I can say with authority that I've done nothing of the kind. There is nobody who loves and cherishes women more than me, Rebecca. I've promoted women all of my career. I prefer working with women over men. That is the opposite of harassment," I said. I was growing tired of this meeting. I wanted her to hand me the file, and then I wanted to go to Mr. Thompson and have her fired.

"You call her cell phone five times a day, both during work hours and in the evenings. You text her sometimes fifteen times per day. You are angry she will not go out with you, Mr. Strom. You are angry that someone has told you no, aren't you?"

"Of course not. I'm calling her for work-related issues. She is assigned to many of my accounts," I said.

"You are clever, Mr. Strom. No voice-mail messages except to call you, no threatening texts. Just to contact you. Why is it so urgent that she call or text you, all the time? What work-related topic, Mr. Strom, could possibly require that type of constant communication on weekends even?"

"We are a busy agency, Rebecca. Surely you know that clients don't care if it's after hours or on the weekend, not if they need things," I said. Everyone has needs, I thought. I wondered what Rebecca needed. Unfortunately, she was not my type. We both knew that.

Rebecca had put her glasses back on and opened the file again. She appeared to be reading some sort of printout, a list of some kind. "This is Caroline Fisher's personal cell phone record from last month. She has not turned over any other communications from you to me, and won't if you cease." I wonder what I was forgetting about, what else Caroline might have from me. I swallowed. Rebecca stared at me and waited for an answer.

"Sure, fine. I'll immediately assign Andy Pool to my accounts and replace Caroline Fisher. He's a great kid, much better at his job than Ms. Fisher, actually. Maybe she will enjoy working on the technical manuals? Those high-tech clients just churn through our young people. You should place her there," I said. "My accounts will be fine. They'll love working with Andy."

"Great. So glad we understand each other," Rebecca said. "This is your one and only warning, Mr. Strom. As you know, we have a zero tolerance policy in regards to gender discrimination and sexual harassment. You are a director of this company and you should be setting the appropriate example. You have not. Unfortunately, without more proof or evidence from Ms. Fisher, I cannot fire you today."

Rebecca stood and placed both hands on top of my file. She glared at me through her ridiculous glasses. And said, "But I assure you, I know the proof is there. If you go near

her, threaten her, call her, or otherwise just cause her to have
a bad day at the office because of your actions, your career is
over here. Understand?"

I realized that I had never been threatened by a woman
before this moment. I had a new feeling inside and I didn't
have a name for it. Suddenly, I felt claustrophobic. There were
too many potted plants crowding the back wall of her office
and the smell was disgusting, like a moldy jungle. The plants
seemed to be droopy, either from lack of sunlight, overwater-
ing or pure boredom. Otherwise, her office was unadorned.
The walls were white, the shelves barren, except for a few
books about HR policies and procedures. Boring manuals for
boring rule-following people like her. Everything about Rebecca More was drooping, musty and irritating. I was anxious to be done with her. And she was waiting for my answer.

"Understood, Rebecca," I said, standing and leaning ever
so slightly toward her over her desk. She startled and stepped
back, bumping into her chair, which knocked into a potted
tree. A leaf poked through her hair and that made me happy.
I had said her name as if it were toxic, a poison making my
tongue thick by its mere presence in my mouth. And then I
turned and walked out of her office, never expecting to be
summoned there once more only three short months later.

I told myself there would be no more empowering Caroline Fisher. A shame, really, after all I'd done for her. After all
we'd worked on together. I also reminded myself that there
would be other young women drawn to the agency, that I
had a great wife, a brilliant life and two sons who everyone
said were the most handsome boys they've ever seen. And
of course, there would always be someone new on the side,
someone like Gretchen, a young woman who would simply
cross my path at the right time. Although I hadn't met her

yet, I knew she was out there. There were always Gretchens. I mean, look at me. Women love me, almost all women. But Caroline? She never even put out—such a tease. Who needed Caroline Fisher?

Mia interrupts my reflections. "Excuse me. I just need to powder my nose."

Of course I stand as she pushes her chair away from the table. The waiter is faster than me, though, and pulls her chair out for her. She smiles up at him sweetly before walking away from the table, the champagne-colored silk of her dress shining in the candlelight. I watch the waiter as he refolds the napkin and places it on the table, as if she were never there. He ignores me completely. That's fine. My thoughts are elsewhere.

8:45 P.M.

15

Turns out I did need Caroline Fisher.

It is my fault, I know. But I thought if we could just talk one more time, she'd see what she was missing. It had been more than two months of no contact and two long months of watching my back. Or, more precisely, two months spent on full alert, watching to be certain that no one would see me watching Caroline. Rebecca More was not a fan of mine, of course, she had told me as much. I had no way of knowing who else in the office she had turned against me, who else was watching me.

As for Caroline, if I saw her walking down the hall, I'd duck into someone's office before she could see me. Andy had taken over all of her accounts, and the transition had been seamless. Caroline's new cubicle was on another floor of the building; she was handling our automotive accounts with a senior account executive, a ballbuster woman named Judy. Fine.

But for some reason, I couldn't get my mind off Caroline. I couldn't stop myself from stealing a glance at her as she walked into the office each morning from the parking lot, for example. It was something to look forward to, a moment I cherished, catching a glimpse of Caroline stepping out of her car, looking lovely. This particular November day, there was a chill in the air, and Thanksgiving was just a week away. Somehow, we ended up alone together in the same elevator. I swear I hadn't planned it. It just happened. Serendipity. She wore a tight-fitting navy knit dress and high-heeled leather boots, and she smelled like apricots. She tried to get out of the elevator when she spotted me, but it was too late and the doors closed.

"Hello, Caroline," I said. Friendly, nonthreatening salutation, but my voice was husky with desire, I'll admit.

"Paul," she said. She nodded but kept staring at the doors as if willing them to open.

"Good to see you, it's been a while," I said.

Caroline kept her gaze on the closed elevator doors. "Yes, it has."

"Drinks tonight, for old times' sake?" I asked. That's all. I promise. I may have added, "You look amazing," or "God, I miss you," but that's it, really.

She turned her head and looked at me as if I'd grown horns. Her face was white, her eyes wide as if she was afraid, which was ridiculous. How could she be afraid of me? "You are unbelievable. You're sick. You really are sick," she said, and as soon as she stepped out of the elevator, I knew I was in trouble.

It took Rebecca an entire week to summon me to her jungle-like lair that last time, which is why for seven days I had convinced myself that Thompson or Payne had saved me.

We were the good old boys. We did what we did, and we got a slap on the wrist. That's what I had thought. In the end, I didn't get anything more than two months, Mia is correct.

Rebecca stroked a fat green leaf on one of her plants and smirked as I walked toward her desk. She'd won, she knew it. "Mr. Strom. Have a seat."

I closed the door behind me, but it opened again immediately. A stout short guy dressed in a rent-a-cop uniform appeared behind me. "You've got to be kidding me," I said.

"I can assure you this is no joke, Mr. Strom. It's over. You're fired. Your things will be shipped to your home address. The partners have generously given you two months' severance, although I recommended against it given the severity of your crimes."

Rebecca was enjoying this. I was not. "Crimes. Really? I've been a loyal employee, I've made this place what it is."

"We're finished here. Please escort him out." Rebecca smiled, a tight-lipped smile. I felt the meathead's strong hand around my arm.

I shook him off. "Big mistake, Rebecca," I said, and walked out the door, my head held high, a smile on my face until I reached my car. Inside the Flex, I began to formulate my plan.

I have been draining my 401(k) although minus the company's match for last year. I lost that when I got terminated. I'm considering it to be my severance package. I lost a lot in penalties using it, but it is what it is. Back then, when it happened, it wasn't long before Christmas rolled around and Phyllis and Donald's gifts rolled in. I had imagined we could make the 401(k) money stretch to another Christmas, get the gifts from good old Phyllis and Donald again. That was as far as I'd gotten, back then. Oh, and my special credit card. I know now it was not a solid financial plan. This money thing is my only weakness, I told you that.

My wife reappears at the table, and I scurry over to pull her chair out before the waiter can. I'm not a barbarian. After I settle her in, I pat her shoulder once before I return to my seat. She tenses under my touch. We need to move on to a nonfinancial topic. We are locked in a no-win conversation. I'm eager to change the subject, to set her mind at ease. She hasn't ever worried about money in her life. There's no need for her to start now. She has all we will ever need, already.

"I have a plan," I say. And I do. But I don't know why I just said that. It's the corner I'm in, I suppose. My plan is for me only. I will not share it with Mia. She will find out soon enough. Perhaps beginning tonight.

"What's the plan, Paul?" she says, extracting her napkin from the table, unfolding it before it disappears onto her lap.

The waitress whom I waved over appears at our table and thinks I want her to pour the champagne. The bottle is empty. I finished the last of it when Mia was in the bathroom. I would like to ask her to be our server, but instead say, "I'll have a Tito's on the rocks with a lime. Mia, anything?"

"Ah, sir, I'll get your waiter," the waitress says, although I know in a place like this she has been trained and told to help out whenever asked, whatever is asked by a customer.

"Mia? A chardonnay?" I ask.

"Yes, please," Mia says. When the woman leaves, she adds, "So far it appears that your plan is to drive us into debt. I took a look today, and all of the credit cards are maxed out—did you know that? Do you have a secret pile of cash somewhere you aren't telling me about?"

You, dear, are my pile of cash, I think, but I don't say it. I know I should feel shame, but I don't. We will be fine. She is loaded and things will work out.

"You're overthinking this, Mia," I say. "We are fine, we're a team. I will take care of my family, my boys. I expect to take an offer next week." I also expect her to smile and nod, but she doesn't. I will take the stupid job, just to show her I'm wanted. I soften my tone, tilt my head to the side. "Honey, I can't believe you'd doubt me, after all we've been through. I'm a good provider, a good husband. You know this. Everything will be fine. So you see, this conversation is a waste of time. It's causing too much drama. Stress is bad for you, bad for your health. And you know how I hate drama. Now let's get back to a nice evening. Sound good, honey?" She needs to help me douse the flames. *Please, Mia. Help me help you.*

Mia tilts her head, mirroring me, and tosses her hands in the air before dropping them to the table as a new waiter, perhaps someone's assistant, appears at our table with my drink and Mia's wine. I am pleased. I've decided to drop the entire working for John thing. It doesn't matter, not anymore. For one thing, she knows everything, which she should have told me sooner. For another, well, I do have a plan.

I hear Mia let out her breath, a quiet whoosh. I wonder what else she's heard about me, what else she has been waiting to question me about. Is this the first raindrop leading up to a torrential downpour, or is this little shower, this little job situation, all she has been worked up about, the cause of all the tension in the car? At this table? *Ping.*

My house salad arrives with mild fanfare, silver cover removed with theatrical flair. I take a bite. The lettuces are dark green, arugula, kale and perhaps even a dandelion green. I taste sweet onion and tangy blue cheese. The dressing is vinaigrette, not too tart. Appreciation of fine food is an important facet of successful men like me. I have this down. It's an art I like to teach younger people, younger women especially. Gretchen has been a quick study.

"Pepper for your salad?" a voice says. Our waiter has returned from Siberia.

"Yes, please. Two rounds," I say, making eye contact with him. I'm challenging him nonverbally. Lucky for him, he submits. He quickly finds something very interesting in my salad to look at.

"Ma'am, you need anything at all?" he asks. Who is this guy? Some sort of guard dog for distressed restaurant diners? If she said, *Yes, I need a better, kinder, wealthier, truer husband,* would blue eyes here be able to deliver? Is that type of man on the menu here, or anywhere?

No, he isn't. We're all like me, ladies, just differing degrees. We are more than willing to put up with your emotions, as long as you keep your end of the bargain. Look good, take care of the kids, maintain a clean home, have sex when we want it and for God's sake, don't question us or our motives. Never do that.

9:00 P.M.

16

In lieu of ordering a better version of me, my wife smiles and says to the waiter, "I'm doing fine. Everything looks wonderful. Thank you for your kindness."

What the hell is going on? *Your kindness?* Has she lost a limb, or did she just have a minor spat with her husband? Everyone is going crazy around here but me. I take another bite of salad and chew slowly, trying to figure out what conversational topic would be most tame. *The boys.* No, they are at a movie, with a sitter, and that is a reason for my wife to stress until they are back home, safely tucked into their beds. *My job.* Nope. *Her job.* Nada. *I know. Lakeside.*

"Honey, aren't you excited to be back at the cottage?" I ask. This is safe and happy ground. This is why we're here and having the best day possible. "Everything looks great and soon, your gardens will be in full bloom. Even the strawberries."

Mia exhales. Her face is pinched. She looks terrible. She

sounds exhausted. "I guess the first step is to fix the cottage up and put it on the market," she says. This, now, is her sadness. It's not over money. It's that we may have to give up the cottage. Ridiculous. At least now I finally understand. Relief floods over me, leaving only smoldering embers.

"No, of course we're not selling the cottage. I'm not letting that happen. Everything will be fine. I promise. Remember when you thought we couldn't buy the cottage in the first place, but I surprised you, handled the mortgage all by myself? Please don't worry about the cottage, it's ours. Everything is under control," I say. I'm so happy to know the actual cause of her distress isn't me, but the thought of losing her second home. She's not upset about my job or our pesky money problems. She just doesn't want to give up the lake. Perfect. She's still my sweet Mia. I can't really explain it, but I feel like jumping up out of my chair and grabbing her face between my hands and kissing her firmly, taking her, right here, right now.

But that would be Tom Cruise–ish weird, and not my style. I turn on my biggest smile instead.

"Trust me. You'll have this cottage for as long as you live. Heck, the boys will inherit it. It will be a Strom family asset, for generations," I say, not adding, *just like the Boones*. Greg Boone was upset because I'm a better card player than he is. Beat him every time they invited us to the lake. That was the entire problem, if you want to know the story. He called me a cheater. *Au contraire, Mr. Boone, I am a winner.* In the heat of the moment that night, though, I might have called Greg a thing or two, with my hands clenched by my sides. I know I can appear threatening but most of the time, my bark is worse than my bite.

"Just like the Boones," Mia says, as if once again reading

my mind. Her face is soft, though, and she takes a thought-ful sip of her wine.

Mia and I never did discuss why Greg and Doris stopped inviting us to the lake. It wasn't like a big blowup or any-thing, and it wasn't as if I'd hit on Doris, I would never do that. I mean, have you seen her? Short, short hair, too perky, too annoying. Like I told you, the only thing I can think of is because I beat Greg at euchre all the time. Maybe Mia did something wrong, I don't know.

"You talk to Doris a lot still, don't you?" I ask. This is a new realization on my part—Doris and her role in my life both here at the lake and back home in Grandville. And it's time to ask Mia about it. My salad is finished, fork at four o'clock on my plate. It occurs to me I didn't offer a bite to Mia, but then again, she's having salad for dinner.

"Not a lot, really, not since her kids started private school, but she's a good friend. It's helpful, you know, since I didn't grow up here like you did, like she did. Since she's lived in Grandville forever, she knows where all the skeletons are bur-ied," Mia says. She glances out the window, or perhaps she is checking her own reflection, a candlelit mirror.

"You look lovely, honey," I say, pondering her friendship with Doris and what interest she might have in Grandville's skeletons. Do they discuss my wayward brother, my family of origin? Does Doris share her love of mall spying with my wife?

Mia smiles and seems to blush a little, acknowledging I caught her looking at herself. It's funny, Mia just isn't one of those women who checks herself out in every mirror she passes. I've often admired her lack of vanity, except when I wished she'd pay a little more attention to herself. Tonight, though, she seems drawn to the window. I already checked. There is nothing out there beyond the glass. Just inky darkness.

"I do see Doris around the neighborhood, and of course, up here," she says. I realize she is still talking about the Boones. Interesting. "I miss spending time with them. They're a fun couple and great neighbors, here and at home. Doris has been good to me, despite our falling-out as couples."

"Yes, I'm sure she has. And as for the couple time, their loss as far as I'm concerned. I've never figured out why they stopped inviting us. But hey, I'd be open to hanging out with them whenever you'd like. Maybe next weekend? The fantastic foursome, reunited just in time for summer," I say. I'm magnanimous. Forgiving. Easygoing. A gentleman.

Mia's mouth drops open. She's shaking her head back and forth as if she's having a stroke. She covers her face with her hands and I hear a muffled sound like a cat mewling. She drops her hands on the table. I reach to hold one but she yanks it away.

"Ugh. You're ridiculous. You know there won't be a reunion, and you know why."

I arrange my expression into one of mild curiosity. "Do I?"

"Of course you do. Greg says you cheated at cards, that when you two stepped outside so he could talk to you about it, you yelled at him and took a swing at him. You sucker punched our neighbor, our friend. That's what you did. Of course, Doris and I didn't have a clue, didn't hear a thing. You came in the room, told me it was time to go. Thanked Doris for a great evening and left her husband bleeding on the back deck of their home. Incredible," she says.

Now I tilt my head, blink my eyes. "I'm hurt, Mia."

She looks at me, her mouth open. "You're what?"

"You heard me. I can't believe you'd actually think I was

capable of such a thing. Greg is a tool, a sore loser, that's all. He lost in euchre and instead of taking it like a man he's telling stories to make me look bad. Disgusting. And, honey, if you did believe his story, why didn't you ask me about it sooner?"

I pause as the waiter approaches the table, with two other members of the waitstaff. They place our dinners in front of us and remove the silver tops with a flourish again. So dramatic.

Mia smiles at the waiter, not me, and then looks back at me. "I stand corrected, Paul. I'm glad we got that out in the open. Doesn't dinner look wonderful?"

She believes me, my wife believes me. Of course she does. "Well, thank you for that, honey. And yes, my veal looks and smells divine. Bon appétit." I take a bite of my entrée and savor every taste exploding in my mouth. There's nothing better than young tender meat. Mia's salad looks like a fancier version of the one she ate at Sloopy's for lunch. It's too bad her tastes are so limited. My only complaint, if you could call it that, is no one has brought us bread yet. I'm assuming the blue-eyed guard dog should have that duty, but I could be wrong. He appears at our table again and I watch as he peppers Mia's salad before I interrupt. He is doing it, grinding the pepper for her, very kindly.

"Could we have some bread?" I ask. The waiter stiffens, pepper mill gripped in his hand, nods slightly in my direction and is gone. "It seems this waiter is quite upset about our earlier spat. Do you want to tell him we're fine? Shall we hold hands as he brings the bread basket?"

Mia smiles. "Are we fine, Paul? I'm not so sure." Her eyes dampen, but she looks down at her salad, her hair falling in front of her face like a privacy screen.

"Hey, I thought we'd gotten past this. Didn't we just talk

things out? And aren't we here enjoying this gourmet meal?" I lower my voice to its most soothing register. "In my opinion, honey, we're more than fine. We're blessed," I say.

The basket of bread appears, with a healthy slab of butter on a small china plate alongside it. I reach for it before remembering to offer Mia a slice.

"Bread?"

She looks up, her silky hair parting and revealing her face. "No, thank you. You're right. We are blessed. I just want to feel better, to get better. I'm tired of being sick, that's all," she says. And she smiles again. "Of course we're fine. Let's eat."

"Let's," I say. Suddenly, I'm starving and can't wait to tuck into the meal in front of me. Mia smiles and takes a bite of her salad. We're good, so good. We both chew our food, gazing at each other across the flickering candlelight. It's as if everyone else in the room has disappeared and we're back to the two of us, the two of us against the world.

"You know what it is, what I miss?" Mia asks.

"No, what do you miss?" She looks so beautiful, so happy just now. I again have an urge to reach across the table for her hand, to remember this moment, this look forever, but I really want to finish my meat.

"I miss the feeling of being carefree. Free," she says. She then pokes her fork through a mound of greens and puts the whole mess in her mouth, realizing too late it was much too much for her to handle. She covers her mouth now, with her hand, to continue chewing.

I chuckle, a small laugh. I have an image of my wife as a cow, just then.

"Well, you're the one who wanted children," I say. "You can kiss freedom goodbye once they arrive, as you know."

"I do. But it's not just the boys. They don't make me feel

less, less free," she says. She looks up at the ceiling and then turns to face the window. Finally, she turns back to me. "I was also remembering when we first met at the office. You were so fearless. Boldly asking me out after we'd only just talked once in the conference room, even when it was against policy, even when you were my senior. What if I had said no that day in my office? How would you have reacted?"

Mia looks at me with the love and admiration I'd seen on her face the day we met. The look that told me she was mine for the taking.

I beam at her from across the table. She is so sweet, so innocent. "Women don't tell me no, honey. You're living proof of that. Once I set my sights on you, you were a goner." I slip the last piece of veal in my mouth and prepare to savor it.

9:15 P.M.

I'm making the most of my last bite. The taste of veal is singular, rich, thick. Sure, every time you order veal it's a little different, but they share common traits. Subtle flavors, pliable flesh, deep enjoyment. I finish my bite and smile. I think back to the seduction of Mia, how easy it was compared to some others I've encountered lately, most notably Caroline.

Caroline felt it, though. The chemistry, the surge. My power. But now I need to focus on Mia. That is the task at hand. Operation Make Mia Love Me Completely Again Tonight. What is going on with her? I wonder. Why the trip down memory lane? I swallow and soften my approach.

"You wouldn't have said no, Mia," I say. "It was an instant connection. Such chemistry. I know you felt it, too."

"I felt it," she admits, her voice quiet. I lean forward to hear her. "But with all the rules, well, if I had turned you down,

what would you have done? Would you have been embarrassed? Tried to get me fired? You did hold all the power. I
was brand-new at the agency. What would have happened?"

"I'm not sure I see the value in hypothetical conversations.
But if you'd said no, I would have kept asking until you agreed
to go out with me. I knew we were meant to be together. I
couldn't imagine a different outcome," I say. I'm so good at
this. "Our story is a romance novel. Love at first sight. As
you wish and all that happily-ever-after."

"I don't read romance novels, but I do know most people
are driven by fear and shame. Most guys would have been nervous to ask a new, young associate on a date, especially since
there are rules about that. But you didn't have any fear, not at
all. You don't have any shame either. It's interesting," she says.
Apparently, she has finished pushing greens into her mouth
as she places her fork at four o'clock and slides the bowl an
inch forward. Impeccable manners, another reason I love her.

"I know what I want and I go for it. There's no shame in
that, Mia. Not to me," I say. "I am what I am."

"True," she agrees. "I thought you were so unique, when
we first met. You just wowed me. I remember huge bouquets
of flowers arrived all the time. You tucked sweet love notes
into surprising places at my desk. You swept me off my feet,
like a movie, like how I dreamed. Before I knew it, I was ignoring my friends, my family and spending every moment
with you. I was intoxicated by you. I thought you were so
special, I thought you were the most handsome, most intel-
ligent, most romantic man I'd ever met. And the sex, well, I
had never been with a man. You taught me everything." Mia
pauses, takes a drink of water. Her eyes are shiny with love.
"But now I know you're a type."

"A type?" What does that mean?

"May I clear your salad?" our waiter asks Mia, rudely interrupting when she was clearly trying to say something, something about me or about us, I'm not sure.

"Yes, thank you, I'm finished. No dessert for either of us, right, Paul?"

"Correct. The veal was perfect," I say to the waiter, who ignores me.

"Coffee?" he asks Mia.

"Please," she says.

"No," I say at the same time. He will bring her coffee, I know, even though she knows I hate sitting through a coffee. When a meal is finished, it's finished. I don't like to linger at the table. I think you know why now: green beans.

"My family and friends couldn't believe how fast I fell for you, how quickly we became engaged, just six months after our first date," Mia says. "That's really fast. I would kill Mikey or Sam if they did that. And then, bam. I was pregnant. It was all such a whirlwind."

"But it was right," I say. "I didn't consider it too fast. Is there a rule about pre-engagement, honey? I don't think so. When it's right, it just is."

"You'd had a chance to experience the world, move around, live on your own. I basically went from my parents, to college, to you."

Yes, that's what made you so perfect, I think but don't say. I roll my head from shoulder to shoulder and hear a pop on the left side of my neck. What is she poking around at the past for? It is what it is. It led us here. It's why I selected her. "Yes, I suppose you did. But that's a path many women choose to walk, a lovely path."

"Even when I discovered you'd been unfaithful, during our engagement," she says as the waiter delivers her coffee cup and begins to pour the hot black liquid. The smell reminds me of morning, of the office, of Caroline. I know I'm scowling. The waiter hates me even more now. Why is Mia airing our past in front of this ice-eyed stranger?

"Sugar? Cream?" he asks. The way he says it has me imagining that he is saying to her, "Date, tonight?"

"No, thank you," she says. After he bows and leaves, she glances at me and blushes. She must know I'm fuming, the fire starting.

"I don't mean to upset you, Paul. It's just that this time together, well actually, the past few months, I've been thinking a lot." I don't like it when Mia is thinking a lot. I just want her busy at home, taking care of the children, the house, keeping her parents happy and sending cash. She just needs to stop thinking, and stop talking to nosy neighbors like Doris and Buck.

"Honey, there's nothing to think about," I say. I shake my head intently, hoping she'll just drink her damn coffee. Why is she rehashing a meaningless one-night stand from a decade ago?

It's like she doesn't hear me. "We'd already sent the wedding invitations out, the ceremony was days away when I found out about her. Someone at the office left that note in my desk drawer: *Your fiancé is having a fling with a client.* I still remember holding the index card the note was written on. My hands were shaking but even as I read it, I knew it was true. I'd watched you flirt with the woman at the office. I saw how she looked at you.

"I was too ashamed to call it off. But you knew that would be the case, didn't you? That's why you admitted it to me when I showed you the note. It was a power play. You proved you could do whatever you wanted and I'd marry you, stay with you. All those years ago, you'd already won."

Yes, I always win. But still, I realize I'm clenching my jaw. The past is just that. If she wants to dwell on it, she can do it on her own time. I don't feel guilty about my fling with that woman client. It was a last hurrah before the old ball and chain. Plenty of guys do it. But I do wish I could remember her name. It seems to me she moved to Michigan or something. Oh, well.

"Mia, has that really been bothering you all this time? As I told you, it was a mistake. I wanted to confess to you myself, to start our marriage in honesty and trust. I'm not proud that someone else got to you first and remember, I apologized on bended knee." I think back to that awkward moment in her office. I'd instantly decided to admit my culpability while blaming it on the client, and begged for Mia's forgiveness. It had worked perfectly. I'm good at thinking on my feet, a smooth pivot.

"Remember, honey, she came on to me, that client. You saw it yourself. My only crime was a lapse in judgment. I wanted to land the account too much. It was stupid and as you know, it has never happened again. And of course, our wedding went off without a hitch. Everything worked out, right?" I say. But I don't want to hear her response right now, so I add: "I'm glad. Look at us—we're perfect together. We have two amazing sons, and the best life. I love you. Happy best day ever."

Mia takes a sip of her coffee, stares at me over the cup. After a moment, she returns the cup to the saucer, breaking our eye contact. "That's right, the best day ever. What else is on your agenda for us tonight?"

"I have a few more things up my sleeve," I say, remembering the cigarettes in my briefcase, the matches in my pocket. The surprise in my glove box. "Ready to go?"

"I'll ask for the check," Mia says, knowing she can attract our waiter.

"I'll need you to give him a credit card. I, um, forgot to make that transfer," I say. I know my face is full of love, and happiness. I reach for her hand across the table. She ignores the gesture.

"Yes, I figured," Mia says, smiling a fake smile and tilting her head awkwardly. We must look like some freaky couple from a 1950s advertisement for the good life, all stilted and perfect. Except the guy would be paying, I know.

"It's all going to work out, don't worry," I say.

She shakes her head before she removes her purse from the back of the chair, opens it and extracts a platinum American Express card, one I have never seen before.

"I got this for emergencies. Thank goodness I did," she says as the waiter appears and she slips the card into his hand.

"This is hardly an emergency, Mia," I tell her, crossing my arms across my chest. "It's a temporary setback, like every challenge in life, honey."

"Oh, it is, is it? How exactly do you plan to solve our financial situation, Paul?" she asks.

Fortunately, before I have to formulate an answer, the waiter returns with the receipt in a black leather folder. I watch as Mia opens the folder, reclaims her platinum card and adds a 25 percent tip for her guard dog before scribbling her signature: *M. Pilmer.*

9:30 P.M.

It's official. That was the longest dinner I've suffered through since the green bean fiasco, I realize as we stand outside the restaurant waiting for my car to be pulled around. I wonder if Mia purposefully stretched it out, our time together here—but why would she? The parking lot is almost empty but not quite. There are actually people suffering through a longer dinner than I had. Remarkable.

"The stars are beautiful here," she says, looking up at the sky. "It's one of my favorite things about being up here at the lake. The city lights can't drown them out. They shine full force." She pulls out her phone, and I watch as she uses her stargazer app to name the constellations. It is such a childish pursuit, but I smile despite myself.

"Oh, look, it's Orion," she says, holding her phone screen up in the air so that now all she sees is the screen, not the stars. *Ridiculous.* "The hunter." She drops the phone to her side, looks at me, and then looks back up to the sky.

"What's he hunting?" I ask. The parking lot is eerily quiet, just the two of us. The few diners still left inside the restaurant are barely visible inside, tiny dots of heads through the windows.

"Don't you remember your Greek mythology? You took that class in college your senior year, didn't you?"

"Yes, yes I did, but I'm afraid I didn't pay much attention to the professor," I say, staring at my wife. I had other things, like Lois, on my mind. But she doesn't know that.

"Orion is sort of a narcissist, actually. He thinks he's the greatest hunter in the world, but Zeus's wife kills him with a scorpion," she says. "Scorpio hasn't risen yet, it doesn't rise until the early-morning hours when Orion goes down." She isn't looking at me. She's still staring up at the sky.

I'm not looking at her either. Not anymore.

"Wow, a shooting star! Did you see that?" she says, slapping my shoulder with her hand. Finally, the valet pulls our car up.

"Sorry for the wait. Somebody had blocked your car in, and I couldn't find the keys, and sorry," he says, rushing to open Mia's door. Meanwhile, Mia is still staring up at the stupid hunter. "Ma'am?"

"Oh, yes, sorry," she says, sliding into the car. I'm already inside, more than ready to get going. The valet holds the passenger door open, no doubt looking for a tip.

Mia notices and rummages in her purse before handing him a bill. The guy grins and says, "'Night. Thanks." He slams the car door.

"Big tipper tonight, eh?" I say. I usually appreciate a good tipper. People know you're somebody if you tip well. I've always tipped well. It's what a man like me should do. Mia, on the other hand, should not be spending money we do not have.

"Poor boy was out of breath," she says. "Anyway, what a

fabulous thing to see a falling star. It blasted right through the middle of Orion's belt. Too bad you missed it."

"I saw it," I say. I am lying but I don't want to feel left out. During our drive back to the cottage there is one more subject I need to discuss, but I had hoped Mia would have had more to drink by now. That would make her more likely to talk without thinking. Regardless, like most women, she is putty in my capable hands.

"Hey, honey, has your father mentioned anything about your estranged uncle, his brother? The one in Texas?" I ask. I know this is coming out of left field, so I add, "The stars—Lone Star State—helped me remember to ask you."

"Um, no, we don't really discuss Uncle Derrick. You know that," she says. "Why?"

"Oh, nothing. I just thought about him, the other day, at work—well, during a job interview. One of the agency's biggest clients was based in Texas. Made me think of him," I say. "Wonder how he's doing."

"He's a drug dealer or something. But he always was a lot of fun at parties when I was little," Mia says.

I notice she's holding the side door handle, as if she were anticipating an accident. It's a pose you'd assume if you knew something was coming at you head-on at any moment.

She adds, "I should reach out to him, find out what he's up to. You're right."

"No, don't do that. I mean, it's never a good idea to shake the family tree. And if he's a drug dealer we don't want him near our boys," I say quickly, my heart thudding in my chest. "I just brought him up because of the stars, that's all."

"Oh, good point. You just never know. He could be really bad news," she says. Mia seems to let the subject go, thankfully. We enjoy a comfortable silence for the rest of the drive back to Lakeside. I am thinking about how wonderful it is not to have to get home, pay the babysitter and then coerce the boys to sleep. I am thinking about how peaceful this moment is, just the two of us in a darkened car, silently compatible. It's like we could be playing Scrabble or another friendly board game and growing old together. *Bored game*, I think with a smile.

Sure, sometimes I imagine that I could continue on like this, feel content and make myself believe I have enough. Just the two of us, and our boys, blending in with the rest of the people who work boring jobs and then come up here on the weekends and fish for walleye. I'll become head of advertising for the city magazine, even though they'll call me Chief Revenue Officer. Mia, tired of working from home for John's agency, will go into John Larson Advertising's small office in Hilliard three days a week. She will barely make enough to cover the childcare expenses she'll incur when in-office meetings are required by clients and run over into school pickup time, but she'll feel productive. She'll have lunch with her coworkers—there are only three of them besides John—and the receptionist will tell her that John has a crush on her. She'll smile at the silly woman and tell her he's just a friend. She'll dream about the weekends at the lake.

Meanwhile, at the magazine, I will report to the publisher, a woman with the vision of a mouse. She wants to be the best magazine in the city; it is the only magazine in the city. The publisher has teased her rodent-brown hair—to make it appear fuller—and has had too much Botox, so that her face is frozen in a mask of skewed aging perfection. She barely manages a wink in my direction as she escorts me out of our directors' meeting and asks me to grab coffee with her. She trails her pastel pink fingernail down the side of my Italian suit jacket as she makes the suggestion. I tell her I'm happily married, but that I'm sure I'll meet her revenue projections. She tells me she doesn't care about the revenue. Later, that afternoon, she'll insist I go to happy hour with the team, just one of her many team members. She'll keep me in my place.

I shudder, and hope Mia doesn't notice. I was never made for that kind of linear, predictable and ordinary life. Guys like me don't grow old peacefully. No, we fight it every step of the way. I suck my stomach in, the only flaw in my otherwise youthful facade. I'm like Orion, shining in the sky. Don't get too close or I may burn you. As I pull onto our street, I note that our cottage is lit up and glowing, as welcoming as the Boones', and maybe more so. I didn't realize we had left so many lights on, but I guess we did.

Beside me, Mia stretches her arms in front of her and then covers her mouth as she yawns. I'll need to convince her to have another glass of wine or perhaps a cup of tea.

It isn't bedtime yet.

10:00 P.M.

19

I hear Mia's footsteps upstairs. She is in our bedroom changing out of her dress and heels. I don't blame her. I'm reminded again of how lucky men are that we don't have to prance around on tiptoe just to get attention from the other sex. Actually, I've never had trouble in the mating game, as you now know, but some women and men, well, they need to employ all the tools of the trade, respectively.

While she's upstairs changing, I go back outside and retrieve the plain white envelope from the glove compartment. It's an old Thompson Payne envelope, business-sized, with the agency's logo and return address on the upper left side. Just a plain old envelope sealed tight with a little something special inside.

I've parked the car in the garage, to make Mia happy, and after I get what I've come for, I'll need to push the button on the wall and then run out of the garage without tripping the sensors. If I keep this cottage, I will definitely fix the actual door to the garage. It has been wonky since we bought the place. I push the garage door button and sprint through the garage, hopping over the line where the sensor beam will detect me, and burst out of the garage into the night. Somehow, I've managed to keep the envelope in my hands. The universe is making up for the croissants again, no doubt.

Still sprinting, I make it to the back door in record time and rush into the kitchen. It's empty.

"Mia?" I call.

"I'm still changing," she answers, her voice floating down the stairs to me.

"Great. I'm going to make us a nightcap," I say, sticking my head around the corner and talking to the stairs.

"Sounds good," she says. "Be down in a minute."

Quickly, I pull down two crystal tumblers. From the liquor cabinet—aka the cupboard above the refrigerator—I grab the brandy. We aren't really after-dinner drink people, but tonight is special. I pour the brandy into each glass; the strong odor of the liquor stings my eyes. Can brandy go bad? I wonder. I don't have time to change course, so I grab the envelope from the counter and carefully tear off the corner, ripping through "Thompson Payne" in one satisfactory motion. Typically, I wear gloves but there is not time for caution now. I pour the contents into a glass, crumple the envelope and toss it into the sink.

There is a candle next to the sink—its green-checkered wrapper is country and screams "cottage candle." A gift, I believe, from Mia's mother. I reach into my pocket and pull out the matches. I strike the match, light the candle, and then light the envelope. The paper takes forever to catch fire, it seems.

"Paul? What are you doing?" Mia asks, appearing in the kitchen suddenly and causing me to jump.

I turn my back to the sink, blocking it, and say, "God, Mia, why do you sneak up on me like that?" I am willing the envelope to finish disintegrating behind me.

"What's burning?"

I turn to the sink again, and see the envelope fully engulfed. "Gosh, I dropped the match in there after lighting the candle. Must have been a paper towel." I turn on the faucet, dousing the flames, the white envelope now a charred mess that easily rinses away down the drain. I wash my hands with soap, and dry them with a paper towel.

"Smokey the Bear would be proud," Mia says. She is wearing sweatpants now. They are gray and make her look like a lazy housewife who eats too many Oreo cookies while watching daytime TV. To complete the ensemble, she has added a gray sweatshirt with the word *LAKESIDE* printed on it in white. *Charming.*

At the sight of my expression, Mia lets out a little laugh. "I know you hate me in sweats but there's a little chill in the air tonight. I'm so much more comfortable now."

"You look it," I tell her, trying to hide my disdain with a smile. "Let's go sit, enjoy our drinks. Light a few more candles."

"Sounds wonderful," she says. I hand her the tumbler of brandy and follow her into the family room.

I pull the matches out of my pocket and light the three candles on the coffee table, then take a seat next to my wife on the tan couch. It's wonderful to be home, alone, sitting on our new luxurious, decorator-selected furniture. Here we are relaxing in the family room of our lake house, sharing an after-dinner drink after an expensive dinner out. We are

a successful, enviable couple. I am handsome, Mia is holding up well—although you wouldn't know it with the outfit she has on.

"Cheers," I say. I hold up my glass of brandy, clink my
crystal tumbler against hers. "To us."

She takes a sniff and recoils at the smell of the strong alcohol. Her head snaps back as if she saw a ghost. I think the
hand holding her glass is shaking, almost imperceptibly. Is it?
I drink a sip of my own brandy, careful not to shudder, and
smile. Sure, the stuff is strong but she is really overreacting.

"Oh, come on. I know you don't love brandy, but it's the
only after-dinner drink we had in the cupboard. It's a special night. Drink up, honey. It will help warm you up, and
then I'll finish the job," I say with a wink, taking another sip.

She smiles feebly. "Okay, Paul, I'll try it." I watch closely
as she puts the glass to her mouth.

There is a knock on the door. Mia lowers her drink, places
the glass on the coffee table and looks at me with concern.
This is odd. No one knocks on your door after ten o'clock at
night, not in Lakeside. Not even in Columbus.

Mia's eyes are wide as I stand up. "Stay here. I'll get it," I
say. I am brave. I am the man. I make my way to the front
door and turn on the front porch lights. Their glare reveals
Buck. *He has a lot of nerve.*

I yank open the door. "I know your wife is dead and you
may not remember this, but when a man has a date night
with his wife it isn't okay to come over. Not before. Not after.
What part of this aren't you getting?" I say. My hands are on
my hips, and I know my words are cutting and mean. I know
this, and I like it. He has crossed me one too many times.
"What? Why do you think you can just show up here at all

hours? Or is this about the strawberries? They're fine. Been fine. Don't need you, Mr. Green Thumb. So, good night."

I slam the door in his face before he has a chance to respond. Hopefully, I made it clear he wasn't welcome. He couldn't take a hint, but now he has got it, surely.

I look out the half-moon window cut into the front door, expecting to see Buck's back as he is walking away. But he is standing on the porch, looking back at me. He isn't leaving, it appears.

"What the—" I say, about to yank the door open again. This time I'll use a fist to get my point across. I like the idea. Mia appears next to me, grabs my hand and pulls the door open instead.

"Buck, so good to see you twice in one day," she says. "Is something wrong?"

I'm seething, Mia is holding my fist, I want to punch Buck but they are talking on my porch.

"Yes, actually. There's a burglar on the loose. The sheriff came by earlier, but you guys were out. Thought I'd come relay the message myself," he says. What a Boy Scout he is.

"Wow, thanks for letting us know. Can you come in for a nightcap and tell us more?" Mia asks.

"I'd love to," Buck says. He takes a step toward me. He has a lot of nerve. I turn to my wife. This is her fault, too. She needs to stop disrespecting me.

"Mia, this is our special night. The best night ever, for the two of us only," I say. I yank my hand away from hers like a toddler about to have a tantrum at a crowded mall. I reach for Mia's arm. I will pull her back inside away from Buck if I have to, but just as quickly she moves out of my reach.

"Yes, it is a special night, Paul. But Buck is looking out for our well-being. If there's a security concern in the neighborhood, I want to know what to do about it and Buck has the information we need," she says. She is calm, her face flushed, but her voice is firm. We are in a standoff on our front porch. Mia says, "Come in, please. Join us."

No, that isn't it, what you're thinking. She didn't mean join us for anything other than talking, an after-dinner drink. We aren't swingers or "alternative lifestyle" or "it's complicated" people. No, we're above average normal people. Well, sexually I'm above average. I have a gift. One woman just isn't enough to handle all I have to give, but I make each woman feel like she is. Does that make sense?

I need to focus.

My head is reeling, I'm losing control of my home, and I'm not certain what to do. My busy mind tries to come up with a response as Buck walks through the front door, cutting between Mia and me. I'm glaring at my wife, but she's ignoring my stare. Mia follows Buck inside. I have no choice but to follow, too. I step inside my cottage, close the front door behind me, and wonder what I can do to get rid of this unwelcome guest.

"Drink?" Mia asks him, following him to the family room. I have no choice but to trail behind her.

"Sure, what are you having?" Buck asks. He's wearing a LAKESIDE sweatshirt just like Mia's. His is navy blue. He has washed denim jeans on and the kind of tennis shoes they call boat shoes back East. Very nautical, very annoying package.

"Paul fixed me a brandy, but I'm just not in the mood," she says, pointing to the drink she didn't touch sitting on the coffee table.

"That stuff tastes like lighter fluid," Buck says. "How about a glass of wine? Red or white, I'm easy."

"Sure," Mia says. "Paul? Could you open some wine and pour Buck a glass? I'll have one, too."

What is happening? Now I am supposed to serve my wife and our unwanted neighbor wine. My hands become fists until I force them into my pockets and stretch a smile on my face. I stare at the two of them as they settle in around the coffee table.

10:30 P.M.

20

No doubt a shift has occurred in the room with Buck's arrival, specifically between Mia and me, but I cannot put my finger on it. Yes, Mia has invited the man across the street into our house, into our romantic evening together once again. But it's more than that. I know it is, but I cannot figure it out.

And she isn't drinking the brandy.

I stride into the kitchen and reach above the refrigerator, extracting a bottle of passable pinot noir. I don't care if it's a cheap bottle, it's for Buck. I unscrew the top—yes, it's cheap—and pour a glass for Buck. Mia has a drink, one she will enjoy with me. The same as me. Mine.

I walk through the dining room and stop for a moment. My wife and Buck are talking together, their faces close, close enough to have kissed while I was in the kitchen. He is sitting in a chair, one of the ones across from the couch. She is in the other one. Both chairs are blue. Both are being used.

I'm being used.

"Your wine, Buck," I say, walking into the room. Mia stands quickly, as if she just realized she was nose to nose with another man in my family room. She comes to my side and we sit at the same time on the couch.

"Did you bring me a glass?" she asks.

"You have brandy, Mia," I say, and I reach forward and hand her the tumbler. She hasn't even had a sip.

"I really don't think I can stomach it," she says. "I'll just go get some wine." She's up and out of the room before I can even react. With her, she's taken the glass of brandy.

"Allow me," I say, standing. As I begin to follow her, Buck stands. We are face-to-face, man-to-man. All I can imagine is shoving my fist into his dimple, or his nose, or—

"No, really, both of you sit. I'll be right back," Mia says.

Buck narrows his eyes, but a smile forms on his face. "Let's do what she says, okay?" he says. "Far be it from me to refuse a lady." He keeps his eyes locked on mine as he sits down on the edge of the blue chair.

"What are you doing here?" I say, sitting lightly on the edge of the couch across from him. The candles I lit for our romantic evening are flickering, contorting Buck's anchorman looks.

"I came to warn you about the burglar," Buck says. He takes a sip of the wine. "Lovely." I can tell he knows it's cheap, knows it is anything but lovely—the wine, the situation.

"Bullshit," I say.

Mia walks back into the room, no doubt assessing our standoff. We are, us men, predatory. And we are protectors. Like the guard dog waiter at dinner, somehow Buck has caught a whiff of something, the scent of trouble, and he's on the trail like a bloodhound. But he's wrong. And the only person who can tell him how wrong he is would be Mia, the supposed prey, as it were.

My father—he was a wonderful role model as I mentioned—loved this game. The standoff. Come to think of it, I like it, too. I liked it when I had to pretend to police that I was shocked to discover my parents dead in their bed when I dialed 9-1-1. But by now you know pretending was easy. I simply reminded myself it was their fault. They should not have said no to babysitting the night before. It was their one role in life, supporting my children, treating them better than they'd treated me. How hard could that be? When I had to face Rebecca in the Thompson Payne office, I played the game. Amateurs. People try to look at me as a suspect, but I'm good, I'm not easy to catch. I honed my skills at an early age, allowing me to withstand the scrutiny of Donald Pilmer, although, truth be told, there was no stopping Mia from marrying me, no matter what her old man said or dug up.

I sat calmly on the other end of the phone line from Donald, a situation much like this, with this sort of underlying tension, and told him I was marrying his daughter. I didn't so much ask for his blessing as tell him that it was happening. I didn't flinch when he yelled about it being too soon, dishonorable and the like. My voice was calm and strong. I was confident. I was raised to handle tests, to outsmart everyone. My mom told me I was special, even when my dad tried to beat it out of me. So I thrive in situations like this one. The only problem tonight is, I don't understand what is going on. Why is Buck here?

"Mia," I say without turning to look at my wife. I hold Buck's gaze. "This is not about a burglar, is it? Why is he here?"

"All right, Paul," Mia says, and then I hear a drawer opening and I see out of the corner of my eye that she has opened the drawer of the coffee table. I didn't even know there was one. Interesting. "I agree it's time to talk. I should start by telling you I've made a decision."

"And this so-called decision needs an audience, beyond me?" I ask. I'm still staring at Buck but I can feel Mia's eyes on me.

"Yes, it does. Buck is here to support me, as a neighbor and as my friend." She takes a breath, lets it out while an eternity seems to pass. "I've done a lot of thinking, soul-searching. But still, this is so hard," she says.

Across the table from me, Buck smiles and then catches himself and clenches his handsome jaw. His hands are both flat on his thighs. His fingers still.

I don't look at my wife. I stare into the candle flame reflected in Buck's eyes.

"What are you trying to say, Mia?" I ask. I don't turn my head to look at my wife. I continue staring at Buck.

11:00 P.M.

21

"This is hard, even though you've lied to me, about so many things, for so long, Paul." Mia's voice cracks and I believe she may be crying. But I cannot break my stare-a-thon with Buck.

"For God's sake, look at your wife," Buck says. He shakes his head and loses our match, shifting his gaze to Mia.

I win. I always win.

"Of course. Mia, honey, what are you talking about? What's so hard? We have a great life," I say. Now I shift on the couch so I can face her. She is crying—I knew it—and I still don't know what she's holding in her hand, but I suppose I'm curious. "What lies are you referring to exactly?"

Mia meets my gaze squarely. "Uncle Derrick? Just tonight. At what was supposed to be our special dinner, you lied. I know you stole that letter, Paul. I know you are investigating the mineral rights. You're trying to steal them from me."

Hmm. Mia as Sherlock Holmes. How interesting. The role doesn't suit her, though; she simply isn't clever enough.

Well, perhaps she does know more than she lets on, but that's fine. I was doing what I did for both of us. For the kids. For the future.

I need Buck to leave. Now. "I will not discuss private family matters with a stranger here," I say. I'm calm, but in charge. The man of the castle. The one in control, as always.

I wait for Buck to move, to leave. But of course, he has his primitive guard dog juices flowing, and he's not budging.

"I want him to stay," Mia tells me. "I feel more comfortable if he's here."

"'I feel more comfortable if he's here,'" I say, mimicking my wife and her miserable weak tone. "Come on. Are you a child? These are private matters, family matters, between a husband and wife, and I refuse to discuss anything further until he's gone." I take a sip of brandy and it burns my throat.

"Paul, you need to calm down and allow Mia to speak," Buck the widower asshole garden gnome says.

"You need to go back to your empty life and leave my wife alone," I correct him. I am so close to hitting him I can feel it, feel the throbbing pain in my knuckles as they remember the blow for days after like they did when I dropped Greg Boone, another nosy neighbor. I'd aim for his nose, but be happy with knocking out the stupid dimple. "Unless you're fucking my wife. Then we have other things to discuss."

"Don't be crude," Buck says. He picks up his wineglass and drinks. He doesn't appear to be leaving.

I should have seen this all along. They are having an affair. And now she is coming clean, telling me everything, even though it was supposed to be our best day ever. That's fine, though. I suppose I knew it somewhere deep down. Best to air the dirty laundry, get readjusted, and then figure out next steps. I have my plan, and now I know she has one, too. Impressive. Mia has played me perfectly. I've fallen into her trap, even as she slipped out of mine. I will not allow her surprises to end the night, though. I will win.

But what exactly does she know?

Mia slides a piece of paper in front of me. I recognize it, of course. It's the letter from her uncle. The one I opened and hid.

"Recognize this?" she asks. The cottage seems very quiet. I feel Buck lean forward, looking at the document.

"I do. But again, why is he here?" I say. "Why are we discussing a letter from your crazy uncle in front of our neighbor? This is a private family matter, nobody's business but ours."

I see Mia send a look to Buck. A look she should be giving me. We're the team here.

"Look. We can talk about everything once we're back home," I say. "It's late, past eleven. We never stay up this late. I'm calling it a night, and that means you are too, right, honey?" I stand up, feign a yawn and pop my knuckles. It's a bad habit, a low-class habit, I know.

"Paul, I know you tried to claim my mineral rights, the ones Uncle Derrick wrote to me about," Mia says, her voice quavering. This is hard for her. Poor Mia. Maybe I'll tell her a little story, just to calm her down.

"I was just researching things for you, but if you'd like to paint me as a criminal, go ahead," I say. I walk around the seating area until I'm standing directly behind Buck. His neck is exposed, just within reach if I take a step forward. I can feel his flesh in my hands, his neck snapping nicely.

Mia has become unrecognizable. It's as if she changed overnight into a sneaky, manipulative woman who hides things from her husband. Meanwhile, Gretchen always treats me nicely. She is the perfect woman for me, I realize at this instant. It all starts with chemistry, which we had that day at her store in the mall. And then it deepens as I test her to see how receptive she is to my rules, my way. Will she pick me over a movie night with her girlfriends, for example?

Gretchen does not disappoint. She's a better listener than Mia even. She wears skirts and dresses, as I request. She'd never wear ridiculous sweatpants that made her look like a hog. Whenever I spend time with her, she treasures it. Sometimes, after a particularly intimate lovemaking session, she cries when I must leave and go back home. She's hooked on me like crack. I know she wants more, deserves more of me.

I tell her I love my wife, but Gretchen knows there are issues between Mia and me. I mean, I'm with Gretchen every day, as long as possible. When we aren't making love, we're cooking a gourmet lunch together because unlike certain people she's actually a great cook, or plotting vacations to faraway lands. I tell her stories about television commercial shoots in Hollywood and assure her she'll come with me the next time I'm on location. I see how her eyes sparkle with those promises. We both know it's just a matter of time, I guess.

Gretchen is the reason why I'm more comfortable letting Mia go now. I often wonder what she'd think of raising the boys with me, although I haven't asked her yet. She'd be great, I know. She's very patient. I'd get her a large home in the suburbs, a different suburb, and we would raise the boys there together. Mia would never see them again.

Oh, I don't mean that. Don't worry; it's the tension I'm feeling with this stranger in our home.

"Paul," Mia says. "Sit down. Please."

"I'm tired, Mia. I've tried to make this the perfect day, the best day ever, but you've insisted on ruining it, every single step of the way. I'm over it. I'll see you upstairs," I say. "And *he* should leave. Now. I'm finished with this little ménage à trois."

I take a step toward the stairs.

11:30 P.M.

22

It's frustrating being forced out of the comfort of your cozy, designer-decorated family room by an irrational woman and her sidekick, the garden troll, but the circumstances leave me no choice.

As far as the mineral rights, Mia is correct. I want the rights in my name, and I've been working good old Uncle Derrick to help him see the light. We almost have a deal, Derrick and me, but Mia need not know that. Derrick is so easily manipulated. He believes everything I whisper in his ear about how close I am to his brother, Mia's dad, and how I'm working for their brotherly reconciliation.

And, just as easily, when I tell him of his brother's pretend betrayal, he'll believe me and want to make sure no other Pilmer inherits the land. It's a clean slate with a Strom, this Strom, in charge. I've almost tied up this loose end.

M. Pilmer. My wife signed her name that way at the Italian

restaurant. I stop at the foot of the stairs. I suddenly see everything very clearly; my busy mind focuses on one thing. Mia.

I turn and look at my wife. She meets my gaze. From across
the room, she says, "Paul, I'm leaving you."

I shake my head. "No, Mia, you're not. The mineral rights
aren't worth more than five hundred dollars a year at this
point. It's nothing. I was just simplifying things, getting a
handle on them, and then I was going to share the good
news," I say. My heart is pounding. People don't "leave" me.
I "leave" people when I'm finished with them. She has gone
insane. She's jealous of the fabulous life I lead without her,
and I'm to blame for that.

"It's not about the mineral rights or Uncle Derrick," Mia
says.

I watch as Buck stands. He has positioned himself between
my wife and me. I must lean to the right to make eye contact
with her, to direct her and coach her as I typically do.

"Can you get out of our house now?" I ask, moving rapidly
toward Mia. I cross the family room and find myself face-
to-face with Buck who, instead of moving out of the way,
has become a human roadblock between my wife and me.
We are the same height, but I have more weight on me, and
more anger. I have the fire.

Something has come between us, dear, I think, *and it's the fucking neighbor.*

I take a step to the left. Mia is now directly in front of me.

"What is wrong with you, Mia? Do you need help again?
Do you remember when we had to take you to that psy-
chiatrist? Postpartum depression or whatever? You're fragile
and you need rest," I say. I'm speaking with my kindergar-
ten teacher voice. "I shouldn't have given you so much freedom and space. You're sick again. I'm so sorry. This is all my

fault." I've taken a step back, and I can see my wife clearly, even with the stupid neighbor between us. He isn't budging. He hasn't moved at all. I decide to speak to him, reason with him, man-to-man.

"Buck, my wife is bipolar. Well, the diagnosis is unspecified, um, but clearly with the delusions and the like, well, it is manifesting again. I'm sorry to be angry with you," I say. I drop my gaze to his feet. I'm apologetic, contrite. "My apologies. And if you'll excuse us, I'll get her to bed."

"How did I marry this?" Mia whispers to Buck. I hear her loud and clear. Her words are directed at me. Her words are about me.

I watch as Buck pulls her into his side, wraps his arm around her waist. Both of them now locked together, facing me. I am disgusted. I take a step toward my wife and Buck steps them back, as a unit, as if they're going to backstep out of my cottage. They will not.

I look at Mia, at her shaking, whispering, sneaky, sweatshirt- and sweatpants-wearing self, and I am disgusted. *How did I ever love that? Unthinkable.*

"Look, Mia. You're upset, and you have clearly gotten your bulldog Buck on your side here. Not sure what you did to earn that, but fine. I'm not going to imagine you two fucking. Instead I'll choose to be glad you made a new friend. Here's what's going to happen. I'm going upstairs to sleep. In the morning, we will talk. No one is leaving anyone, you understand? What we have together is special. Think of our boys for once, why don't you. We've had too much wine, too much stress for one day, that's all," I say. And then, I hold my hands up, as if I'm in a bank robbery, and take several steps backward. I hope I don't run into anything.

"Come on, Mia, you're strong, you've got this," Buck says

to my wife, who wipes a tear from under her eye. A black river rolls down her left cheek. She isn't wearing waterproof mascara. Obviously, if she'd really known what she was going to be doing tonight she would have worn waterproof mascara. Poor Mia. She's under Buck's spell.

As if reading my mind, Buck says, "You're in control now, Mia."

Silly man. He doesn't realize I hold the power for both of us. Her power doesn't exist. I started taking it the moment we met.

Mia chokes out a sob, as if to confirm my thoughts.

She looks horrible. She has streaks of mascara running down her cheeks, and her nose is bubbly with snot. She opens her mouth, as if to talk, but nothing comes out. She turns and buries her gooey face in Buck's LAKESIDE sweatshirt.

Why don't they just fuck in front of me? I wonder. Whatever. I don't really care at this point. I want to go upstairs, to my bedroom. I want to reconfigure some things. I have climbed three steps up from the family room when the blob speaks. I stop and turn my head to look at my pathetic wife.

"Paul. I'm worth more than this, more than the way you treat me. I have been a faithful, loving wife and mother. I've done everything you've asked of me, and more. I've given up my career, my friends, most contact with my family, all for you. I loved you once, Paul. Deeply and with my whole heart. But you don't deserve that love anymore. I am leaving you, effective tonight. I have papers for a separation, there, on the coffee table. And I want you out of this house," Mia says. She delivers these very strong words in a very tiny voice. She has pointed her finger at me, but the effort of that seems to have wiped her out. She's again leaning against the anchorman. The garden gnome who put her up to this, I now realize. Of course, she would never have attempted anything like this without someone pushing her into it. That's why I've kept her parents far away from us. Unfortunately, I underestimated Buck. In fact, I didn't give him any thought at all. My mistake.

"Oh, Mia. I'm afraid your plan just doesn't work for me. This is my cottage. You are my wife. Get control of yourself," I say. I shake my head at the silly woman and turn and resume my climb up the stairs.

12:00 A.M.

23

I'm still shaking my head as I reach the top of the stairs of *my* lake cottage.

Of course Mia's net worth is more than mine. Her daddy is worth more than you and me and the state of Tennessee combined. So what? Wealth can be measured by so many things: intelligence, social IQ, sales ability and, well, so much else. Intelligence is picking the right suit, the perfect car and the young wife, all designed to make you look your best. Virile. Enviable.

The goal is to find your soul mate, and then convince her that she has found hers, too. That Mia had money was a bonus, that's all.

Oh, who am I kidding? We know each other so well by now. That Mia came from money was everything to me. I'm good at finding money, attracting money, as you can tell. I'm not as astute at holding money, building wealth. But now that I have Mia, I don't need to worry about money ever again. That's why I can screw around with beauty, even though Gretchen is poor. Mia is my golden ticket. So really, this minor weakness has been overcome. Of all the world's weaknesses, it's the one I'd choose. It's not even a weakness, actually. I'm simply overly generous. And now I can afford to be, thanks to my little Pilmer piggy bank.

I stop at the top of the stairs. To listen. The walls of my cottage are quite thin, as I noted.

What did Mia mean by her comments about me not treating her well? I have cherished her, provided for her, given her sons she adores. What is she trying to tell me? I hear Mia sob. Am I the weak one, running away? Perhaps I am, but Buck is to blame.

Why are they together, at what my Apple Watch confirms is midnight? How did I allow my family to get so out of control, out of my control, that my wife is with another man in my family room and my boys are not to be disturbed? How did that happen? And, in fact, now that it has, shouldn't I, the responsible parent, be the one who returns home to claim the children?

If she abandons me, she abandons them. No one likes a mother who neglects her children, most especially not me.

"Mia, I'm so sorry. Let's leave the papers. You can stay at my house," Buck says, his voice quite clear from where I'm standing at the landing.

Nicely played, Buck. Although any man that would want my wife in her gray fatness and sobbing sadness is a weak, pathetic excuse for a male.

Mia says, "I have so much I want to say to him. What kind of man tells his fiancée he is having an affair with a client days before the wedding, but says he still loves her, that it was just a fling? He actually convinced me at the time that she forced herself on him. Who does that? And why did I still marry him? I never should have believed anything he told me." I can't see them but I imagine her pounding her fists into his chest, like the actors do on *Days of Our Lives*.

"How you treat your spouse is who you are. He is a bad man. You deserve to be cared for, supported and loved. Not controlled, deceived and stifled. You know this," Buck says.

Well, actually, she doesn't, Buck. There is a reason I selected her. And Lois. And Gretchen. I know their kind. It was as if I was bred with an extrasensory perception of people I can control. Specifically, women I can control. I can smell them, feel them. I know it the minute we bump into each other, the ones I can get. Just as I may be a type, so are they, only they don't know it. By the way, I don't tell anyone these things, so please don't say anything or share my secrets.

Buck's also wrong about another thing. It's not how you treat your spouse that shows people who you are. It's how you treat yourself, how much you care about yourself. Mia became selfless with me. It's her fault, not mine.

"Paul. Please. I know you are listening from the top of the stairs. We're over. I need to give you these papers, you need to sign them, and then I need you to leave. Otherwise, I'll call the police," Mia says.

For obvious reasons, I don't want the cops here. Although I've never made their acquaintance, and small-town, hick-filled police departments don't concern me, I'd just rather not have that type of encounter tonight. You know, you start to get on the radar of a police department, even if it's tiny Lakeside PD, and it could become an issue. Mia's voice is firm, threatening. Tonight, at this moment, I don't think she is bluffing.

I have no choice. I start walking back down the stairs. This situation is uncomfortable. Made doubly so by the pretty boy in the corner. Pretty boys have haunted me, always. I was just as handsome, mind you, just not equipped with the right stuff. They seemed to know I didn't have the right pants to wear for sixth grade dance club, or the money for the best equipment for football in seventh grade. My mom was different than the other mom volunteers, less put together, always nervous, inferior. My family was a step down from the rest of the families in my friend group. I was the poor boy. Even though my parents bragged about making the move to Grandville, buying their first home in what they thought was the best suburb in town when it wasn't back then, I was acutely aware that we lived in the cheapest house in the neighborhood. I knew we were barely hanging on. With every beating I repeated to myself: I will never be the poor boy again. Never.

I feel my hands clench by my sides. I work to open them by the time I reach the bottom of the stairs. I stretch a smile across my perfect white veneers.

12:15 A.M.

24

Buck looks at me from a position of strength, preening like he's a rooster winning the cockfight. He's a fool. Doesn't he know all the animals die in those games? He has resumed his position standing between me and my wife. I can't believe both of them, wearing their stupid matching Lakeside tourist sweatshirts. Did they plan that, too?

"Paul, sit down," he says. He points to the spot on the couch. I defy him, a little victory, and sit down in the closest blue club chair. I'm tired. And bored with them. I yawn.

"Are we boring you, Paul?" he asks.

"Cocky asshole, yes, you are," I say.

Mia steps forward, closer to me. She's back. I think I've won her back. I smile my most winning smile and feel her being drawn toward me. I'm a magnet. I can almost reach out and touch her arm as she points to the documents on the table. Her red, blotchy, tear-streaked face is hideous in the candlelight. But I still love her, poor thing.

"Paul. Here is the separation agreement. I need you to sign it, and then leave and go to the hotel room I reserved for you at the Lakeside Inn. All of your belongings have been taken there already," Mia says. Her voice is quiet, shaky. I think maybe Buck has talked her into this whole ridiculous exercise. When I get her alone again, I'll smooth everything over. She stands and backs away, stopping next to Buck. From there she adds, "Except I kept a couple of things you won't be needing."

How dare she rummage through my things? When did she even have the time? When I was at the store purchasing items for her, from her grocery list just to make her happy? Bitch. But still, there is nothing of note hidden in my belongings, I'm sure. A little folder about the Texas land, that's all. I wonder again what else she knows, what is making her take this step.

"Mia, you surprise me. You've turned sneaky. Conniving. A planner. Everything you hate in the world. Bravo," I say, raising an invisible glass in a mock salute. "I've taught you well."

Mia shakes her head. I'm unsure what to do next. Has she gone through my briefcase? What does she have? For a moment my heart thuds in my chest as I remember the special envelope. I think back to the sink fire, relieved.

Mia walks back toward the table, coming closer to me, holding a pen. "You will keep the home in Columbus as your primary residence since it was yours when we married. The cottage will be mine. You'll see I've been more than fair, about everything."

I wonder how many of her daddy's expensive New York City attorneys billed time against this document. It doesn't matter, really. I know it will be airtight, unbreakable. I am signing the end to this gravy train.

If I sign.

I pretend Buck is not in the room, and address only Mia. "Look, honey, it's late. We're all tired, a little worked up. Why don't I go on over to the inn and we can look these things over in the morning? How's that?" I ask.

Mia looks at Buck, Buck stares at me.

He says, "No. That doesn't work. We need this signed tonight. I don't trust you to come back over. I don't believe anything you say."

"Who are you anyway, and why are you here?" I ask for the umpteenth time tonight, standing once more. Mia jumps back and hides behind Buck. The fire in my soul is starting to burn. "I want you out of my house now. This is between my wife and me."

"Paul, calm down," Mia says. She has stepped toward me again. Buck stops her, placing a hand on her shoulder. She turns and looks up at him. She's a traitor.

"May I?" he asks her.

Mia looks at him like a lost puppy dog and nods a silent yes. Clearly my mutt needs a little retraining.

It's Buck's turn to take a step toward me, putting himself between Mia and me, his favorite position tonight. "Sit back down and I'll tell you everything. And then you will sign, and you will leave. You can even go back to Columbus tonight, if that's your preference."

It's an interesting idea. Maybe I will do that. Head back home, enjoy the drive without Mia's nonsense in the passenger seat. She can be stranded up here with Buck and her strawberry babies. I'll be home by three, climb into bed and wake up with the boys in the morning. After Claudia leaves, I'll begin explaining to them why they won't ever see their mommy again. They'll have a new, young brunette mommy named Gretchen. Or, if for some reason I can't finagle anything out of Mia, perhaps I'll find another woman with money. It'll all work out. I know women. This is my favorite subject.

I think about that option. A new, wealthy lover. It's enticing. Especially if I agree to leave, Mia will take most of the assets. I'm sure that's in the document. She doesn't know about the second mortgage on the Columbus house—I needed some emergency funds a while back. Without Donald's Christmas gifts, or Mia's seemingly endless gravy train from her parents, cash will be tight for the boys and me. Except, I remember, they have a trust fund. I smile and sit down in my favorite chair as Buck takes a seat in the other blue chair. Gretchen could work, as long as I have the boys' trust fund. I have choices, many choices much better than this one.

Mia seems to be hiding in the corner, a trapped gray creature. She looks like a rat, a sneaky rat with shiny, beady rodent eyes. The room is hot, I feel sweat trickle down my back and I'm the only one not wearing a ridiculous LAKESIDE sweatshirt. Why isn't Buck sweating, too? He seems calm, almost too calm. He leans toward me, resting his elbows on his thighs, his chiseled chin on top of his clasped hands. I fight the urge to deck him then and there.

Curiosity stops me from punching him just yet. I need to hear what good old Buck has to say.

12:20 A.M.

25

Buck says: "I know you have Googled me, trying to figure me out, isn't that right, Paul? No need to answer.
Mia told me you did it together. What did you find?"

"Not much. Just that you sold your company. Your wife
is dead. Besides that, you haven't had a very notable life,
I'm afraid," I tell him. If you Google Paul Strom, you'll get
pages of accolades. ADDY Awards for advertising campaigns
I helped lead, civic awards for the community activities I've
been involved in and, of course, links to my very famous
father-in-law, too. I'm all over the internet, as I should be. Of
course I also made an appearance in my parents' obituaries,
the favorite son who lived right next door. So loyal. I didn't
include Tom in the write-up; he didn't deserve the acknowledgment, the ghost.

"Some people prefer to be hidden," Buck says. "My company, the one I sold last year, handles security for high net

worth individuals. Neither my clients nor I wish for any personal publicity and we allow only very carefully controlled public information out in the world."

"Oh, so you're some sort of spy, is that it?" I ask. I was right about him. My instincts are finely tuned. I remain one step ahead of this imitation James Bond.

"Actually, former special ops, but that's not important now. What you do need to know is that we've been watching you," Buck says. "For a while now."

The candle closest to me sizzles out, a plume of dark smoke announcing its demise. The other, in the middle of the table, had burned out sometime earlier. That leaves only one candle flickering on the coffee table. In the corner, I see Mia open the hutch and pull out another candle. It's reflex. At Lakeside, there are often severe thunderstorms that can knock the power out for hours, or days. We've stocked up on candles, and they are tucked everywhere. Of course, tonight is cloudless, and the lights are on, although dimmed, ironically by me for our romantic after-dinner drink.

I focus my attention back on Buck and his "special ops" announcement. I know it is a threat. A warning not to get physical, but I still have fire in my core. Sometimes rage can overpower training.

"You've been watching me? How charming. Why?" I say. He knows I don't find this charming, but I'm also a bit disturbed. Something in the back of my mind is trying to push to the front.

"Because from the moment I met you, I knew something was off. Really off. Greg confirmed it. You know, your former friend, Greg Boone?"

What is it with these idiots, the Boones? Why can't they

mind their own business? "Greg Boone is a sore loser. A loser, period," I say.

"Be that as it may, I have the resources to check people out. And you are not what you seem. Or, more precisely, you are part of the one percent."

I don't think Buck is referring to income. Clearly he must be aware of our current financial squeeze. "One percent?" I ask.

"Classic malignant narcissist, possible psychopathic. All the definitions really blend together, but it's you. You have no conscience, have a psychological need for power and control and you think you are more important than anyone else. You lured Mia into your web when she was young and inexperienced. You lie constantly and you have no shame. You won't take responsibility for any of this, will you?" Buck says. He pauses and we smile at each other.

What does he expect? Should I pretend to be shocked? I know who I am. I'm special, unique. "Whatever you say, Buck. Why do you think you know so much about this subject? Takes one to know one, am I right?"

Buck doesn't answer me, just shakes his head as my wife appears from behind him. Her hand is on the back of the chair but I know she wants to touch his shoulder. She better not. She knows she better not touch him like that in front of me. Ever. I am staring at her. I am waiting for her to make a big mistake.

"I asked Buck to help me because I thought I was losing my mind," Mia says. She walks over to the coffee table, where we are locked in our little tête-à-tête but stays as far as possible away from me. She lights the new candle with the flame of the old one, places it in the holder and sits down on the couch, much nearer to Buck's chair than mine. She has dripped wax on the table, so sloppy.

"Ever since the boys started school, I've felt so un-me, so needy. If you had let me out of the house maybe things would be different, but I don't know. And then, I got sick. But it doesn't matter. It's your pattern that's the problem. I mean, what is so wrong with me that you had to find lovers during our engagement, and then during our marriage? How many were there, Paul? You lie about everything, you try to steal my money? How did you make it all seem like it was my problem? Like something was wrong with me. I just didn't understand. I was trapped in this world you'd created, a prison. You're the lunatic, Paul, not me."

"So you two are doing it?" I say, my eyes roving over my wife and then over Buck. I sound like a teenage boy in the sports locker room, I know. It's for shock value. It works.

Mia puts her hand over her mouth. Her eyes bug out at me. Ha. Buck starts to stand. Will he come at me? Mia holds her hand up and he stays seated but he's seething. Good.

He says, "Don't be crass. This isn't about me. This is about you. Mia and I worked on the garden together last summer, do you remember? She had two weeks up here without you. Just the boys and gardening. I saw her relax, come to life. I gave her some suggested reading materials." Buck looks at Mia and nods, prodding my wife like a shepherd herding his lost sheep. It works.

Mia leans toward me and says, "I learned about what you are, that there was a name for this. I learned it wasn't me. I am not the crazy one. But still, it took me all winter to get the courage to leave you. When you got fired, and when I found out why, that sealed it. But I knew you wouldn't let me leave without a fight."

"That's where I come in, me and my people. We've been tailing you, Paul," Buck says.

I squint my eyes, staring a hole in Buck's forehead. Why do he and Mia seem to finish each other's sentences, like an old married couple? It's getting annoying. But it doesn't matter. What could he possibly have seen if he was following me? Nothing, of course.

"I fail to see why anyone would want to follow a successful businessman going to work each day and returning home to his beautiful family in their gorgeous suburban home," I say.

Buck is smirking, I am almost positive, though his expression remains stoic. "Nothing is ever what it seems, you know that, Paul," he says. "We follow you every weekday as you visit your lover Gretchen."

How dare he say her name in front of Mia? My brain registers this daunting fact and then I realize she probably has seen photos. *Poor Mia.* I'll need to give her a really big hug.

Mia's head has dropped into her hands.

"She has no impact on us, Mia. I love you. You're my wife. She is just, well, for sex," I say.

"Oh, God," Buck says.

On the couch, Mia is shaking again. I start to stand up, to go comfort her.

Buck places his hand on my thigh, squeezes my leg hard and says: "Sit down. Now."

12:25 A.M.

26

I lower myself into the chair again, but he can't make me stay here. Nobody can make me do anything. I feel the fire surging inside me. I will not be forced to sit for long.

"You've got quite a history with women, haven't you, Paul? We know about Lois, your first wife. I spent an afternoon with her. Lovely woman. Still terrified of you. Funny how you never mentioned to Mia that you'd been married before," Buck says.

"Not relevant, not at all." How dare he stomp around in my business? I know, I never told you I was married to Lois. It was a short, messy affair. Best to just move on and that's why I never discuss it. I had made a very rare miscalculation. I thought I should marry young; it was part of the package of an up-and-coming successful advertising executive. I had the vision of how my life would look in my head. I just needed to fill in the actual people to play the roles.

The moment I met Lois in class I knew she was perfect prey. She would fit the role of wife exactly as I imagined. I worked my charms, waiting for her after class with an armful of her favorite white daisies, for example, and later, leaving little love notes in her backpack each morning for her to find during class. It was all romantic, and no surprise that she fell for me, hook, line and sinker. But I had that regrettable lapse of control and allowed my mask to slip. That would not happen again. No, best not to tell anyone about Lois. That story is over. The end. Lois's divorce papers were simplistic, but I'd gladly signed. Good riddance. And I'd never discuss it now, with this man.

"Lois, Caroline Fisher, Rebecca More—all of these women and others, both you and I know about, are terrified of you. None of them knew about your pattern of behavior, that it has been going on your entire life. They all do now. If you think you can get away with hurting any of them or threatening them again, you are very wrong," Buck says.

"I don't know what kind of picture you're trying to paint of me, but I resent the implications. I've never laid a hand on my wife, on Mia. She will confirm that, right, honey?" I ask. I look over at Mia, now curled up in a ball, her feet tucked beneath her, in the corner of the couch. I want to go hug her and strangle her, all at once. It's a pleasant sensation that I allow to brew inside me. I do not believe that Buck can match my fire. I can take him if I choose to.

You've probably figured it out by now, haven't you? My little plan for our best day ever. My sickly little wife, my secret stash of powder. The two are related, of course. But what would hurt my wife the most at this point, given these new facts laid out by her lover? What would hurt her most—her death by my hand or never seeing her children again? It's an interesting question. I'd planned the former, but now I may need to regroup.

There are always options when you are smarter than everyone. Gretchen and I will sell the Columbus house, use whatever proceeds I make to start over. I read that Nashville is booming, one of the fastest growing cities in the country; maybe we'll move there. I've read it's more than country music now, much more. Lois likes it there and it will be fun to run into her again. I like my new plan.

"So, the little meeting tonight is to get me to sign these papers, to give up the cottage, which is fine with me, given the neighbors—no offense, Buck—and I get the Columbus home. Is that correct?" I ask.

"Yes," the gray ball in the corner of the couch says. "As long as you agree to leave me, the boys and my family alone."

My laugh breaks the silence of the room. "Mia, you're hysterical."

The boys will be with me. They need a father figure. They've outgrown all of that mommy care. It's time for them to become men, which I have talked to her about incessantly. Does she forget everything I've taught her? It's natural for the boys to begin pulling away from their mother and turn to me, their father. It's expected. And so of course, they'll be with me. Mia is staring at me and so is Buck. I want to reassure her that this is the way it is all meant to be. And it is.

"You'll be able to visit, don't worry. You've done a good job with them. Now it's my turn," I say. It's as if I'm talking to a child. We review the same points, ad nauseam. It's frustrating. I feel my right hand clench. I push a smile onto my lips, running my tongue across my teeth. "I'll be with them tonight, as soon as I get out of here. Nothing to worry about."

Mia uncurls, puts her feet on the floor, leans forward and says, "The boys will be with me. Period."

I fight the urge to reach for her. To slap her, hard, so hard she flies across the room. A gray ball flying into oblivion, her head cracking against the floor.

"It's all here, in the agreement you will sign," Buck says. I know he is redirecting my attention to him. Foolish man to get in the middle of my life, to get with my wife. He had better watch his back.

"I will divide the property, but I will not consent to giving up my children. Who would ask that? That's wrong. Boys need their fathers. Look at the terrorists. Look at the prison system. The prisons are filled with boys without male role models," I say. It's true, we all know it.

"Sometimes no role model is better than a terrible one. It may have taken me too long to see you for what you are, but they're still young enough to be saved. You haven't revealed yourself to them, you haven't used them or hurt them, and for that I'm very grateful. You should know, if you had touched them, hurt them, I would have left you. But you know that already, don't you? That's why you haven't laid a hand on them, I suppose. They've been sheltered from your life outside of our home, from the truth of who their father really is.

"I've researched this, Paul. They don't have to end up like you, with your temper and other issues. They won't, not if I can help it. My dad will be a much better role model for them, among others."

Did Mia just look at Buck? I'm going to kill him.

For some reason Mia is still talking. She adds, "And they're going to be fine. They will both become good men, despite you." My wife crosses her arms in front of her chest and smiles.

How did I not see a browsing history of these types of things? I wonder. She must have deleted her history. She must have hidden her reference books. She must have become like me. I think back, trying to remember if she was acting differently around me recently. She wasn't jumpy or anything at the dinner table, she didn't look at me with suspicious eyes. But she had been happier lately, despite her illness, her weight loss. I just thought it was acceptance. Turns out, it was awakening. I missed the signs. I squeeze my hands into fists. She's droning on again.

Mia says, "They'll get counseling, financial security from my parents, until I get on my feet again. It's all worked out."

Ah, yes. Her parents. There better be a big payout in those papers for me. Two children. Boys. White. Smart. Blue eyes. They are worth a lot these days. We're almost a minority.

"So, what are you proposing to pay me, you and your dear father, Donald, to steal my children, to buy my sons, from me?" I ask. This is a game. I enjoy playing games. I enjoy the look my wife gives me as we discuss our children like property. She looks ill, suddenly. All the color has drained from her face.

"You are a sick bastard," Buck says. If I punched him quickly, in the temple, I could stun him long enough to reach for Mia. It's an intriguing and exciting thought.

I see the candle drip wax onto the coffee table. I'd like to push the candle over, start a fire and torch this cottage. It would go fast, with the old wood, all the wood floors, shingled roof. Poof. All gone. It's tragic that Buck and Mia perish in the fire. But sometimes, cheaters get what they deserve.

"I understand who you are, Paul. The sad thing is, people like you don't change, even with intense counseling. Somehow, you walk around in the world among us, hidden, manipulating others, hurting others. Even the people you claim to love. I know you don't feel love, you couldn't and do what you do." Mia stops, bites her lip. She shakes her head slowly. She looks at me with pity, her face drawn. I won't stand for this.

Mia holds her hand up, pointing her finger at me. "I know you're trying to poison me, that you have been poisoning me. I opened the glove box to freak you out during the drive up today." She pauses, then tilts her head. "It worked, didn't it?"

12:35 A.M.

27

The room is silent, as if none of us were breathing. I stare at my wife, incredulous. My mouth has dropped open and I feel the cool air of the room hitting the back of my throat. As for it working, if she is referring to the poison I may or may not have given her, clearly it didn't. Instead of just watching her waste away, I should have killed her in one big dose. A miscalculation, for sure.

At first, I rather enjoyed the disintegration of my wife, the slow disappearance as she wasted away despite her "clean" diet, healthy lifestyle. Ironic, isn't it. And, of course, I picked this path because small doses are easier to hide. I never had to worry, though. All of the fancy doctors she consulted, regular and hippie, never did the special urine test for this particular poison. It's the only way to detect arsenic poisoning and even then, it must be within three days of the dose.

I was finished with Mia, yes, but I didn't want an abrupt

"end." Gretchen and I had grown so close and, well, the wife felt like the proverbial ball and chain. At the same time, I know that a sudden death is so hard on children. Mommy slipping away slowly is much better on them. The long goodbye, so to speak. I was thinking of the boys, as always. I never had to worry, there was a firm timeline to my plan. Sure it shifted, I'll admit. But this weekend, this final time together, well, it was precipitated by my need for resources. My dwindling supplies and, of course, my love for my boys. They deserve the finest in life. Their inheritance will assure it. It had to end tonight. But still, I had wanted a romantic final day with my wife, my little Mia. She deserved it, she did. Until this, the best day ever, turned into something else, turned into this.

Until Buck. The bastard. They're both staring at me. Mia's mouth is open a bit like she's trying to speak, trying to think of something to say. But now I have the floor. She asked me a question.

"You never *freak me out*, Mia, to use your childish phrase. Look at you, sniveling, scrawny, unkempt with mascara streaks down your face. How could you ever think you have any power over me?" I ask.

"Time to sign the papers, Paul," Buck says. He reaches over to the coffee table and picks up the pen. Shiny and silver, it seems expensive. I wonder who it belongs to. Maybe Mia's father, maybe Buck. If I sign, I will take it with me, as a reminder of this moment, of the inferno inside me. And of the revenge I'll extract. It will be a touchstone for revenge.

"And if I don't?" I ask.

"I'll press charges. Attempted murder," Mia says. "We have the proof. Photos of you with the envelope, photos of you pouring the powder into my brandy."

I think of the kitchen window over the sink. It doesn't

have curtains or a shade. I kick myself for my complacency, for my lack of caution. I never imagined someone could follow me successfully, not without my spotting a tail. Now I realize there was someone watching us at the restaurant, as well. It was probably Buck. That's who Mia was smiling to through the window. Of course.

"You ended up lacing your wife's brandy with sugar, sport," Buck says. He is smiling at me. As if he has won. He has not. He doesn't know me. He doesn't know anything.

"You followed us tonight, to the restaurant. You bribed the valet, switched my envelope for yours, that's why it took that punk valet so long to find my car," I say. I typically figure things out quickly. In this case not quickly enough. They have the evidence, the arsenic. "Well, you'll have trouble making any of this nonsense stick."

"You're denying it, Paul? We have proof. You were trying to kill me." Clearly, Mia is agitated again. She's shaking and mucus is running out of her nose.

"Mia, it's okay, calm down," Buck says. He doesn't make a move to comfort her. He knows better. Knows not to turn his back to me right now. He should also know I'll be back for him later. I will be.

"Sign this. And get out of here." Buck jabs the pen into my thigh. I take it from him. I imagine stabbing him in the neck. I could do it, too.

So, if I sign this, I realize, I'm agreeing to give up custody of my children. What they don't realize is I will tell the court I was threatened, forced to sign this agreement against my will. I will not go quietly into the night, not at all.

I pull the cap off the pen. It is a very nice pen, heavy in my hand. I reach for the papers.

"You can read the documents if you'd like, but we've explained the contents. This will be a separation, followed by a complete dissolution of your marriage. Like it never even happened. Papers will be filed on your behalf. Sign the agreement where marked," Buck says. "Here. And here."

He's so helpful, good old Buck. But still, I smile and do as I'm told. I scan the words—sole custody, property, rights, dissolution. As I expected, she keeps everything except our home in Columbus. But that's fine. There is plenty left to liquidate, even with the second mortgage. There is a treasure trove of expensive furniture, antiques and art from her parents. I'll be fine starting over. And I'm good at this, beginning anew and being patient about revenge. I know there is always more than one way to skin a cat. Now probably is not the time to tell you about my own pet's premature demise. Tommy was heartbroken. We'll save that for another time.

I finish with the papers and pen and Buck collects them from the table. I sit back in my chair and watch the show. Without breaking eye contact with me Buck holds the papers in the air in my wife's direction. He says, "Mia, take a look. Be sure we didn't miss a signature line."

I watch Mia reach for the papers. With steady hands she slowly turns each page. She places the document on her thighs. "All signed." I watch as she swallows. She looks relieved. She's no longer crying. She looks at me unblinking, unafraid. She places the pen on the coffee table.

For now, she has won and she knows it.

"Time to go, sport. You will check in and stay the night at the inn. Understood?" Buck says. He stands and stares down at me.

"Fine. I'm happy to get out of here. Where did you say you took my stolen belongings?" I ask. I grab the pen and stand. I am eye to eye with Buck, nose to nose.

"The Lakeside Inn. The nice one on the lake. Talk to Scott. He is holding your things behind the front desk for you until you check in," Buck says.

I take a step back and then turn and walk toward the kitchen. Foolishly, my wife has left the unconsumed snifter of brandy and sugar on the kitchen counter. I start to reach for it as a firm hand yanks my shoulder backward, holding me in place.

"Don't even think about it. You know as well as I do that even though we allowed you to lace her drink with sugar, it's still evidence." Keeping his hand on my shoulder, Buck forces me to the back door, opens it and almost pushes me outside. He tosses my car keys onto the driveway. Rude. These are things I will not forget. Ever. I hear him slam the back door shut behind me and turn the lock in the knob. Like that type of lock could stop anyone from coming inside. He's dreaming. I roll the heavy pen in my pocket.

I'm tired of both him and my wife. Good riddance. I stand in front of the closed garage door. Surely he will know, if he has been doing good spy work, that I cannot enter my garage through the broken side door, that I must enter by pushing the button inside the kitchen.

Ah yes, he's watching. I hear the garage door moan, and start to open. I stand with my back to the house, waiting for my chance to escape. Still, as I climb into my car and back out, I see Buck watching me through the kitchen window. I wonder if he'll sleep there, at my cottage, with my wife, tonight.

I wonder how confident Buck will feel about closing his eyes, now and forever.

1:00 A.M.

28

I drive, too quickly, down our street, checking my rear-view mirror to see if I've been followed.

I'm almost certain Buck will remain with Mia, comforting the poor woman. She is a mess, that's for sure. Good riddance. I turn my blinker on to take a left at the corner, pausing for a moment to stare into the Boones' now dark cottage. I guess the party is over for tonight. I wonder if Greg lost at euchre again. If I had more time, I would go inside and have a little talk, or something, with Greg and Doris. Perhaps demonstrate to them the trouble you can get into when you're a gossipy nosy neighbor. Unfortunately, they will need to learn their lesson when we're all back in Columbus.

I take a left onto Second Street and drive to the old stately inn. We stayed here once with the kids, before we were owners. It's a passable place to stay for some people, once you get past the musty smell. I will not be a guest. I just need to collect my things. I park in a spot out front labeled "check-in only" and turn off the car. As I step outside, I look around, checking my surroundings. The lake is behind me, just beyond the expanse of green lawn that belongs to the inn. A large stone fountain gurgles water, making an oddly eerie sound in the otherwise silent night. Across the street is the beginning of the park, and farther down, I see the outline of the boathouse and the dock. It is very dark, very still out here.

There is no one else around; I'm certain I haven't been followed as I make my way up the steps and into the lobby. Directly across from me behind a large wooden desk with a sign that says Reception, a bored teenage boy, cheeks covered with acne and sallow-looking, stifles a yawn and says, "Hello. Are you checking in?"

His lack of tension makes me realize I've been holding my shoulders tight and I smile and relax a bit. "Hello, son. Some friends of mine kindly dropped off my suitcase and belongings here, but I'm afraid I can't spend the night," I say. I am using my best and friendliest face, my most polite words. I am imitating the waiter from tonight. I am overly kind.

"Oh, I'm sorry. Okay, then, do you want your stuff?" the boy asks. He is wearing a name tag that says "Scott." The name tag is gold and shiny. The word is printed in black.

"Please, yes, Scott," I say. I'm friendly. Just a patient, weary traveler who needs his shit now, Scott.

"Your name? And I need to see some identification, too," Scott says.

I wonder how many people drive up to a hotel at 1:00 a.m. and try to retrieve a stranger's things. In Lakeside? I suspect the risk is low, but Scott is only doing his job. I tamp down my brewing impatience and slide my driver's license over to him.

"Be right back," he says, barely glancing at the license. I

collect it and slip it back into my wallet. I realize I have not a dime to tip this kid, nor do I have a working credit card for gas. This is not the best scenario as I must hurry back to Columbus. I look around for a camera, but of course I don't see any. Lakeside Inn is a trusting, folksy place devoid of crime and suspicion, apparently. Slowly I walk around the counter, and see what must be the cash drawer, slightly ajar, just in front of where Scott had been sitting.

I reach over, open the drawer, and extract all of the twenty dollar bills and the one fifty dollar bill in there, shoving them into my front pocket. I push the drawer closed and return to my original place in front of the reception desk, making sure my face is still kind, and friendly.

Only once I'm safely back in position on the customer's side of the desk do I realize I should have stolen his tip. Oh, well. Poor kid will just have to survive on my smile.

"Here we are, Mr. Strom," Scott says, appearing through the same door he'd disappeared through a moment before, now rolling out a luggage cart containing my suitcase and briefcase. "This is your stuff, right?"

"It is. Thank you, son," I say as he pushes the cart around to my side of the desk. I grab my suitcase, yank up the handle, slide my briefcase on top and, nodding to the helpful boy, roll quickly to the door.

"Sir, are you sure you won't be checking in? There's still a room reserved for you." Scott calls to me as I am almost through the door.

"No, son, change of plans. But thank you. Have a good night," I say, with another big smile for the lad. I feel a little terrible he will be accused of stealing the money in his drawer, and no doubt be fired. But it's a good life lesson. He should have been more careful, should have locked that cash drawer before he left his post. You just never know who you're dealing with, despite appearances.

As I roll my bags to my car I realize I should check and make sure Mia put everything back in my suitcase, but I'll have to do that once I arrive back home. I pop the trunk, shove the briefcase and suitcase inside, fight the urge to look around again, and quickly climb into the car. I lock the doors, turn the key in the ignition. Before pulling away from the curb, I consider my options. What I know I should do, what I want to do, is start driving, head for Port Clinton, and then the highway to take me back home. But another part of me wants to circle back to my cottage, have what you might call the final word with Buck and my wife. That is what Buck will expect, I'm sure, especially if Scott tips him off that I'm not checking in.

Maybe I'll just drive by the cottage one last time, you know, on my way out of the gates. It will give me time to think things over, although glancing at my gas gauge, I know I don't have much time to think without filling up. As I drive down Second Street heading toward my cottage, I smile remembering my petty theft. If I'm lucky, Scott won't check the cash drawer for the rest of the evening and whoever replaces him on the morning shift will assume Scott took the cash. He is an untrustworthy teenager, after all.

If I'm unlucky and Scott notices the missing twenties, surely he won't think of the kind stranger, dressed nicely, obviously successful and from the city. No, it would have had to be someone else, earlier in the night. I was nice to him, although I didn't tip him. If I had taken the cash, surely I would have tipped him, he'd reason.

Unless Buck has told him things about me, spreading more rumors darkening my name. I will need to get in front of

Buck and his lies. I drive slowly around the corner at the Boones' cottage. It's dark and unmoving, as it should be at this time of night. In contrast, across the street, my cottage is awash in light. There are two squad cars parked in my driveway and through the brightly lit windows I see too many people walking around inside my family room. I spot Mia through the window, sitting on the couch, my couch, drinking a cup of tea, feeling all smug and secure. She's surrounded by cops, telling the little sob story of her unhappy life. Poor little crumpled, gray Mia. Her husband was such a bad man. He gave her a big house, two healthy boys, a life of leisure beyond most people's wildest dreams.

I touch the shiny pen I placed on the passenger seat. It's cool, like my wife.

Unlike me, Mia is a spoiled brat who got everything she wanted, everything she deserved. I put the pen in my pocket, turn off the headlights and park one house down from ours on the same side of the street. There aren't many streetlights in Lakeside, none near our cottage. The stars are obscured by clouds. It's dark, very dark on our street. Mia complains about that, but I am a creature of the shadows. I'm comfortable here, as you know.

I spot my target near his precious strawberry garden, the very thing that caused all of this. Buck has let his guard down because the cops, country guys who should be home banging their wives or swilling moonshine, are protecting her. One of the officers even sports a soul patch on his chin, so three years ago. I turn my attention back to Buck. Buck's retreated to the garden, my garden, letting the authorities comfort my gray blob of a wife. He's such a loser. It's so easy.

I creep into my yard undetected. He doesn't even know what's hit him from behind, until I do, my rage overpowering his supposed training. I have him in a choke hold. Buck fights like the tough guy I know he is, but I'm stronger. He skids the heel of his shoe down my shin, but he's wearing tennis shoes, lame. I squeeze his neck tighter, hear him gasping for breath. I pull him to the ground behind the strawberries and straddle his chest. I punch him in his pretty face, direct contact with that dimple, that perfect jaw. The sound is thick, satisfying.

My hand stings. I love it. It makes me feel alive. I kick him in the side, once. I hope to crack a rib. That should keep him from humping my wife for a while. I stand above him. He rolls to his side, tries to stand but I'm not letting that happen. My shoes are dress shoes, with a pointed toe. I aim at his temple, then his ribs, and I kick his throat. He moans and then is still. Take that, tough guy. I'm done here. I won't kill him. No, that would be too easy. I feel the heavy pen in my pocket, imagine it sticking out of his neck, piercing his artery. I like the image, but I want him alive. I will make him pay for what he's done to me, slowly, over time. But I assure you he will pay for ruining my life, for stealing my wife. When he least expects it, I'll get my revenge.

I hear voices and duck behind the strawberry bed. The cops are heading out, walking to their cars. The idiots are going to leave Mia alone, in our house. I cover my mouth with my hand; my white smile could give me away. I'm like a shark, lurking in the depths, waiting to strike.

The two police cruisers flip on their headlights and pull away.

I turn toward the cottage. Mia stands in the window, staring into the backyard. It's almost as if she knows I'm here. I begin to wave. She's not looking for me, though.

At my feet, Buck moans. So much for special ops guys. Ha.

I kick him in the ribs. "Shut up," I say. My voice is firm, commanding. I really don't have time for this garden gnome. I need to rescue my wife, from herself, from this story she's concocted in her mind. Poor woman.

"Hello, Mia," I whisper, looking toward the brilliantly lit cottage. "Don't worry. I'm home."

I take a step toward the house as a hand clamps on my ankle. Fucking Buck. What is his problem? This time, I yank my foot out of his grip and kick him in the head. There's a satisfactory thud, and blood flows out of his ear. It would be so easy to off him, I think, squeezing the pen in my pocket. But I need to get to Mia.

I run to the back door, kick it open. I told you the lock was ridiculous. That was easy, and I'm definitely not special ops.

Mia screams from the other room. She's going to be so happy to see me.

I hurry through the kitchen, to the family room. She's running to the front door. I grab her hair, stopping her dead in her tracks. She stumbles back, her hand grabs mine and she spins around, a puppet in my hands. What now, little Mia?

It takes me a moment to see the knife. She slashes at me with the fury of a feral cat. She comes close to my hand and I release her hair.

Mia is shaking, the knife is barely capable of slicing an apple, but she points it at me, acting heroic. "Get out of here, Paul. I've pushed the panic button. Help is on the way. And Buck is just outside."

"Buck is a little busy with the strawberries right now, poor guy." I smile as Mia's eyes get larger.

"What have you done to him?" she hisses.

"Nothing he didn't deserve. But let's talk about us, shall we?" I smile. I say, "Panic button. Really? What panic button, honey? You really must be losing your mind. There is no panic button. That's for the movies. Besides, you couldn't have anything like that, not without me knowing about it. You have nothing without me. You are nothing without me." My hand is throbbing from punching Buck. I like that.

"Get out of here, Paul. I'm serious. You don't want to be caught breaking in here." Mia's little knife is wobbling again. It's cute.

"Mia, this is my cottage, our cottage. We own it so I couldn't possibly break in. I think you've forgotten how many good memories we've made here, even in one short year. Remember the champagne toast on our new screened porch when we first bought this place, and how happy we were?" I'm smiling, Mia is not.

"And all the while you were poisoning me," she says, shaking her head.

"Oh, honey, don't be silly," I say. I haven't been poisoning her the entire time, silly woman. "Come here. Let me give you a hug. You seem so distraught. You're lost without me." I take a step toward my wife and she backs into the corner by the front door, slashing the air between us with her little cheese knife. Perhaps I'll teach her a little lesson.

It's at that moment, as we're studying each other, contemplating our next moves, that I hear sirens. The sound is faint but growing louder. Definitely coming toward us.

Mia must hear her rescuers in the distance and finally manages a smile, possibly the most genuine smile of the day. It's the half-moon kind of smile, like the one she gave me this morning, like she gave me when we first dated, a smile of love. But then her face falls, as if that smile is not for me, not anymore. "Wrong, Paul. I am much more than you. And

I'm so much better off without you." Her ridiculous paring knife is clutched in her hand pointed at me. It would be so easy to grab it, turn the blade toward her, plunge it into her traitorous chest.

The sirens are closing in. She does have a fucking panic button. Now I must decide. Finish what I started with the poison, or get out before the Keystone Cops arrive, grab my kids and start over. Because clearly, she hasn't thought of everything. Our kids, our precious boys, are at home asleep. Blissfully unaware of all of this strife, like little lambs just waiting for their shepherd to save them.

Red and blue flashes are lighting up the street. I've got to get out of here.

"This isn't over, Mia, but for now, good night, honey. Sleep tight. We'll see each other again soon. Perhaps when you least expect it," I say before turning and running out the back door, through the yard to my car. The cops drive past me as I sit low in my front seat, flying into our driveway at speeds that could only be considered excessive. You'd think there was an actual crime taking place inside. Instead they'll find a crazy woman huddled by the front door with a tiny knife, and eventually, a former special ops guy knocked out by his precious strawberry plants. Losers. Both of them.

My poor little wife. She thinks she is so clever. Outsmart Paul Strom? Never.

I push the gas and drive by quickly. Decision made. I find myself constantly checking my mirrors, rearview and side, until I escape through the Lakeside gate.

I know I'm driving too fast, even if all of the cops from this entire little township are busy at my cottage for now, and I pull my foot back from the gas pedal. I need to conserve fuel until I make it to a bigger town where there will be an open gas station. It would not be prudent to run out of gas somewhere in the middle of these dark country roads tonight. I have too much more to take care of for that.

1:45 A.M.

29

I haven't noticed another car on the road with me for miles, and believe me, I've been looking. At night, if you are aware, you can spot a tail. It's easy when you have to keep your lights on to see. And out here in the country, you need your headlights. If Buck or his people were following me, they aren't anymore. I tighten my grip on the steering wheel, remembering how Buck's people followed me around Grandville, spied on my life. How could I have missed them?

The gas station is a still life. Pumps ablaze in too-bright fluorescent light, but everything is eerily motionless except for a large moth diving in and out of the scene. I roll to a stop and climb out of the Flex. It's interesting to me how much my palms are sweating, although I hadn't registered in my mind anything like fear. My body feels tense, on edge. I remind myself to breathe as I look around. I'm the only one here, except the person working in the station.

As I walk toward the silhouette of a man sitting behind the counter, I smile and notice the camera. That's fine, too. We are all being videotaped all the time now. If anyone cares to retrieve that tape it will simply prove that I decided to drive home instead of spending the night in the musty inn. No crime there.

The gas station door is locked. I shake the handle as the employee, a burly man whose other job could be biker, leans forward and presses a button.

"Need gas?" the voice booms through a speaker.

No, I just wanted to stop by and say hi, my busy mind thinks. I wonder why I don't just move to another country. People here are such simpletons. His brother is probably one of the cops assigned to protect Mia. Equally effective. So stupid, all of them.

"Yes. Pump 1. Forty dollars," I say. I've located the after-hours pay drawer. I pull out my wallet as he slides the drawer open. I place two crisp twenty-dollar bills in the drawer and he closes the hatch.

I wonder if he feels safe, locked inside a fully lit glass building. He shouldn't.

"Pump 1 is on," he says. His voice is impatient, as if he has better things to do than supply gas to late-night drivers. But that is his only function. I shrug him off. I'm the one in a hurry, I remind my tense body.

Turning my back to the thug, I return to my car and begin pumping gas. I'm now standing in a pool of light, exposed to anyone who drives by on the country road. But who would be looking for me now? Buck and Mia have handled everything, they think. Meanwhile, Buck is watering the backyard with blood and Mia is cowering with a knife. The authorities either know I've left Lakeside, or they think I've checked into the inn. Or, they think I'm lurking somewhere in the darkness, ready to strike again. No matter what, they are wrong. All of that extra police security is totally unnecessary. I'm here, pumping gas at a desolate country gas station. I'm a tired man just hoping to make it home to his boys soon. Sunrise isn't until about 6:45 a.m. I have plenty of time.

My boys. The joys of my life. Mikey and Sam will be so happy to see me. I might even sneak into their bedrooms, give them each a fatherly hug. They loved having me take them to school this morning, begged me to take them to the lake, too. Their disappointed little faces haunt me a bit right now. I'll make it up to them. Maybe a trip to Disneyland? Gretchen would like that, too. Maybe I'll bundle them up and put them in the car and take them to her apartment tonight. It would be such an adventure, way better than Lakeside. We could get on the road before sunrise. I smile at the thought. The four of us, Gretchen, the boys and I, headed to the happiest place on earth. The boys would be thrilled.

The pump stops. I pull out the nozzle, screw the gas cap on and hurry into the car. As I pull out of the bright white light of the gas station and back onto the country road, I wonder if it's too late to call Gretchen. She has called me four times since I left on my trip with Mia. That's not like her. For my part, I've been declining her calls. She knows better than to leave me a voice mail. It's against our rules.

As I pull onto the interstate, I feel a flood of relief wash over me. I've escaped the country bumpkins. No one has followed me. I sigh, relaxing. I know it's late, but I call Gretchen. The phone rings loudly over my car's Bluetooth system. One ring, two rings.

"Paul?" Gretchen says. She sounds sleepy. I wish I were in bed next to her.

"Hi, my love," I say. It's important to have different terms of endearment, I've learned. Mia is *honey*. Gretchen is *my love*. Caroline, well, she is now the bitch. Before, she was *babe*. Lois was *sweetie*, until she wasn't. Buck talked to Lois, my busy mind recalls. I need to deal with Buck. I should have killed him in the backyard of my cottage earlier. Soon I'll finish him off. He thinks he's so cool, so tough. He's not. Did you notice how fast I took him down? He dropped like a rock. All talk, no substance.

"Why didn't you take any of my calls today?" Gretchen asks.

"You know why, love. I had to be with Mia," I say. "But I've got some good news. I've left her. Everything you've dreamed of for the two of us can come true now."

"Paul, some man came to see me early this morning. He said his name was Buck. Said it was urgent that we talk. So I let him in," she says. Her voice is sounding awake now. Urgent. I should have taken her calls. "He wanted to talk about you. He... Paul, he said such ugly things. And he had photos of a woman's face all beaten up. Said you did it."

Fine. The bastard tried to convince her I'm evil. I will convince her otherwise.

"Oh, love, I'm so sorry. Buck is crazy. The guy is totally jealous of me. He's our neighbor up at the lake, and he is not right in the head. It seems he's developed a fixation with me. He actually wants to ruin my life with lies and innuendos. Please don't think twice about it. You know I would never hurt a woman. No one loves women more than I do. No one loves you better, right?" I say. My hands grip the steering wheel once more. I want to turn around, drive back to the lake and kill Buck, even though I'm not that kind of guy. It takes everything inside of me to keep heading home to my boys and Gretchen. "This is just some cruel game Buck is playing. He's twisted. You don't actually believe him, do you, love?"

"I don't want to, Paul," she says. Now her voice is shaky. I imagine her sitting in bed, knees pulled up under chin. She's naked. Maybe I'll drive there first, pick her up and bring her to my house. "I just don't know what to believe."

What I cannot believe is how Buck and Mia have messed with my life. They will not get away with this. As much as I want to go comfort Gretchen, and I may still, I realize the true power play is back at home, asleep in their beds waiting for their beloved dad to come home.

"I know you're frightened, my love," I say in a soothing voice while checking my rearview mirror. I pass a semitruck, but no one else is on the road. No one is following me, I'm certain. "It was reprehensible of Buck to involve you in his ridiculous vendetta. He's a sick man, he needs help. How about this, love? I'll bring over breakfast in the morning, we'll talk all of this through. You've been dreaming about going to the beach together and now we can. Sound good?"

"I need to think," she says quietly. "I need some space. I'll call you in a few days. Don't call me, Paul. Okay?" She is crying. I hear a big sob as she hangs up on me.

My mistress just hung up on me. How is this happening? Somehow, in the space of one day, my wife leaves me for another man and my mistress tells me not to call her. This is all Buck's fault. I should have shoved the pen in his neck or stomped on his trachea in the garden. I want to scream or throw something at someone but I'm driving and that would be ridiculous. I need to calm down and focus. I'm sweating and I crank up the air-conditioning. I tip my neck from side to side until it cracks satisfyingly. I am still in charge of the situation, or I will be as soon as I am home with the boys. Maybe we'll leave for Disneyland tomorrow? If Gretchen changes her mind, she can join us.

I forgot to tell her about Disneyland, I realize. I push the button for Gretchen's number. Her contact information is disguised as a restaurant named Savory. Clever, I know. The Bluetooth kicks in and the phone rings. One. Two. Three. Four.

"This is Gretchen," her voice mail announces. "Leave a message."

I cannot believe she is ignoring me, ignoring my call. How dare she. This is not acceptable. Rage overtakes me as I hurl my phone at the passenger window and hear the thud as it falls into the crevice between the door and the seat. The only sound in the car now is my ragged breath. I squeeze the steering wheel as my jaw clenches and I stomp on the gas pedal. I'll listen to my playlist. I push the button and my favorite song, Bobby Darin's rendition of "Mack the Knife," blasts through my sound system as I sing along.

I glance in the rearview mirror and see the flashing lights of a police car. I am out of control. I will make a mistake. My heart is thudding as I slow down to sixty-five miles per hour. This is not the time to be pulled over. The lights are behind me now, and I can hear the sirens. The cop car speeds past me. It's a sign. My shoulders relax, I loosen my hold on the steering wheel, and I turn up my song. Smooth jazz: calm and structured and in control. Just like me.

2:45 A.M.

30

The bright lights of downtown Columbus are a welcome beacon in my agitated state. I am making great time; there are hardly any other cars on the road, just long-haul truckers and me. I check my watch obsessively. I am anxious to get home but I realize I may have a couple of other things to attend to before I am reunited with my boys. I mean, they're asleep, so they're happy, but I am not. There are still at least three hours of darkness left tonight, giving me enough time to tie up some loose ends.

Ironically, the freeway exit I take isn't just the way home; it's the exit for my office, too. It was convenient, driving from my stately suburban home to my gleaming office building in under ten minutes. The two worlds, home and work, close in proximity but so very different. The office building is a square of glass and steel, situated on a hill with direct views of the downtown skyline. It was a convenient location and the partners were hailed for building here when they did. It made sense, of course; a quick turn onto the freeway got you downtown or to the airport in minutes, while a few minutes in the opposite direction led to home. Very convenient if you forgot something or wanted to check to be sure your wife really was taking a nap with the kids. For the record, she always was doing exactly what she told me, my sweet Mia. After a few years, I didn't even need to check in on her so often. Funny, how one becomes complacent, accepting things at face value. When did she stop asking if I'd be home for lunch? Possibly work got in the way, or perhaps it was Caroline's fault.

Caroline is no Mia.

Mia never lied to me. Well, not until now. Caroline did from the very moment I met her. She flirted right back. She felt the heat between us in that elevator, and she knew what we could be together. I wanted to be what she needed. We had that potential. But all along, she had Chadwick.

Chadwick. What kind of name is that? I guess it's better than Paul, as far as Caroline's concerned.

And here we are, my old stomping grounds. I park in one of the two Thompson Payne partner-only spots—pompous jerks—and scan the rest of the lot. Empty. I reach across to the passenger seat floor to retrieve my phone, relieved the screen didn't break when I threw it across the car. I need to make sure to keep myself under control. This is a time for calculation and calm. The fire can come out later.

Of course, I know there are security cameras trained on this parking lot, on the building entrances. But the partners are both pompous and cheap. I also know they reset every morning at 6:00 a.m., recording over the past evening's tapes if the alarm wasn't triggered.

It won't be. I slip my key into the door and, as predicted, it opens. Yes, Rebecca made me hand over my key. Yes, I'm savvy enough to have made a duplicate years ago. I hurry to the security code keypad, type in the same four numbers the company has used since it was founded—a combination of Thompson and Payne's birth dates—and the beeping stops as the little button turns green. I'm a go. I knew they wouldn't change the code, or rekey the whole building. I was a token fire, a take-one-for-the-team-because-we-take-sexual-harassment-seriously dismissal. I'm not a threat, not really. I'm just a sad footnote in the otherwise spotless equality history of the firm. Right.

It's nice to be back home, I realize, stepping inside the stainless steel elevator, pushing the button for the top floor. My floor. Also on this floor: the partners, HR and, yes, precious Caroline. I hurry down the luxuriously carpeted hallway, past the numerous framed awards lining the walls, many of them for campaigns I worked on, campaigns I created. I stop for a moment and stare at my office, now filled with someone else's possessions. I know Rick Jacobs got the promotion, took my job. He was the only guy who wrote to me after I left, the only one who said he missed me. I move on.

Rebecca's office door is locked. Of course. She is the only person in this entire company who would actually lock her door. But that's fine, because my position came with many privileges, not the least of which was a master key. Her door swings open and I recoil from the smell of manure. Good God, who allows this woman to create a jungle in her office? It is against common courtesy, I mean, the poor folks on either side of her. What is she subjecting them to with all of this pesticide use, this damp musty air caused by her incessant watering? I'm probably saving someone's life, I realize, as I yank the first plant out of its pot, tossing it on her desk.

She considers these plants to be her kids. I'd heard that somewhere, not long after our first meeting. She's worse than Mia with her strawberry daughters, a sick woman.

I quickly eliminate all of her children, making a leafy green pile of debris on her white office chair, her desk. I squish a particularly large, mushy green plant into her area rug—from her trip to India, I hear—the stain adding a touch of forest green to the otherwise tan and brown carpet. I'm an artist.

Finished gardening, I pull on the file drawer, and it's locked. This I don't have a key for, this is not part of the master plan. Rebecca is such a mistrustful, nasty woman. I don't need her files anyway.

I'm out in the hall and inside Caroline's office. The small space smells like cinnamon and jasmine, the scent of the candle she always had lit on her desk, and I take a moment to breathe her in. I sit down in her chair and close my eyes, resting both hands on her desk, feeling her energy. Such a missed opportunity, such a stupid girl. We could have been so great together.

I open my eyes and stare at the framed photo next to the candle. It's Caroline with her arms wrapped around the waist of a jock. He's blond, at least six-four and an idiot, I can tell. He's wearing his football jersey from their college team. *College sweethearts, how lovely.* But she told me she was single, didn't she? Yes, I'm sure she did. And when I was still here, there was no Chad on her desk. That I would have noticed, of course. I am the first one to respect a boyfriend/girlfriend relationship. So here we are, Chad, Caroline and me. What could I possibly gift to the happy couple that they don't already have? A potted plant perhaps? Well, unfortunately, we're fresh out of those at Thompson Payne. I do need to leave her with something, some way for her to know I was here, and that she picked the wrong guy.

I grab the frame and pop the photo out. On the back, in Caroline's writing: "C&C forever." I fight the urge to rip up the ridiculous photo but instead I pull out my new pen, scribble out the C&C nonsense and replace it with P&C forever, adding a little heart. I smile as I place the photo back in its frame and position it perfectly next to the candle.

All she had to do was tell me she had a boyfriend, the slut.

I swivel around to her computer and it is on. I click on a file on her desktop, CC, and voilà, it's all Chad and Caroline all the time: hundreds of photos of the happy couple. I open her email and search my name. At least fifty emails load. I scan through them. Some are account-related, to me or from me. Some are not. I refine the search to Paul and Chad.

"There's a guy here, older, named Paul. He scares me. He's always watching me, pretending to bump into me. Creepy." Caroline typed this to Chad. I scare her? I wanted to make love to her. Bitch.

I exit out of her email and open her web browser. She must be lonely without Chad. He lives in Virginia, and although they've discussed marriage, he wants to finish law school before he proposes. How sweet. This should keep her busy in the meantime. I watch as my chosen site loads, and as I keep clicking, like a nasty virus porn explodes across her screen.

And I open more sites, and the debauchery keeps loading. I don't know how much her computer can take but I'll keep giving it to her until she can't handle any more. I smile as I hear the computer running hard. I want to be sure she shares her secret sex perversion with everyone. I create an email, you know, between her and Chad. I attach some of the most interesting photos to her love note. And then for fun, I blind copy everyone in the office. Oops, Caroline.

I schedule the message to send Monday, early afternoon.

HR has a strict no-porn rule. Everyone might understand, I suppose, that poor Caroline was alone, her boyfriend two states away. What was a girl to do? But still, a rule is a rule, even for perfect Caroline. Rebecca, still grieving the loss of her plant babies, will be forced to fire her. I can almost imagine the scene, the rent-a-cop's arm on Caroline's shoulder, ushering her out the door as her tears fall on the dark green stain on Rebecca's rug.

I check my watch. It's time to go. I step into the elevator one last time and ride to the first floor. I am at peace with this place now. Perhaps I'll even send a postcard to the team once I'm settled in Florida, or maybe not. I reset the alarm and stroll out into the still-black night. It's truly amazing how much one can accomplish in a day when one is committed to tying up loose ends, when one has a plan.

Gretchen will be happy to see me. Sure, she's confused— thanks to fucking Buck—but once she sees me, she'll realize who she can trust, who she can believe in. Fortunately, her apartment is a block from my office, and I am in front of her building in less than two minutes. I hop out of my car and hurry up the familiar walkway. Gretchen's building is one of a series of old brick brownstones, charming and decaying at the same time. Gretchen has planted pink geraniums in the window box next to her front door. Her next-door neighbor, an elderly woman I've said hello to a couple of times, has chosen to plant red ones. The look is homey, very Americana.

I wish Gretchen had given me a key. She keeps forgetting to ask her landlord, she says. She also says she'll remember when I remember to divorce my wife. Cute, huh? A little bit of a power play going on with her, I realize, and feel my fists clench. I take a deep breath, calming myself. I need to hurry.

I knock softly on the thick front door, imagining Gretchen sleeping in a soft silk nightie. I don't want to frighten her, but I need her to wake up already. I resist the urge to bang my fist on the door, deciding to go around back. I walk between the carports, my feet crunching on the gravel driveway. Her window is sheltered by a large pine tree that she likes for privacy, but it scratches my face as I push my way inside its branches. She doesn't even have a curtain on her window, relying on the pine tree to shield her from prying eyes. I need to tell her that isn't safe; I mean, all it takes is breaking a few branches off and you have a clear view.

I tap on her window a couple of times, harder with each tap, and watch as she stirs. She sits up in bed, looking toward the window but not seeing me. I knock again. *I'm here, my love.* She turns on her bedside table lamp, her eyes squinting in the bright light. She's disoriented, poor thing. She picks up her phone, perhaps checking the time. It is late, or early, depending on your perspective, almost four thirty in the morning. I myself have been fighting waves of exhaustion whenever my adrenaline rush fades.

I knock again, three times, and then wave a hand so she'll know it is me, a friend, a lover, not a Peeping Tom or some other creep. She stands up, her short nightie revealing her gorgeous legs. Gretchen has her phone gripped in both hands in front of her. Too late I realize she may be dialing 9-1-1.

"Gretchen, it's me, love. It's okay, no need to call the police," I yell through the glass. Fortunately it's the old leaded glass, beautiful but thin. No storm windows, of course, since her landlord is cheap.

She leans forward and then takes a step toward the window, trying to see me in the dark, phone still positioned defensively.

"Paul? What are you doing here?"

"Hey, yes, it's me," I say, relief flooding over me. "I came to whisk you away to the happiest place in the world, my love." Even to me that sounded a bit corny, but women love this sort of thing.

"I asked you to leave me alone, to let me think." Gretchen steps back. "You need to go now, Paul."

Buck has done this. He has poisoned everyone with lies. I may need to make a stop in Nashville, just to say hello to Lois, make sure she isn't going to do anything crazy. But first, I need to get Gretchen back on team Paul.

"My love, listen, let me in. Let's talk. I'll help you pack up. We'll have so much fun!" I put one hand on the window, enjoying its cool smooth texture. I want to touch Gretchen's cheek, feel her warm body beneath mine. I smile my winning smile, adding a wink.

She does not return my enthusiasm and takes another step back, toward her bedroom door. "I'm not going anywhere with you. If you don't leave now, I will call the police."

Lights suddenly flood the driveway and carport area, and I am illuminated as if it's daylight. Next door, the old lady's brownstone pulses with light as her back door opens.

"Who's out here? I'm gonna call the cops."

She's an idiot. If I were a bad guy I would jump her now that her door is open, bash her head in and take any money she might have around. But the old lady has balls. We are feet away from each other, but my pine tree is protecting me.

I look back through the window at Gretchen. She mouths two words: "Go away." Fine. I hear her, loud and clear.

The old bat closes her door and turns off the outdoor floodlights, and once again I'm shrouded in darkness. I'm fine. I don't need Gretchen. She's not even rich. No, it's best to start over, just the boys and me: the three musketeers against the world. Fuck you, Gretchen, my love. I flip her the bird but I don't think she saw me, retreating as she did into her living room.

I cut through the yard on my way to my car, and for good measure, for fun, I pop my head into her living room window.

"Boo," I say, with a wave goodbye.

The look on her face is priceless, and I laugh all the way to the car.

Women are so predictable, so easily manipulated. I'm glad we didn't have any girls. Boys are transparent, easy to read, easy to raise. They'll have so much fun in Florida, or Nashville, wherever we end up.

I pull away from Gretchen's apartment thinking fondly of all the great sex I had there, enjoying the little zip of desire that courses through me as I make my way onto the familiar street that leads to home. Norah Jones sings "Come Away with Me" as I cruise down Lane Avenue. The street takes me on a straight path through my beautiful suburb, a place filled with high-end shopping, cozy restaurants, country clubs, lucky children and spoiled housewives. My boys will carry memories of this place forever. Come away with me in the night, boys. We'll build our new home in the sunshine.

That's the only negative thing I can tell you about Grandville—I mean, it is never sunny. From October to the end of April, it's perpetual gray. And then, when the sun does start to shine, it's great for a couple weeks until it turns to unbearable heat and humidity. We'll be better off someplace else. Anyplace would be better than here.

The light is green and I turn onto my street. I haven't seen another car since I left the office and I still don't. It's just the Ford Flex and me, cruising my neighborhood, heading for home. I only have one more little detour to make.

I pull over to the curb, and turn off my headlights. The Boones' Grandville home isn't as special as their cottage. Like you, I've checked the value of all of my neighbor's homes on-line and I know ours is one of the top two. The Boones', on the other hand, is in the middle of the pack. In fact, if you'd never visited their lake house, you would think they were barely hanging on.

Maybe they are. It seems Greg made a bad business invest-ment, and he's overleveraged. One little thing could push them over the edge, especially since they cut their homeowner's in-surance to a minimum. I don't know that for a fact, it's just what I hear, since we share the same insurance agent. I was only asking for myself, of course, since I'm in a bit of a pinch and wanted to save somewhere. My agent, Bob, took me to lunch, but advised against cutting coverage as much as my neighbor.

"What do you mean?" I asked, sipping my too-hot diner coffee—Bob's a big spender—scalding my tongue in that an-noying manner that makes you unable to taste food for the rest of the day. Thanks, Bob.

Bob leaned forward in the booth, conspiratorially. One good buddy to another and said, "Your neighbors, the Boones, well, confidentially, he cut his insurance to barely anything. I mean, he's totally exposed. I wouldn't recommend that." Well, thank you, Bob. Great guy. Bob was such a helpful font of information. "Don't say anything, please."

I smiled, happy to have this newfound knowledge, my taste buds a small price to pay. "Oh, of course not. Not a word. What policy would you recommend, if I were to cut back? I know, not what the idiot Greg Boone picked."

We laughed and then Bob droned on about his recommendations, of course, but all I could think of was how exposed Doris and Greg were.

"You've convinced me," I said once Bob finally stopped talking. Our eggs had arrived, signaling the end of his diatribe. I couldn't taste anything of the meal, but it was very satisfying. You know I don't believe in gossip, but sometimes it comes in very handy.

Like now. The Boones' home is lifeless, all of the family members nestled in their grand cottage at the lake. Unfortunately for them and lucky for me, the nearest streetlight is a house away, across the street, so their home is masked in darkness. I'm familiar enough with their home to maneuver in the shadows, of course.

Like most of us in the neighborhood, the Boones had a cord or two of wood delivered in September, preparing for the winter ahead. And, like most of us, the Boones hadn't burned through all of the logs yet. I reach the side of their yard, and the neatly stacked pile that's shaped, ironically, perfectly for a fire, tucked up against the house, kept dry by the overhang of the roof. With the warm, dry May we've been experiencing, it wouldn't take much kindling for this to combust. I need a slow burn, though. I don't want to draw attention to this little flame until it has made its way into the walls of their home, fingers of fire pulsing along the electrical wiring, shooting up the walls.

I glance up and notice the back door, with its intricate stained-glass window pane perfectly positioned for a break-in. This will be easier. I pull off my shirt and wrap my hand. I punch through the window, reach down for the doorknob and welcome myself into their kitchen. Greg is too cheap for security monitoring, another cut he shouldn't have made, and he'll be sorry. I find the designer knife set displayed on the counter in a wooden block and grab the large serrated knife. I pull out the stove, find the hose connecting the appliance to the gas line and easily cut through it, smiling when the familiar mercaptan chemical scent begins to fill the room. It doesn't take me long to find a candle. I light it with my Frank's grocery matches, bringing back such good memories of my time there waiting in line with the little people and the man with the yellow hands. I swallow and look around.

The candle looks lovely here, burning bright on the honed black granite island. I take a moment to appreciate the kid art tacked to the refrigerator door. A small handprint dipped in paint pushed onto construction paper to make the shape of a tulip. Precious. The little Boones are quite the artists, but not as good as my boys. I look around once more, appreciate the flickering candle and the strong smell coming from behind the Viking stove: only four burners compared to our six-top. But still, a nice brand. Kudos, Greg.

My work here is done.

Time to go home.

4:45 A.M.

31

I'm just half a block away and I still haven't been able to figure out how to let Claudia know I'll be coming in the door. No doubt she has set the alarm and I don't want it going off and waking the entire neighborhood at almost five in the morning. There is about a minute before the thing blares, but that means I need to hope she hasn't dead-bolted the back door, or the door to the garage.

There really isn't a choice, though. I need to see my boys, get my boys. Take my boys. And no one is going to be able to stop me, that I can promise. Between the Boones' house and ours there are plenty of streetlights illuminating the street, something missing in Lakeside, so it seems lighter, happier here. I will appreciate this place more now, I vow to myself. At least enjoy it until I sell. Enjoy the final hour here until we leave. I check my watch. There isn't much time left before sunrise.

In the driveway I turn off the headlights. Again, I don't want to scare Claudia by shining my headlights into the guest bedroom. Who knows how a druggie would react to that? Our guest room is above the garage, around the corner from the boys' bedrooms. I decide against opening the garage door, as I know that sound will alert her. Instead, I will check the back door. She is lazy, Claudia. Perhaps she didn't lock it at all.

I put the car in Park and get out of the car. It's nice to be home. Slowly I walk to the back door. I take a moment to admire the green grass and the trimmed bushes, the tulips blooming in celebration of spring. I look to my right, at my parents' former home, dark and filled with sleeping strangers. Good old Buck didn't know that part of the story, I realize with a smile. He has underestimated me, as usual. He shouldn't.

The alarm isn't set. The light of the panel is green. This is brilliant news, even if it is news that would lead me to fire Claudia under normal circumstances. These aren't normal circumstances so I'm grateful for her lack of competency, the druggie. I push the key into the lock and hear it click; I twist the knob and walk into my home. I flip on the back hall light and I'm momentarily thrown off by the simple fact that the back hall table, an expensive antique that was a gift from Mia's parents, is gone. This is the spot where I place my keys every day after work. But it is not there. I am certain it was here this morning when we left.

This is odd. Why would Claudia move a table? I wonder. I walk slowly, quietly down the hall and arrive in the kitchen. Here, everything seems to be in order. I swallow a growing feeling of unrest, of concern. There is no mess here, no dishes. No signs of little kids. No blocks. No booster seat at the kitchen table.

Where is Sam's booster seat? I leave the kitchen and head for the stairs, taking them two at a time. I start to go to the master bedroom, but think twice and instead quicken my steps to Mikey's room. I quietly turn the handle of his closed bedroom door, and push it open gently.

The room is completely empty.

"What?" I say aloud before hurrying through the Jack-and-Jill bathroom connecting the boys' rooms. I throw open the door to Sam's room. It's empty. No furniture, no Sam.

Where are my boys?

"Claudia!" I yell, marching to the guest room. There's no one in the guest room, though. The door is open. The furnishings—furniture, lamps, paintings, even the small Picasso nude from Mia's parents that we hung in the room to impress guests, everything—are gone.

I stand there, in the empty guest room, in shock. For a moment. I rub my hand through my hair before pulling my phone out of my pocket. I dial Mia's number. My call rolls to voice mail.

"Mia, what have you done with my boys? Where is my furniture? My antiques? My artwork? Where is my Picasso? The Alice Schille beachscape on the wall, it's gone, too. I need an explanation. Call me immediately," I say. My voice is calm. I am in control. She will be as alarmed as I am. She will obey me.

I walk at last into the master bedroom. The bed is still there, as are the side tables. The walls are bare, gaping holes where art used to hang. The happy family portrait, the four of us posing in the gazebo at the lake, that was hanging just inside the door is missing, too. I touch the spot where it should be, where it always was. Who could have done such a thing? Violated our private spaces?

I storm into the walk-in closet. Only half of the room is full. All of Mia's things are gone. On the bathroom counter there is a red envelope with *Paul* written on it in Mia's writing. I grab it, feeling the thick texture. This is a love note, of course. And, perhaps, an explanation. Maybe we are moving somewhere together, and this is all a big surprise.

I tear open the envelope and pull out the letter.

Dear Paul,

By now I'm sure you're anxious to know what's going on. It's hard being one step behind, I know. Trust me. Because of you, I've learned. So welcome home, and welcome to your new reality.

The boys are safe, in hiding with my parents, and so am I. As you have been told, there must be no attempt to find me, or the children, and no action threatened or taken against anyone who helped me. All we want is to live in peace, away from you. This day, everything that was orchestrated, was the only way I could make sure of that.

Since you are reading this, you have already signed the agreement. I cannot be sure what else has happened. If you have hurt me, or Buck, my parents will press charges. They know what you are capable of doing. I've told them everything I know. And it is a lot. I'm not going to waste time here outlining everything we've discovered about you, your past and your present. You know who you are, what you've done. I can promise you one thing, though: your future will not include us.

Please know that the boys and I are out of your life forever.

Don't lie anymore, Paul. So many people are watching you now.

Mia

She has taken away my whole life. I grip the red envelope in my hand and begin to rip it to pieces, but instead I crumple it into a ball. Her letter of betrayal I will keep. It will remind me never to trust a woman, ever. I fold Mia's stupid note into a little square, shoving it into my pocket. I cannot believe she got the upper hand. I can't believe I allowed this to happen, allowed her to win. It was a foolish mistake, and it won't happen again.

Everything will be fine. I'm a survivor. I will simply pivot and start over. Nobody can keep Paul Strom down, not for long. Sure, she's taken my boys but I can make more. There are plenty of women who want what I have, who would like to be Mrs. Strom. Not Gretchen, she's poor, and certainly not good old porn-watching Caroline. Lois is married, and not rich. I believe I'll set out for greener pastures. I don't need Disneyland to find the happiest place on earth. No, I just need wealthy women, preferably young widows. Palm Beach, here I come.

I walk back into my closet and pack my favorite lightweight, warm weather suits and some bathing suits and shorts. I'm like the Phoenix, rising again. I change into a pink polo—perfect, right?—and some comfortable jeans and driving loafers. I'll look the part of a successful businessman on holiday. I'm just a lonely man trying to recover after losing his entire family—wife, two sons and the in-laws—in a terrible plane crash last month. Private jets, you just never know. And no, their bodies haven't been recovered yet. It's tragic.

I check my reflection in the full-length mirror, and glance at my watch. Sunrise is in fifteen minutes. I need to get going before daybreak, before all hell breaks loose on our street, too. I grab my designer suitcase and make my way down the hall.

There is someone standing at the top of the stairs. What the heck? I shove my hand in my pocket, satisfied the pen is there. But still I'm on edge. I don't have a long-range weapon. I rely on the power of surprise. And right now, there is no-where for me to hide.

"Hands up where I can see them," a male voice says as a flashlight blinds me. I see the end of a gun pointed at my chest. "Officer Clark, Grandville police. We received a call about a burglar, breaking and entering."

"I'm the homeowner. I live here," I say. Who the hell called the cops? Who knows I'm here? Mia does. I should have finished her off long ago. So much for being patient with her demise.

"I'll need to see some identification. My partner, Officer Miles, will extract your wallet. Don't move."

As I stand in my almost empty home, my hands raised, my pockets violated, I know this will not be the end. I cannot let Mia win. I will not let Mia win. I should have finished her off, her and Buck. The officer pulls my ID out of my wallet and shines a flashlight on it.

"His address on the ID checks out. But what's all this?" asks the second officer who is violently pulling the cash out of my back pocket. He's taken Mia's love note out of my front pocket, too. I hear the pen fall to the floor. The cop ignores it as I fight the urge to bend and pick it up, perhaps jab it into his thick sweaty neck. I examine Officer Miles's face, scarred and pockmarked from bad acne episodes. Simply hideous. He could never have another life; his options are so limited in this world compared to mine. Maybe I should end his suffering.

"I asked you a question, sir," pock-face Miles says.

"Ah, that is a love note, from my wife, Officer. It came sealed in a red envelope, the color of passion. It's special," I say. "It's personal."

He tosses Mia's note to the ground. "I'm talking about this," he says, waving the wad of money I borrowed from the inn in front of my perfectly smooth, masculine face. My five-o'clock shadow has become a small beard by now I'm sure. It has been a long day. He's still staring at me, now examining the bills as if he's never seen so much in one place. Poor fellow.

"It's cash. Money. I know that you don't make much, but that's what it is," I say. Really, the caliber of people they have protecting and serving us is ridiculous.

"You're so funny, asshole," says Ugly Face. He's fortunate to work the night shift. He would scare small children in the daylight.

I shrug as the cop keeps my wallet and keeps his hands around the cash, stepping back from me. He'll pocket my money, I know he will. It won't even make the police report. The other cop has the gun trained on my heart, which I now realize is beating rather quickly.

"We had a report of a theft up at a place called Lakeside, at the hotel there. Someone robbed the cash drawer tonight. Know anything about that, Mr. Strom?" Officer Clark asks.

Oh, this is ridiculous. I am not going to be tripped up by a petty theft.

"I have no idea what you're talking about," I say. "Can I put my hands down?"

"Weren't you just there, in Lakeside, sir?" the ugly guy asks.

Why does he insist on calling me sir, like I'm an old man? Sure, he's young but look at that face. I'd rather be me. "They relayed your license plate number. We know it was you, sir. That you were there. There's a camera in the lobby." Interesting. I didn't see that. Those cameras are getting smaller every day. Looks as if Scott will be off the hook for this one, after all. Fine. Everything is beatable, escapable. You just need to use your brain, and mine is second to none.

"Put your hands behind your back, Mr. Strom. We're taking you to the station," Officer Clark says. What choice do I have? It's two of them against me, and I'm unarmed. I know what you're thinking. I handled Buck deftly, although I should have finished him off. Could I take these two? Most likely. But I'll be released as soon as I post bail. Why make a fuss now? Better to go to the station, get these peons off my back, climb in my car and drive off into my future the next day. Heck, I'm already packed. I look longingly at my suitcase, a Rimowa dark gray, very stylish, and decide to comply.

They handcuff me and lead me out of my house. Thankfully it's still dark. Thankfully my boys did not witness this embarrassment. I'll never tell them about it either, when I see them again. And I will see them again.

As I slide into the back seat, Officer Clark pushes my head down, roughly.

"Hey," I say. "Don't make me file a brutality charge."

"I'd zip it if I were you, Mr. Strom," Officer Clark says before slamming the car door. He reappears in the driver's seat, as Officer Miles slides into the passenger seat. I see now that there are two more squad cars parked on the street in front of my house.

"Hope you enjoyed your last day of freedom, scumbag," Officer Miles says.

I will not go to prison for petty theft, no matter what Ugly Face wishes for. The prisons are not for people like me. They are for dumb druggies and inner-city people. Mia and Buck won't tell them anything else, because they want me to just go away. And I will, at least for now. I know how badly I hurt good old Buck. Maybe Buck is dead. One can only hope.

Suddenly, the car is rocked by an explosion and the sky briefly fills with a flash of light. I allow myself a smile at the perfect timing.

"What the hell?" Pock-face is alarmed. He hops out of the car and disappears into the night. The two squad cars that were staked out in front of my house flip on their sirens and drive off. When Miles returns he's out of breath, so excited. Nothing bad ever happens in Grandville so this is big news.

"A house just down the street exploded, man, I called the fire squad and they already were dispatched. You should see it, Clark. The house is like totally gone. Gas leak or something. Stuff we read about, man, hope everybody got out."

Despite the childish description, I'm pleased. As he climbs back in the car, two fire engines and two emergency squads blare down the street, full lights, loud sirens. They won't need the paramedics, but only I know that.

"We have to take this guy in," Clark says in a commanding voice.

"Yes, all the neighbors will be awake now. Let's get moving, shall we? I'd like to deal with this little misunderstanding and get back to my life," I say. And it's true. Up and down my street the neighborhood is coming to life, lights flipping on, housewives in bathrobes and men in boxers spilling out of their happy little homes. Tragedy is such a magnet, isn't it? These are my neighbors, drawn like moths to a flame, or in this case, drawn to a gaping foundation where a tidy home

used to be. Soon, these same neighbors will be gossiping about
me, about our marriage falling apart. I don't like failure and
this, my empty, loveless house, feels like defeat.

"Buddy, with the size of that explosion, your visit to the
station won't even make the news," Pock-face says. As if I
want to make the news.

"What a shame," I remark. But he is wrong. I am important. Our family's deconstruction will be the talk of the town.
After Greg and Doris Boone's unfortunate slip into poverty,
that is. "Can we go now?"

Officer Clark laughs as he flips on the bright lights of his
squad car and we roll out of my driveway and into the still-
dark night. Through the window of the police car I see two
bright stars, the cat eyes of Scorpio's tail, rising in the sky.

Mia's a Scorpio, did I mention that?

ONE YEAR LATER

EPILOGUE

One of the best things about standing along the shore of Lake Erie on a brisk May evening is the color of the sparkling water as it reflects the setting sun. Tonight, the water is swirled with purple and orange as it laps the rocks lining the shore.

"Mom!" Sam yells. He and Mikey are playing on the swings in the park just behind me. I turn and look at my little boy and smile. "Look how high I'm going!"

"That's great, baby," I say, twisting my guardian angel bracelet around my wrist. I had tucked the lucky bracelet into the glove box of Paul's car that day, hoping to protect myself, and as a reminder you're never alone. It was a token of faith, and a symbol I'd started believing in myself again. I haven't taken it off since. My heart is full at Sam's happiness. He is seven now; his blond hair grows just a bit darker every year. But ever since my separation from Paul—our exorcism from Paul, as I think of it—at times, everything else about Sam is lighter. It's the same with all of us. I guess I didn't realize how strong denial is, how much I had put up with from my husband.

It wasn't just the multiple infidelities that ground me down, it was the little ways he made me feel insignificant and small each day. Checking on me to make sure I was at home with the kids each day, making sure I didn't find time to keep up with my friends, coming between me and my parents. I let it all happen and I feel such shame, still, for putting my children through it, for the close call that I barely survived. Because even though he never physically hurt my boys, he damaged me at the cellular level and my boys felt that. I'm not just referring to the poison. I'm so much stronger now.

"I'm higher," Mikey says. He's about to turn nine, and he has to be the winner of everything the two boys do. It's usually not a problem. Mikey looks the most like Paul, especially in the eyes. But he is not his father's son. Despite his competitive spirit, he has a kind and giving heart. He is open and honest. He remembers the most about his father's behavior, his authoritarian dominance. Despite my fog of denial, he was watching. He felt my suffering, my isolation, my tiptoeing. My lack of self-confidence was clear, and painful, to my oldest son even as a small child. But there is hope. Our counselor says Mikey will be fine, that both of the boys will be. She worries most about me, my ability to move on past the shame and guilt: because I should have saved all of us sooner. She tells me to focus on the positive. I got away. Some never do.

"You're really swinging high, Mikey," I say. "Can you touch the stars with your tennis shoes?"

"Of course not, Mom," he answers. But the grin on his face makes me think he is imagining just that.

I hug myself with my arms, smiling as I feel the roll of fat that's returned to my center. Now that I'm not being poisoned, I've been slowly gaining weight. I embrace it as a sign of health, and happiness. I'm almost finished with the dialysis treatments, bowel cleansing and IV chelation. I'll be under the care of a doctor to make sure all of the arsenic is cleansed from my system. But I'm encouraged. I'm going to get better. I have color in my face again. I look healthy. The opposite of what I looked like as an attempted murder victim. I still try to eat healthy foods, but I'm not so vigilant anymore. French fries are totally back on the menu. And the kids and I even shared a cheese pizza at Sloopy's for lunch. Turns out, cheese wasn't the culprit, my husband was.

A chill spreads up my spine as I think of Paul. He posted bail the night of his arrest and no one has heard from him since. Buck's guys followed him back to our house, where he picked up a suitcase and headed out of town. They stopped following him in Cincinnati, turning it over to another team who tracked him all the way to Palm Beach, Florida. That explained the pink polo shirt they photographed him wearing as he drove away. But not a lot else.

Why did he pick Palm Beach? we all wondered. The climate? The distance from his past? There had to be a bigger reason. It became clear as the tail photographed Paul with a woman who was his own age—older than his usual and dripping in jewels. He was looking for his next sugar momma. From all the reports, he seems to have found her. Buck's team will try to warn her off if it gets serious, and I know that's the right thing to do. But mostly, I want him to just stay there, stay away from us, from the whole community.

Doris and Greg live in a two-bedroom rental now, the next town over. While most people in town never linked Paul to their home's gas explosion and complete destruction, Buck and I did. Still do. But there is just no evidence. We called in an anonymous tip, but it is to no avail. Unless I came forward and pressed charges about the attempted murder, and the attack on Buck at Lakeside, the police won't take his criminal nature seriously.

Buck's contacts in the police department tell him the cops think Paul was a poor stressed-out guy whose wife dumped him, moved all of their belongings out, took his kids and left him with nothing. He had no choice but to take some cash from the inn. He paid it back. All is forgiven. End of story.

The police have created a very different profile of Paul than the man I know. But I'm not putting my kids or myself through a trial. So instead, I take Doris to lunch often, and have her kids over for sleepovers so she and Greg can have some space. It's the least I can do.

Buck waves from beside the swings and I smile at him.

"We're going to shoot hoops!" he says, one of my sons under each arm. He looks as strong as ever even though he took the brunt of Paul's rage physically, requiring an overnight hospital stay, and a month of rehabilitation. He tells me it was worth it, even the shrouded sucker punch he suffered to protect us.

Buck and the boys are a joy to watch on the basketball court. They embody life's simple pleasures as they laugh and tease each other. It's amazing Buck came into our lives when he did. If he hadn't been our neighbor here, if we hadn't shared a love of gardening, I never would have realized what was happening—the hair loss, the weight loss, the fatigue—until it was too late. He broke through the denial, convinced me to get a urine test. Half a dozen doctors had performed myriad other tests and found nothing wrong with me. That urine test revealed the arsenic poisoning and set my escape plan into motion. I'd called Buck from my doctor's office and told him the news.

"That's it. He's going down," Buck said. His voice was deep and powerful. I knew with him on my side, the boys and I would be okay. "I'm packing some things and I'll be down, get a hotel room in Columbus. You need to speak to an attorney. Make a plan to get the boys out of the house, and out of town. You're going to be all right now, Mia."

I had held the phone in a trembling hand, overwhelmed by the shell of a woman I'd become. Paul had broken me physically and mentally. Buck was helping me rebuild myself, and had been from the moment we met.

"Thank you, Buck. I don't know what I'd do without you," I said.

"Let's not find out," he said. "My team is still on you, 24/7. I'll come around tomorrow. Sit with you during your treatment."

This was what love felt like, I realized that day. Buck and I hadn't even held hands at that point, hadn't done more than share a trowel, but I knew. Buck did, too.

Each day, for the two weeks before Paul and I drove to the lake, while Paul took off for Gretchen's apartment, I showed up at the hospital for my dialysis treatments and bowel cleansings. While Paul made love to his mistress, I focused on recovering my health. They had him under surveillance, Buck's team did, and my job was to make sure I didn't eat anything else that he could have possibly poisoned. At dinner each night, as he sneakily poisoned my food or drink, I would hold my stomach and confess to feeling too nauseated to eat. He tried to hide the poison in my yogurt, in my tea, in so many different foods and drinks. It was exhausting trying to

stay ahead of him. He was careful not to tamper with anything the boys could eat, so I knew I was safe sneaking frozen chicken nuggets when he was out of the house. Dinners
were the tricky meals with him watching me, ready to sneak
powder into my food, my drink.

I could tell Paul was getting frustrated with the situation.
He wanted me to grow sicker, faster, we knew. He was ready
for me to be gone, for Gretchen to take my place. He lost his
job, lost his chance with Caroline and he was finished with
me, with us. And he was running out of money, and the boys,
minus me, were his golden tickets. He'd spent most of the
past six months with Gretchen, so he'd already moved on in
that sense. I was in the way, an obstacle to his future. Even
though my father had made it very clear to him he would
never touch a penny of their trust funds, with my death, Paul
would be the guardian and entitled to a stipend to care for
them. Greedy and heartless.

A chill races down my spine. Paul had grown tired of me,
but instead of punching me in the face and leaving town, the
way he had ended things with Lois, he'd decided to kill me.
Slowly. I still get goose bumps when I admit this to myself.

So I was ready for it to come to a head. It was a relief when
he asked me to spend a weekend together in Lakeside, just the
two of us. Because I knew that would be where he would take
me to die. Away from the boys, away from the neighbors. Just
the two of us, an envelope of arsenic and a romantic dinner.
Sounds perfectly logical if you're a psycho: he needed to give
me a bigger dose of poison. To finish me off. And our new
cottage was the perfect place for a death scene.

Meanwhile, I needed to escape and I would. I needed to
serve him papers when and where I knew the boys would

be safely out of reach. In that sense, we both agreed the lake house would be perfect.

My parents were ecstatic that I'd come to my senses, especially my dad, who hadn't liked Paul from the start of our relationship and had frowned on our brief courtship and quick marriage. He had been right all along, but I had been too infatuated, too foolish to see beyond the lust, beyond the illusion of love.

Paul was great with illusion. I saw him as the grand old-fashioned suitor who brought me flowers, and wrote love notes and took me to expensive and wonderful dinners. The older advertising executive who had traveled the world, who taught me about jazz music and sexual expression. I saw the Paul I wanted to see, the Paul he made sure I saw. That man was a wonderful romantic, a Renaissance man. That man was a lie.

The difference between the act and the truth was clear as Buck sat beside me during a dialysis session. I took a deep breath, took my power back into my own hands, and called my parents' home.

"He's not going to get a dime of your money," my dad said. "I'll call the attorneys as soon as we hang up, the bastard."

"Oh, honey, are you doing all right? How are the boys?" my mom asked. Her sadness made my heart heavy.

"Can they come stay with you, on the day I serve the papers?" I asked. "I'm going to the lake with him on Friday. I'd like you guys to fly into town, take Mikey and Sam back home with you." Buck touched my knee and I remembered to add, "I'm going to have security following you. And the moving van will come and move our things out as soon as we're on the road."

"Of course. We'll be there. Do you want us to come now?"

she asked. I imagined her frightened eyes. I know my dad's were squinting in anger.

"No, we'll stay here until Thursday. Get an early flight. We can't see the grandsons until Friday, Phyllis, or we'd tip that nutjob off," my dad said.

"Exactly, Dad. And, Dad, is there time to draw up a separation agreement with an accompanying dissolution? I don't want any record of being with him, not ever again," I said. I'd been trying to be strong but with those words a sob escaped.

"Oh, honey, yes, we'll screw the bastard," Dad said.

"I want to come hug you right now," Mom said. "Are you alone? We've been afraid he's been isolating you."

I took a deep breath and Buck took my hand in his. "Yes, he has been cutting me off from you, from everyone. But I have a friend here with me. His company specializes in global security. I'm safe until you arrive. And I'll fly to you and the boys as soon as I can."

"Well, thank God. Tell that man—what's his name?" Dad asked.

"Buck, Buck Overford," I said, meeting Buck's eyes as he wiped a tear from under mine. Over the phone line I heard my dad writing Buck's name down to check him out. It made me smile even as I wondered if it would have done any good if my dad had run a background check on Paul before I married him. His record was clean.

"Tell Buck he has our gratitude and to keep you and the boys safe," my dad said. "I need to call the attorney. Check in with your mom and me, every day until Friday. Understood?"

"Understood. And thanks, both of you," I said. I was right not to tell them about the poisoning yet. I knew I couldn't stop my worried mom from coming to town if I had.

Our plan worked perfectly. The day was outlined step-by-step, with the only hiccup being that Paul took the telephone call on our way out the door. I knew it wasn't important, whatever woman of his it was, but I couldn't show my frustration when he finally got into the car. In fact, the entire day was a grand acting job, trying to keep my fear in check as I rode in a car, alone, next to my husband, a man who was trying to kill me.

In hindsight, I'm not sure how I stayed even as calm as I did that day. I'd grabbed a *People* magazine and tried to keep my mind on other people's scandals, but I couldn't. My only consolation was coded texts from Claudia letting me know that my parents had swooped by the school and picked up the boys. I had left a note with the principal, explaining how their grandparents had a special weekend planned. The stop for croissants was to give me a moment to confirm the boys were en route to the airport with my parents. Once I knew they were safe, I felt better.

Claudia let me know when the moving van arrived, and that everything marked had been loaded into the van. In addition to my parents, she was my hero that day, supported by a team of two of Buck's guys. One of the guys was "super cute" according to Claudia. That had made me smile as I spoke to her outside on the sidewalk on Second Street, finally away from Paul for a moment after our lunch at Sloopy's.

I remember how much I wanted to run away from Paul at that moment. The boys were safe, all of my belongings were packed up and driving away. But there was still one more step. We needed him to sign the dissolution papers. And then Paul had walked out of Sloopy's, squinting in the bright sunshine, looking like the handsome man I'd married. Sure, ten years had taken a little toll, and he had a small pouch around his tummy I used to like to tease him about, but still. His smile was bright and it seemed just for me. Part of me still admired the way he walked toward me with a swagger in his step. The confidence. All of those things drew me to him; all of those things almost killed me. In that moment I could almost forget we were enemies. Almost.

The other thing that kept me from running was the fact Buck would be waiting for me at the cottage. Where Paul had swagger, Buck had substance. I realize the difference now. And even though I wouldn't be able to fall into Buck's arms, not yet, I would be able to stand next to him. Absorb more strength with him by my side. As Paul pulled the Ford Flex into the driveway of our cottage I almost didn't wait for the car to stop moving before opening the door. Walking as fast as I could without running, I made it to the garden. And there was Buck, as promised. He smiled, his dimple showing. Calming my nerves.

"Take a deep breath, Mia. It's all going to be over soon," he said. We were standing side by side, pretending to look at the strawberry beds. "You have this. You are safe. Hear me? Are you okay?"

"Now, yes," I said. I could feel Paul approaching us from behind as chills spread down my spine. As relieved as I was to finally stand next to Buck, I knew I had a long night in front of me. I just had no idea at the time how long the night would become.

My finest piece of acting had to be at the restaurant that night. I was forced to leave the safety of Buck's presence at our cottage, and climb back into the car with my husband. It was part of the plan, of course, and necessary to provide Buck with the opportunity to search Paul's things, and to get them dropped off at the inn. He also used the time to make sure all of the cameras he'd placed inside the cottage were working. He tested the panic button he'd installed earlier in the week. It worked, thank goodness.

While Buck set the rest of our trap, I suffered through our last supper. The meal was torture, even with the kind waiter trying to protect me from Paul's ugly comments. Every moment of that supposed-to-be-elegant dinner was an act: trying to pretend I was sitting across from someone I still loved when actually I hated him, hate him still. My mind flashed to the photo of a young woman's battered face, and then to one of Paul holding up a nightgown as he flirted with a different young woman, who I now know is named Gretchen, at a lingerie store. And even though there was no photo of it until after our dinner, as he tampered with my brandy, I saw white powder in his gloved hands, stirred into my evening tea, swirled into my Greek yogurt.

All of his lies, all of his manipulations coursed through my mind during that dinner but I couldn't accuse him of anything, I couldn't tip my hand.

I was in a panic, sweaty and jittery until the moment I saw Buck through the window, standing outside on the deck of the restaurant, watching me, guarding me. I couldn't help but smile, even though I knew Paul thought I was looking at myself in the shiny glass. He would think I was vain. I wasn't. I was smiling about our signal. The thumbs-up sign from Buck meant that everything was in place, that we had Paul and the proof of the poisoning that we needed. The proof meant this charade was almost all over. As I smiled my relief out the window, I felt strong. This day would forever be the start of the rest of my life. The best day ever, in fact, just not the one Paul envisioned.

Sometimes I wish I could have seen Paul's face, confidence shaken when he was taken into custody inside his own home.

Did his heart fall when he discovered his kids were gone, or did he tell himself he'd win in the end? I wish I could have been a fly on the wall when he opened my little red envelope. No doubt, in his messed up way, he thought it was a love note from me to him. I wonder if, just for a moment, he felt sorry about what he had done. Did his heart drop at everything he'd lost? Most of the time, though, I'm glad I didn't see his reaction. It probably would have been my final disappointment.

As Paul was discovering all the surprises I had in store for him at home, I was at the hospital with Buck. The early-morning hours were scary as I saw Buck's injuries and realized exactly what Paul was capable of doing to another human being. I watched as Buck was admitted and hooked up to machines, all the while wondering if the police in Columbus would actually catch Paul or if he'd outsmart us all. I just had a sinking feeling he would get away. The wait was terrifying. The call came at sunrise, informing us Paul had been booked on robbery charges.

"Robbery? That's all?" I said, incredulous. Buck's team had called his phone. I picked up the call.

"It's all they have, ma'am," the man said. "He'll probably post bail in a few hours. Stay safe." Later, I would discover he had secret credit cards. It had taken months to sort out his financial schemes once he was gone.

I looked at Buck, sleeping thanks to some IV drugs, and realized it was fine. We would stay safe. With Buck by my side, Paul wouldn't dare come back. He'd signed the papers. We'd won. His only choice was to scamper away in the night. I fell asleep sitting up in the chair next to Buck's hospital bed, and even so, it was one of the best rests I'd had in months.

The next day, Buck was released from the hospital. I drove

us back to Lakeside. As I pulled into my driveway, a chill
spread down my spine. Buck grabbed my hand.

"Let's go to my place."

I nodded, turned off the engine and hurried to help Buck
open the door. With his bruised ribs, he'd need to take it
easy for a bit and I didn't mind. It was my turn to take care
of him for a while.

Even with the pain in his side, Buck was beaming. It was
a beautiful summer day. Trees heavy with green leaves, kids
pedaling by on rented bicycles. I'd never been inside Buck's
cottage, even though we'd spent two weeks together the summer before, gardening. It wouldn't have been appropriate.
My boys had been with me and, well, I was afraid Paul was
watching. I felt like he always was watching me. Now I know
that was true. As Buck opened the door and stepped to the
side to let me in, walking gingerly, I had been surprised by
his cottage's sleek sophistication. It was as if I was walking
into a home and garden magazine's interpretation of the perfect lake house.

"Nice place you have here," I said. I was taking in the
white linen sofas, the dark hardwood floors, the sleek stainless steel light fixtures and the large white stone fireplace of
the family room.

"Glad you like it," he said. I watched as he closed and
locked the door, sliding in a dead bolt. My husband was
gone, but Buck still was on high alert. My hero. "You're safe
now, Mia."

Buck stepped closer to me, and finally, I could fall into his
arms. In the hospital, he was tended to by his staff and the
nurses. Neither then nor now was the time for passion, of
course. It was time for relief, for appreciation, for freedom.

We simply stood in his cottage and held each other. It was a new start.

I'm stronger now. It helps that we keep tabs on Paul, that we know where he is, what he's up to down in Florida, Palm Beach of all places. I hope there will come a day when I don't wonder if he'll appear back in our lives; I hope there will be a time when I'm certain he has moved on. I want to believe that if I can move on, so can he. As he said the last time we saw each other, I disgusted him. Probably, given everything that transpired, his feelings of disgust have intensified. I just hope those feelings don't turn to revenge. Buck tells me not to worry. They are tracking him. We will be the first to know if Paul ever decides to make his way back to Ohio. He says it's time to heal, to move on.

Together, as a family. This time, my fiancé has my parents' glowing endorsement. Especially since we are house-hunting in New York City, where the boys will once again live close to grandparents who love them. We'll keep the Lakeside cottages for now. The place is still special. Paul can't take that away from us.

"Mom, it's time to go eat," Sam says now, running up to me and grabbing my hand. His face is flushed bright red from playing basketball. He's happy, and hungry. He's normal.

"Did you have fun playing with Buck?" I ask. I love the feel of his sweaty little hand in mine and I hold on tight.

"Yeah! Best day ever," he says.

I swallow at the use of his dad's phrase and smile. "Yes, it was," I tell him. "The best day ever."

★ ★ ★ ★ ★

PAUL STROM'S PLAYLIST FOR THE BEST DAY EVER

"Mack the Knife"—Bobby Darin

"Come Away with Me"—Norah Jones

"Somebody That I Used to Know"—Gotye (featuring Kimbra)

"As Time Goes By"—Frank Sinatra

"Crazy He Calls Me"—Billie Holiday

"The Story Of Us"—Taylor Swift

"Unforgettable"—Nat King Cole

"You Don't Know What Love Is"—Billie Holiday

"We Are In Love"—Harry Connick Jr.

"You Know I'm No Good"—Amy Winehouse

"Cold, Cold Heart"—Dinah Washington

"Every Breath You Take"—The Police

"Bad Romance"—Lady Gaga

AuTHOR NOTE

Paul Strom popped into my subconscious almost fully formed, although I'm not quite certain where he came from. Now that you've read the book, I know that you understand how scary that was. Despite the fact that characters like Paul can give you the creeps while you're writing their story, I thoroughly enjoyed my time with him. Maybe he'll have another story down the line? I love writing, and reading, books with unreliable narrators. One of my previous novels, *All the Difference*, features a female unreliable narrator. She's very scary herself.

You don't have to be a character in a novel to be unreliable. When you think about it, we are all unreliable narrators of our personal stories. We edit. We modify the truth. We try to show the world a spruced up version of ourselves, whether it's to impress a date, a boss or our children. We Photoshop and we brighten. Now more than ever, we harness the power of social media platforms to create a curated view of our lives. We choose the photos our "friends" see, we create our world and present it through our own filters. And we can make ourselves look perfect, happy, blessed to those on the outside looking in.

But we all know that no one's life is perfect. Part of the ongoing fascination with domestic suspense novels in particular is getting the chance to go behind the closed doors of seemingly perfect lives. Paul and Mia appear to have it all. It's only when we get a glimpse of what's really going on that the facade begins to crack.

In *Best Day Ever*, Paul is trying to impress us with his intelligence, his love for his wife and kids, and his unparalleled business success. But of course, we can read between the lines. Sometimes it's more about what a character doesn't say than what he admits to doing. And that's the appeal of writing, and reading, a book like this. Hopefully, you'll agree.

Kaira.

ACKNOWLEDGMENTS

To my family, especially my husband, Harley, who is my first reader and biggest fan, and to my kids, Trace, Avery, Shea and Dylan, with love always and forever. To my mom, Pat Sturdivant, and the extended Sturdivant and Wise families, love you all. To my friends in Columbus, Malibu, and Laguna Beach, and from Vanderbilt and beyond, you add the wonderful to my life and I'm blessed to know you. And, as a note: Columbus is a spectacular, booming city, a great place to live and visit, no matter Paul's snide comments.

Special thanks for this novel's existence goes to my wonderful agent Katie Shea Boutillier, to my brilliant friend Andrea Katz of Great Thoughts, Great Readers who pushed me to pitch this book and never stops pushing in the best possible way, and to Laura Garwood, my first go-to editor. What words can I use to adequately describe my fabulous editor Margo Lipschultz, who sought me out at the same time I was looking for her? Our partnership was meant to be, Margo, and I hope it continues for years to come. Your insights into the story, along with those of Brittany Lavery, made Paul's adventure so much better, so much creepier. Thanks, too, to Tahra Seplowin #besteditorsever. I'm more than thrilled to be helping launch Harlequin's new Graydon House Books imprint, and am amazed by the talent and creativity of the entire team, especially Loriana Sacilotto, Dianne Moggy, Susan Swinwood, Merjane Schoueri, Amy Jones, Ana Luxton, Diane Lavoie, Sheree Yoon, Erin Craig, Michelle Renaud and Lisa Wray. At HQ UK, thanks to Lisa Milton and Charlotte Mursell. At HQ Australia, thanks to Lilia Kanna and Jo-Ann Milne. Thanks to Dilan Swain and Michelle Kroes of CAA who took on the film rights, and believe Paul belongs on the big screen.

Thanks, too, to Laguna Beach Books for their continued support of my stories, to my fabulous author communities including the Tall Poppy Writers and the Women's Fiction Writers Association. Special thanks to Jennifer Tropea O'Reagan from Confessions of a Bookaholic, Marlene Engel from Book Mama Blog, and all of the amazing book bloggers for cheering me on from the beginning.

And finally, to you, the reader. Thank you. I couldn't be living the life of my dreams without your support. I hope you enjoyed *Best Day Ever*.

READER'S GROUP DISCUSSION QUESTIONS

1. Paul Strom is an unreliable narrator. At what point in the story did you begin to realize he may be telling you only what he wanted you to know? How long did it take you to realize he was poisoning his wife?

2. What do you think of Mia? We see her largely through Paul's point of view, and he hardly paints her in the most sympathetic light. Do you identify with her or did you think she should have made different choices in her relationship with Paul?

3. Does Paul legitimately think he is a good husband and father? He says his life revolves around his perfect family. Is he trying to fool you, the reader, or himself?

4. What do you think a young woman like Gretchen sees

in Paul? Is she ultimately a victim, or is she part of the problem?

5. Caroline is the only woman we know of who resisted Paul's advances. Do you think this rejection started Paul on his downward spiral?

6. If Mia's parents weren't wealthy, she'd be in bigger trouble when trying to extract herself from her marriage. If Mia's parents weren't wealthy, Paul would not have been interested in marrying her in the first place. What do you think of that dichotomy?

7. Paul implies that he was abused as a child. Does this justify or account for his behavior as an adult?

8. Do you feel sorry for Paul's mom? Why or why not?

9. What motivates Buck? Is he more than just a protector? What does he symbolize in the story?